# T.I.T.O.R.

# T.I.T.O.R.

J.M. Surra

J.M. Surra
Visit his website at: http://www.jmsurra.com
First Print Edition : March 21, 2013
First eBook Edition: January 31, 2013

22 21 20 19 18 17 16 15 14 13     1 2 3 4 5

Published or pending publication under the following ISBN numbers and formats:

Paperback format: 978-0-9834647-5-4
Kindle eBook format: 978-0-9834647-6-1
Audio book Format: 978-0-9834647-7-8
Multiple formats: 978-0-9834647-9-2

Print and eBook formatting by Quixotry Books.

The main characters in this book are fictitious. Any similarity to any real persons, living or dead, is either unintentional or coincidental, and not intended by the author. Actions, statements, or opinions made by any characters named after real persons are fictitious, and some are historical events documented elsewhere. All are blended together as historical fiction and alternate history. When in doubt, consider any phrase or passage to be pure fiction.

This is not a non-fiction book. No footnotes or citations of any actions, events, or occurrences herein will be given. Though there are informative and educational items of interest in this book, this book is not intended to be an educational book of reference.

# Foreword

Flights of fancy like T.I.T.O.R. don't just happen. The elements needed to create it included two real, controversial legends, each with legions of obsessive, fanatic, and some might say addicted followers. Passion-driven or not, a story being real doesn't make all of the elements true. But what if that story contains compelling—yet unproven—elements that have the power to draw in and challenge the imaginations of an ever-growing audience? In that case, the story will move up the food chain, and every once in a while, one will go a step beyond, and achieve the elusive status of 'Legend.'

The first legend of choice was that of the mysterious and elusive Internet chat room persona John Titor, whose purported time-traveling exploits and predictions fueled the fires of controversy, to the point where chat room attendees fought amongst themselves, taking sides, throwing insults, alternately protecting and attacking Titor, at times to the near-exclusion of Titor himself. Though pushed to the side during the ruckus, he managed to post now and again. And then, at the precise departure date he'd given at the start, he disappeared without a trace, leaving us to speculate.

Was the John Titor we chatted with actually John Titor? Perhaps not, but even if he wasn't, it wouldn't preclude him from being a time traveler.

My second choice of legends was far better known. The legend of the Roswell crash, which occurred around the first of July in 1947, still sparks the imaginations of people around the world, though more than 65 years have passed. In blogs and forums everywhere, it remains the focal point; arguably the origin of our UFO awareness, the Mecca of UFOs.

That gave me an idea.

Few people ever paid attention to what happened immediately after the date something crashed in Roswell. In the summer of 1947, the American military abruptly experienced spasms of growth, separating the branches and adding a new branch with greater funding and (not incidentally, I think) ultimate control over all things UFO, a branch which today we all know as the Air Force. Pandemonium ensued. Thrown into upheaval, military bases, their contents and personnel were moved whimsically around the country. Years passed before the dust settled on the whole deal.

Was it intentional? Would the American military purposely create so much disorder and confusion, just to obscure our view? Sure, they would. It would have allowed them to operate with virtual impunity, right under our noses. Maybe I'm the only one to see it. I grant you, it wouldn't be the first time my hyperactive imagination saw what others don't, or more than they're willing to see. Of a certainty, it will not be the last time. Either way, it's within the realm of possibility.

With two great legends tucked away neatly in my bag of tricks, and an interesting side story thrown in for good measure, it was time to go to work.

Weaving vital, new fabric from the separate legends of John Titor and the Roswell crash was a formidable task. But with a little magic, and a healthy dose of imagination to fill in the gaps, an amazing new legend took shape.

That legend is T.I.T.O.R.

Enjoy, my friends.

J.M. Surra

# 1

The operations command center easily spanned seventy-five feet in width, and every inch of that, floor to ceiling, was occupied by the main view screen, displaying the Earth's northern hemisphere. From the lower right, a glowing white line swept in a perfect arc up and into the black of space, pausing at the last recorded position before the communications blackout.

Technicians remained focused on their monitors, tracking Hop 206 through the so-far routine mission. Meanwhile, the others who comprised the quiet machinery of Hop Ops remained in motion, moving about the command center, carrying files and clipboards, whispering, and watching the mission progress up on the main screen.

Colonel Marcus Clayton sat in the command chair, center rear, overseeing the bustling command center. Signing an order presented to him, he handed the clipboard back, then turned his attention back to the mission. "Mr. Waldron, report. Are they in re-entry?"

Everything was fine when Waldron checked his readings and said, "Sir, outgoing telemetry showed them on-time and on-track, with re-entry in one minute ... *mark.*" Still relaxed, his eyes remained on his screen, waiting for the end of the minute to report Hop 206 in re-entry.

When an object appeared on the screen only a few seconds later, he tensed, typing furiously and checking his readings. "Mixed telemetry coming through, sir. It's them, but they're too early. Their approach is too steep." His calm voice belied the increasing tension in the room when he reported, "We're losing telemetry, sir. The window's closing."

Clayton watched the big screen in alarm, as the smooth, perfect arc made an abrupt turn from orbit and swept earthward in a straight line toward North America. He barked, "All Op stations, condition red. Record *everything*. Keep trying, Jeff. If we lose them, we'll need all we can get."

Waldron said, "I'm on it, sir. People, you heard the colonel."

Ear-splitting klaxon alarms sounded, reinforcing his words.

Running and shouting, people bounced off each other, sprinting for their stations in the mad dash to initiate emergency protocols.

Clayton yelled, "Damn it. Shut that noise off!"

Raising his voice to be heard over the cacophony of noise and alarms, Waldron yelled, "Sir, no luck re-establishing a full stream. We're getting no new telemetry—I'm losing them—" He searched anxiously for any further readings. "Hop 206, people. I've got nothing. Listen up; I want all recorded telemetry forwarded to my station *now.*"

When nothing new appeared, he looked up, visually polling the technicians, station to station, hoping for something. Anything. But he already knew. There was no new telemetry to forward. With each shake of their heads, his heart fell.

The klaxons ceased.

Where just seconds before, chaos had consumed every aspect of the command center, now, even the familiar quiet banter and buzz of background activity were gone. The all-consuming silence that replaced it was far more unnerving than any klaxon.

Clayton expected a report, and Jeff Waldron would have given anything to avoid being the one who broke the silence. But that was not to be, and waiting was not a luxury he had.

"I'm sorry, sir. They're—they're gone."

"Where? When? Can you track them at all?"

"No, sir. There's no new telemetry to track their descent. Using the last known trajectory data, we can project, but we can't know exactly where they're coming down. I *can* say they're headed for the southwestern U.S."

"Date?"

"Also uncertain, sir. Formulating the variance and the, ahh, okay, my best guess—if I had to guess—"

"I need that guess, Jeff."

"Yes, sir. My estimate is … right around July first, 1947."

"First of July, in 1947? Are you sure? Margin for error?"

"Let's see … point-five percent, sir. Maybe point-three."

Clayton said, "I'll take those odds, coming from you. Give me a number based on point-three; another one of your guesses. In days, that would be?"

"Roughly five to seven days on either side of that, sir."

"Jesus. This can't be a coincidence."

"Sir?"

Though clearly rattled, Clayton pressed on. "Roswell. Roswell, New Mexico. Does that fall within your impact projection grid?"

"Roswell, New Mexico—yes, it does, sir. Right smack in the center of it. The unchanged trajectory from our last point of contact places Roswell less than a hundred miles south of the impact point, at the dead center of the search grid. But, sir, I don't want to give you false hopes. More than likely, they—"

"They won't survive," the colonel interjected.

"That's correct, sir. The craft will disintegrate upon impact at those speeds, even if they somehow survive the descent. The odds of anything living through such a crash would be virtually nil."

Clayton responded, "No. I'm saying it outright; they *won't* survive. It was *us.*"

"I'm sorry, sir; *what* was us?"

"What do you *think* was us?" the colonel snapped. "Keep up, Mr.

Waldron. Why are we here? Time. History. Mistakes. Roswell, New Mexico. An unidentified craft crashed there, the wreckage spread over three miles of countryside. Area 51. UFOs. You wouldn't be at that monitor if you didn't know your history."

Waldron said, "Yes sir, we're all well-versed in the details surrounding the Roswell crash—uh—wait. Wait, you're saying—" The color drained from his face. "You're saying that *we* crashed in Roswell? That was *Hop 206* they found?" The implications slammed into him like a train, leaving him breathless. "That means …" he trailed off, his mind racing, unaware that he hadn't finished the sentence.

"That means that *we* caused the nuclear war, Mr. Waldron. We may not have pushed the button, but Hop 206 crashed near Roswell in early July of 1947. And we all know that *whatever* crashed near Roswell on that date set off a chain of events that ultimately resulted in the deaths of five billion people."

In a room packed with dozens of stunned hop-op technicians, the only sounds to be heard were the gentle hums and clicks of computer fans and hard drives.

Clayton broke the silence. "I want an emergency meeting of all key personnel, Mr. Waldron. All personnel with a clearance of four or above *will* be in the conference room in one hour. Mandatory attendance, no excuses, no exceptions. We have a genuine crisis on our hands."

# 2

*New Mexico, near Roswell*
*July 5ᵗʰ, 1947*

Mack Brazel looked out over the rugged New Mexico landscape. His ranch was large, and inspecting any one parcel took several days under optimal conditions. He hadn't inspected this parcel since mid-June, and he saw that the terrain now displayed a long, deep gouge, perhaps a hundred yards in length, which disappeared behind the hill. As he rode around the hill, he saw the long, thin furrow grew wider and deeper, extending another several hundred yards. *That damned Army Air Force,* he thought, *this is the second time one of their contraptions has crashed on my ranch.*

"Vernon. Dee. You two stay right behind me; y'hear? Especially you, Dee; you mind me, now. Don't go runnin' off until we see what we're dealing with." He spoke gently to his horse. "C'mon, Pat, let's see what we have here," and clicked his tongue gently to urge his mount forward. The palomino responded easily to the commands, and moved further down along the length of the dig in the earth. Mack's eight-year-old son, Vernon, and his best friend, Dee Proctor, had tagged along today; as young ranchers-in-training, they were there to help Mack do his work. He paid them the princely sum of twenty-five cents a day each, showing near-infinite patience some days as he suffered their youthful ways, not to mention all the eight-

5

year-old help those four bits could buy.

Brazel wanted to see if he could tell what kind of aircraft it was, so he could at least describe to the authorities what he'd found. Bits of metal and cloth material littered the ground, and he dismounted to inspect some of them. The bright, silver metal reflected the sun like chrome. He picked up a piece, about a half-inch thick, roughly six by nine inches. It weighed practically nothing, which surprised him. He retrieved a piece of the cloth, which had the appearance of light, almost shiny, gray rubber. Like the metal, it too was light—light as a feather, in fact—and though it looked and felt like rubber, he couldn't stretch it at all.

"Hmm." He took the reins, threw them over Pat's neck, and walked away down the furrow. The loyal, well-trained horse trailed patiently alongside, and a single step behind. The debris field was expansive, at least two hundred yards long, though not too wide, except for a handful of odd bits thrown beyond the furrow's edges. It sloped upward to the southeast as he walked, and at the crest, the furrow stopped, but the debris field continued for a short ways. He thought, *Something struck, or at least bumped the ground here. It wasn't a crash, but they didn't get off scot-free, either.* Turning around, he did a mental reenactment of the angle of the impact, and the way the craft—or whatever it was—had struck. *You know, maybe they didn't crash here. Maybe they bounced.* At the end of the shallow ramp, he looked out in a straight line. He tried to imagine how it might have continued, but saw nothing at first. Looking further into the rising hills a few miles out, he saw a glimmer, and thought, *that's probably nothing. And it's quite a ways to go just to find a windshield busted out of somebody's truck, or an old window or mirror someone dumped.*

"What do *you* think, Pat? Is it worth the ride? Something would have had to be going pretty fast to end up clear over yonder. That's gotta be two, maybe three miles, at *least.*"

The horse nuzzled him affectionately from behind, looking for a good scratching. Mack gave in to his faithful old friend, and while he scratched, they conversed. "Yeah? You're curious too? You want to go see what it is? Well, I guess we'd better go see, then."

He said to the boys, "See that gleam on that hillside off to the east there, a bit south? Pat thinks we should go take a look, so let's hit the trail, men." He mounted Pat with one swift, easy motion, a move perfected by spending years in the saddle. Another click of the tongue to Pat, and off they rode, bound for the plateau just off those distant hills.

An hour of easy riding had passed, when they came upon another debris field, more densely covered with bits and pieces than the first; and a wider furrow in the ground, which grew deeper as it went. It ended abruptly against a rock outcropping a half-mile away. They picked their way around the dense debris and through the field. As they neared the outcropping, Mack noticed that Pat was jumpier than usual. He decided to walk the rest of the way on foot, to give Pat a chance to approach at his own pace, and grow accustomed to the unusual objects all around him.

He said, "Boys, I want you to stay right here while I check out whatever this is. Right here. Understand?"

"Yes, sir."

Dismounting, he threw the reins over Pat's neck again, and they walked along together as they had at the first debris field.

"Looks like somebody wrecked a truck, doesn't it, Vernon?" Dee said, excited. "Let's go see what it is."

Vernon wasn't so sure. "We can't, Dee. Daddy said—"

But Dee was already off General Lee's back, and scurrying toward Mack and Pat. Vernon sighed, exasperated with Dee. He dismounted, threw his reins over Caesar's neck, and followed. It wouldn't be the first time he had to ride herd over his impetuous, over-exuberant friend. Most days, those same characteristics made Dee fun to be around.

This situation didn't have that feel of fun to it.

As Mack approached the rock outcropping, his stomach dropped. He could clearly see a vehicle in the wreckage. Walking closer, he saw it appeared to be the nose of a Ford truck. "Jesus, Pat, they hit a truck when they crashed," he said, and drew closer, but now he feared what he might find. He thought, *are there some poor, hapless souls in that truck? And if there are, what were they doing out here on my ranch, in the middle of nowhere? Maybe there isn't anybody in there. With any luck at all, it's probably just some hikers or campers, who don't even know their truck is wrecked yet.*

From time to time, he encountered nature lovers, out and about, enjoying the outdoors, and as long as they stayed clear of the sheep and horses he raised on the expansive ranch, he had no objection to their presence. He was sure he hadn't seen this truck before. For one thing, it was pretty new. Few folks around could afford a new truck. He stepped closer.

Pat whinnied, reared, and pranced away, and then sprinted off about a hundred yards at a gallop. Mack knew the horse wouldn't go far, even if he ran off. But he also knew that if Pat was nervous, there was something to be nervous about. With no other clues, he kept an eye peeled for rattlesnakes as he walked nearer the wreckage.

"Oh, no," he said, encountering a body in plain sight, and then he saw no fewer than three other feet protruding from various parts of the wreckage. Staring intently at the grisly scene for another minute, he committed as much of it to memory as he could bear, knowing he would have to report it.

Just then the wind shifted, and a stench permeated the air, unlike anything he'd ever encountered. Now he knew what spooked Pat. He heard a noise behind him, wheeled, and nearly cried out in fright. The last thing he expected to see was Dee retching on the ground, not ten feet away from him. Standing halfway between him and Dee, transfixed, was Vernon, who couldn't tear his eyes away from the horrific sight before them.

"I thought I told you boys to stay back there!" Mack barked. He rarely yelled, and didn't like to. Under the circumstances, he made an immediate exception to his own rule. "You two get back to Caesar and the General. I mean, right now!"

The boys vamoosed, scrambling for their mounts, while Mack took a last look. Realizing that nothing could be alive in that twisted, tortured mass of metal, he turned and jogged toward Pat, whistling. The horse came forward and met his friend, who swung up into the saddle and clucked twice, reining the animal away from the debris field and toward home.

A few miles away from the crash site, the boys remained atypically silent. They'd seen far more than two eight-year-old boys should have. It wasn't their fault, but it couldn't be undone. Though they needed rest, he felt they shouldn't delay. "I think we can make it home today, Pat. What do you think?"

The horse's ears pointed back toward the man when he talked, though the mount never understood quite what was being said. He knew his friend was talking to him. During the many years they'd ridden the range, their interaction and unspoken communication was always a comfort to him, and continued to calm him as they rode along. Even so, the horse sensed his companion was disturbed, and somewhat unnerved.

"Boys, Pat thinks we should be able to make it home tonight. And I don't feel right staying out here. What do you think?"

The boys responded in unison with not a trace of their normal exuberance, offering a dull, automatic, and more than a little disconcerting, "Yes, sir."

# 3

Colonel Clayton held the respect of his people. He asked nothing of them that he himself wouldn't do. Not to put too fine a point on it; if he gave the order, they'd march straight into hell—or would have, if they didn't already live in it. What he asked of them he expected would be done; no hesitation, no excuses.

The T.I.T.O.R. project had the unenviable task of identifying precise moments in time, points of 'possible divergence,' where a wrong path was taken, or perhaps the wrong person died. Hop machines and their crews traveled back in time to tweak specific situations and events, correcting perceived errors, with a focus on improving the future.

Elite or not, in the dozen years since the inception of the project, his people had never faced a situation as dire as this. Every day, paradoxical consequences threatened all they worked for. Playing with time would always be inherently dangerous; and some went so far as to call it reckless, like giving a box of matches to a child. But *reckless* was a relative term, especially given their situation. One look at the desperate, tattered, post-apocalyptic remnants of civilization outside of the compound walls was enough to convince anyone that the gamble was worth taking. To achieve their mission goals, Clayton often asked for the impossible.

Now he called the meeting to order, and the air was filled with foreboding. One word he carefully avoided using was *paradox,* though it mattered little. This new development was devastating.

Profoundly so.

"The loss of Hop 206 is an unforeseen tragedy, but we're in the business of taking big chances. I want to make sure everyone is clear on just what happened today, and the associated implications—the *known* implications—we're facing. Rose will fill you in on the details. Rose?"

Rosemary Rios stood and walked to the front of the room. "T.I.T.O.R. stands for *Temporal Integral Tactical Operations and Recovery*. The project was founded for one reason; to give the earth a possible second chance. To identify the cause or causes of the war, and hopefully change them. To help the world recover. When we regained access to the hibernating military satellites, we learned that on September 15th, 2015, both the United States and Russia elevated their DEFCON levels, and early in the afternoon, multiple detonations occurred on American soil, followed by a massive nuclear exchange between the two powers. The Board determined that the Roswell incident led to a nuclear conflict. Bits and pieces of information we were able to piece together pointed to the probability that the Russians somehow attempted to seize the Roswell wreckage, which escalated into a nuclear exchange between the two superpowers.

"Precisely how is not known, and we continue to search for any information to give us a clue as to why the situation was important enough to warrant the exchange of nukes. There's damn little information available, so it's not all that surprising that, in all our years of research, we never found a single indication that the wreckage might have been a hop machine. That all changed today, and it may change a whole lot more."

She continued, "Time travel is touchy stuff, and though we live with the dangers of it every day, I don't think any of us ever expected to learn that the Roswell incident was a direct result of our program. Expected or not, as of today, Hop 206 became the focal point of the 2015 nuclear exchange. How do we proceed? How *should* we? The irony of the situation is that it seems—by taking into account our present situation—that, had we never established T.I.T.O.R., the nuclear war might never have occurred."

The room remained quiet as she spoke. "There are too many variables to consider all of them. One would assume that we would have attempted to leave ourselves a message, something warning us to scrap the program. If that did happen, if we tried to send ourselves a message, somebody may have found it, and walked away with it. That warning could be buried in the sand somewhere, or washed out to sea. There's no telling. Whether we tried to or not, we weren't successful in warning ourselves.

"What we *do* know—now—is that we're the only ones who stand any chance of changing what happened today. Essentially, our mission must remain unchanged."

She paused, and said, "But now we know that, whoever started the war, it wasn't alien wreckage they planned to seize. It's unlikely that they could have known that. Perhaps having that knowledge will make a difference for us. Okay; research teams, you'll concentrate on optimal situations, dates, and locations for recovering the remains of the Hop 206 crew. Your focus will remain the same as it was before; to avert the nuclear war. As for the rest of us, it's business as usual, but it's critical that we factor in this new information."

Clayton turned back to the table. "Does anybody have any questions for Rose?" When nobody responded, he said, "Let's get back to it, folks. Work together. Share ideas. Nothing is too small or insignificant. If you have any ideas, we want to hear them. Dismissed."

# 4

Back in the Ops center, Clayton stopped in to check on their progress.

"Mr. Waldron, what have you got for me?"

"Using the small micro-singularity generators in the research lab, Rose and I were able to create a small, stable window of real-time access to the information stream in the year 2000, which they called the World Wide Web. Our original idea was to use it to exchange information with our embedded agents. With any luck, we can use it to gather some information that will help us to identify where the wreckage of Hop 206 was taken. It's limited to how long the generator holds up. It's really designed for small lab experiments and such. Our best estimate is that it may last six months, but it's more likely that we'll get only four months before we start to lose our real-time window."

"Real time? What does that mean?" Clayton asked.

"In the present context, it means that the way this access port works, if it's November first here, it's November first *there*. As time proceeds here, it does so there as well, as long as the stream is maintained."

"So, we have through March, April at the outside before we lose this communications port? Can't you just establish another?"

"It was a lucky accident that we were able to establish this in the first place. It took about a year of complicated work to establish this link. We couldn't do it again, sir. Not quickly. Not anytime soon."

"I see. Didn't they monitor all information flow on the Web around the turn of the century, after a major terrorist attack on the U.S.? Isn't that risky?"

"Yes, sir; they referred to the day of the attack as Nine-Eleven, because of the date, September eleventh of 2001. That's when they implemented Homeland Security and started monitoring everything. We've tried the mid-1990s, but there just wasn't enough information stored on the Web. We've accessed it about a year in advance of Nine-Eleven, and we think we can get some information. As I mentioned, we also have an agent living in that time. Most of you know Flash.

"There's some element of risk, but we have a very narrow window of opportunity. If we're to retrieve Hop 206 before the nuclear exchange in 2015, we're going to have to take some chances; push things a little farther than we normally would. I've met some folks in an online forum called a chat room, and I'm confident I can block any attempts to trace me. I'm going by the name Timetraveler_0, and I'm claiming to actually *be* a time traveler. So far, they're responding to me."

Clayton rubbed his chin. "That's risky. But I can see where most of them won't believe you anyway. Carry on, and keep me informed. Play it close to the vest, Jeff."

"Will do, sir," Waldron said. He and Rose got to work, and he filled her in on his progress in the chat room. "They want to know my real name, and what year I'm from." He raised his eyebrows, and silently extended an invitation to her to participate and share ideas. It was all fabrication, anyway. Her Hop Ops jacket caught his eye, with the word *T.I.T.O.R.* emblazoned across the patch. "How about Titor?" he asked her. "Jeff Titor?"

"That's not bad," she said, but then scrunched up her face a little, leaned her head left and right, and suggested, "How about you use your initial, but change the name? *John* Titor sounds good."

He smiled and turned his focus back to the screen. "Sure, I can remember that with no problem. Works for me." He talked as he typed, "My name is John ... Titor. I ... come from the year 2036, and I'm here visiting my family and my two-year-old self at my family's home in north Florida. There, now I have a name."

She grinned and said, "Two-year-old self? Okay, now you're just having too much fun. Why 2036?"

"I didn't think we should tell them that we're from 2098. I think 2036 is as much as they can handle. Don't ask me why, but I think it comes across better. Besides, I have something in mind for that year."

"Okay, I'm with you. I hope your fingers are all warmed up, because I think you just opened a *big* can of worms. You'll be answering questions for months, you know."

"I know. I had to gain some visibility so Flash can find me. After all, that's the reason we established this link. You know the old saying, the louder you shout the truth, the fewer people who will listen."

"And the quieter you whisper a lie, the faster they'll be lining up to believe you; and you don't want *that* kind of attention," she said.

"Exactly. Striking a balance is what this is about," he said, and held up a photo. "Hey, do you have any more of these old photos of the early hop machines? Didn't you have some user's manuals for them too?"

"Is that one of the first-generation dual micro-singularity models? Sure, I have more photos, and the diagrams and manuals too. You know, classics or not, they didn't work for crap."

"I know."

"They were lucky if they could get you back to last week. I think we even have one or two of them in mothballs around here somewhere."

"We do. Ephraim has a handful of them stashed around the R&D lab. They're mostly all defunct now."

"What do you want the photos for?"

"For the chat room. They want me to post a photo of what I traveled there in, and I don't want to give them anything they can really use. I thought I'd throw them a bone. After all, those first generation hop machines were built for the original program in 2035, which dovetails with my B.S. story. Let's scan the photos and a few pages from an old manual. That'll make them happy."

"Yeah, for about five minutes. Do you really think they're going to believe any of this?"

"That's not important," he answered, "I just need to attract some attention and gain the focus of a few serious people. I'm actually counting on the likelihood that the majority of them *won't* believe me. Whatever happens, it's critical that we give Flash a way to find us and establish contact."

"What about the truck?" she asked.

"The truck?"

She pointed to an area on the photo he held. "The truck that the machine is bolted down to in the photo. Do we want them to know we use vehicles to carry the machines?"

Most of the first-generation hop machines were self-contained, and employed no other means of moving about. They took off from their "peds," spring-loaded feet that also absorbed the shock of setting down. The last few of the first generation featured an innovation which was carried into the newer generation of hop machines. Both were designed to fit inside the bed of a pickup truck.

The reason was simple: camouflage. After dark, the field from a hop machine emanated a fairly intense glow, and could be seen at great distances. During the day, second generation hop machines emitted a shimmering silver field which gave the appearance of solid stainless steel, and another of its properties was that it reflected the sunlight like a mirror. Day or night, in the air, hop machines were visible from great distances, making camouflage imperative; and that meant the ability to blend into their surroundings upon landing. On the ground, the hop machine framework could automatically fold down until it was nearly level with the top of the truck bed, and looked like a stack of metal. Once the framework was retracted, the crew could simply drive away in the truck. A photo which revealed such a detail—if closely inspected—might pose some small risk.

After studying the photo, she made an executive decision. "Go ahead, give them that little tidbit. It won't advance their science any, and it makes our story a bit more believable."

"Enough to get them arguing amongst themselves, anyway. Should be fun," he said, an impish grin spreading across his face.

"Okay, I'll go get them ready for you," she said, and left to take care of it.

Absently watching Rose leave, Jeff pondered their situation. As one of the most important technical minds the Ops program had, from the start he'd dreamed of being a hop pilot. But, being in the wheelchair, he couldn't pass the physical. So, he settled for a position for which he was eminently qualified: lead technician. And, as luck would have it, he had found a good friend in co-worker and scientist Rose Rios. Certified as a hop pilot, she preferred her Hop Ops pilot jacket to a lab coat. Though it lent an elite aspect to the way she was perceived by the others, in her mind the piloting of time travel machines didn't hold a candle to the theoretical aspects of time travel. She saw herself as a scientist and a geek, and loved what she did.

Jeff saw Rose as a breathtaking, dark-haired beauty with liquid black eyes; a brilliant scientist who could interact with other scientists on any level. After her longer shifts, she left her scientist persona behind in T.I.T.O.R.'s tech labs. Once off-duty, she liked to relax with a few drinks and a few good friends at the compound club.

Jeff wouldn't *think* of missing a night off with her. She never commented on his wheelchair; it was a part of him, and she accepted it without a second thought. Rose made this job bearable for him. Without her, the crushing weight of the goals they were trying to achieve would turn him to powder. Few people even knew that T.I.T.O.R. existed, but those that knew and were involved with T.I.T.O.R. thought of Jeff Waldron *as* T.I.T.O.R. Jeff felt differently about that. To him, Rosemary Rios was the beating heart and sentient soul of T.I.T.O.R. She brought focus and determination to the table. He felt that their goals would be unobtainable without her.

He heard footsteps approach.

"Will these do?" she asked, bringing him back from his reverie.

He plugged in the storage device, and brought up the photos, inspecting them for his purposes. He was pleased with what she brought. "Ahh, yes, these are *perfect*, Rose! Half of the guys in there will get all excited, and the other half will be yelling that they're faked. I'll toss in some old theory and quote a few scientists from their time, that'll really get them twisted up."

His delight was evident, and she grinned at him. "I'll give you one thing. You're easy to satisfy."

"Says you," he countered, with a blasé wave of his hand. A wry smile crept across his features as he continued his work, humming a tune under his breath.

# 5

Mack entered the sheriff's office and looked around. Behind the desk wall, he could make out the top of the secretary's head. "Is that you, Marcy?"

Raising her head up and stretching to see over the divider wall, she grinned and said, "Mack Brazel, do you know anybody else who would put up with that man, especially for what I get paid?" When he grinned in response, she asked, "You looking for George?"

"Yes, ma'am, I sure am."

"Well, he's around. I'd try the truck stop first. You know how that man loves to talk."

Just then, the door opened, and in walked a dark-haired man with bushy eyebrows and a ready smile. "Mack Brazel," he said, "Good to see you. How're things out at the ranch?"

"That's why I'm here, Sheriff Wilcox. You got a minute?"

"Sheriff Wilcox? Ain't that a bit formal, Mack? Sure, let's go sit down in my office and you can catch me up on whatever's going on."

The two sat down, but Mack appeared to be agitated, and was obviously struggling with whatever was on his mind.

The sheriff said, "Whatever it is, Mack, just get it out, and we'll take it from there."

Mack nodded. "Something crashed out on my ranch, George. Made a hell of a mess. Debris all over the place. Here," he said, and placed the piece of metal and the rubber it was wrapped in on the sheriff's desk. "Pick this up. Feel the weight. Touch it. Feel it. Try to

21

stretch that material."

Wilcox picked the chunk of metal up and his eyebrows registered his surprise at its lack of weight. He inspected the rubbery material next. "I see what you mean. This is what you found?"

"Enough of it to fill a truck. Hell, two trucks. And George, it looks like this thing struck a civilian vehicle, too. There's a Ford truck tangled up in the wreckage. Nearly new. And ... there are bodies, too. At least three I could count, but I didn't get right up on it. Pat spooked, and we ... I—I backed off when I saw the bodies."

With the word 'bodies,' the sheriff stiffened and sat up, and said, "I thought you look a little spooked, Mack. Probably just as well that you came straight here. They hate when civilians get involved in a fatal crash. C'mon, ride with me, and we'll go to the base. If there are bodies, the military should be involved from the start. We can talk more on the way. You did the right thing, coming in and reporting it, Mack."

Flat New Mexico desert passed by the windows, and still more stretched out to the horizon as the sheriff continued questioning the rancher. "Was there a fire? Was the wreckage burnt?"

"There was no sign of any fire at the crash site. I think that's what bothers me most. Bushes and shrubs were wilted, like they were singed and dried to a crisp, all along the path right up to the wreck, so it seems there must have been some sort of fire. I'm wondering if maybe I've found one of them saucers everybody's been taking about. It's hard to explain. The bodies, they looked like they'd been charbroiled, like all the juices were sucked right out of them, until they were dry. In the one I saw clearly, I mean. The skin was the color of a Jericho cricket, with a texture like brown canvas, as near as I can describe it. I swear, George, other than the way they looked, I never saw any real proof that there had been a fire. But something about it—George, something about it was just *wrong*, you know what I mean?"

"Yeah. I think I do, Mack. I've been a sheriff for a while now. Now and again, I see things that just don't make a lick of sense. After a while, somebody usually comes up with the answers, but until then ..." his voice trailed off.

*   *   *

"What do you think, Major Marcel?" the sheriff asked.

The major shook his head. He, too, was at a loss. "We're not currently running any operations, nor are we aware of any other operations or aircraft losses in this region. You say you saw three bodies?"

Mack said, "Yes, and there may be more. I didn't care to get too close to the wreckage. There was a Ford truck tangled up in the wreckage, too. I mean, I got pretty close, but I didn't dig around any. I saw the one whole body, and three other feet. That means at least three bodies, right?"

"Sounds like three to me," the major agreed, rubbing his chin, his thoughts elsewhere. A few seconds later, he voiced his thoughts. "Most of our operations here are designed to support the Manhattan Project, so this is a little outside my area of expertise. But I think it falls within our purview, and that means we should look into it. I'm calling in somebody from the other side. Excuse me for a few minutes."

After he left, the sheriff said, "Looks like they'll pick up where we left off, Mack. Let's hope so, anyway. I'd rather be doing traffic control and nothing more when there are bodies involved."

"Yeah, I knew as soon as I saw those bodies that this was going to be more trouble than anyone needs."

He had no idea how truly prophetic his words were.

# 6

Operations continued uninterrupted. All hop pilots were briefed with new orders. Any new information related to the wreckage from the Roswell crash was of critical importance and should be pursued, if at all possible. They had done just that from day one, but overtly pursuing this information during any one of the forays exponentially increased the risk of discovery. It was a calculated risk, and one that Colonel Clayton deemed to be worth the consequences.

An ordinary hop was just that—ordinary. In the early days of aviation, airplane pilots referred to short flights as 'hops,' and when applied to the pilots and techs of T.I.T.O.R., it stuck.

A hop crew's job might simply be to travel back to 1992 and save a life, which could be done as easily as a crew member throwing up an arm on a New York City street corner to prevent the subject from wandering out in front of a bus. Or perhaps a hop back to 1976 to gather a few lines of source code from a certain computer, or to pick up an encyclopedia. Beyond the parameters of his or her mission, a hop pilot rarely knew all the reasons for their actions or the items they picked up, moved, or destroyed. Those details were reserved for, and decided upon, by individuals far above their pay grade, with far higher clearance.

The reason for that was simple. What you don't know, you can't tell.

Twentieth-century historical events were scrutinized by the research teams, and then by the Board, reviewed down to the last detail. Should an historic event—or the results of that event—be identified as a mistake or a wrong turn, that event might be scheduled for a do-over. The mission goals were evaluated and prioritized, and the operation would be planned according to how critical the issue was. A mistake or a wrong turn meant that the event—or some aspect of it—had the potential to push that timeline to the brink of nuclear war. If there was the remotest possibility that it might contribute to the war, the event was viewed with jaundiced eyes, and subjected to the missions committee, also known as the Board of Overseers. The Board convened in Port Angeles, in Washington State, the post-war capital of the United States. The Board was granted total power over the program, and whatever the situation, their word was final.

Occasionally, successful operations might not 'stick' as planned. Time itself was obstinate, with its own ideas about things. When somebody died, time, for its own reasons, may have wanted them to remain dead. Say the aforementioned hop crew member threw their arm up, to stop a subject from being killed by a bus. But then, a week or two later, the same subject was killed by a runaway car or a fall from some height. The situation would be tagged to be evaluated for a recycle, but in such a case, the Board might well elect not to send another hop crew.

Call it superstition; call it erring on the side of caution. The dangers were clear. If manipulating events in time was tantamount to a kid playing with matches, then going back to repeat their actions might be akin to throwing a bucket of kerosene on it. There was no telling who or what might be consumed in the ensuing blaze. Any isolated action or incident could result in a paradox of epic proportions. Until today and the Hop 206 tragedy, they'd managed not to make anything too much worse—taking into account the dubious prospect that things could possibly go more wrong.

Common sense would tell anybody that they shouldn't be dabbling in time travel at all, but their situation left them without any other options. They lived on a post-apocalyptic Earth that displayed ever-fewer signs of recovery. All indicators showed the planet rapidly losing ground. Weather patterns were failing. Air quality was steadily declining. They faced a grim reality; in the not-too-distant future, Earth would not support human life at all. The humans had well and truly used up all their earth-mother had offered them. Mankind would soon be gone entirely. The present generation had perhaps a decade left. Perhaps.

The ancient earth mother would live on; this she had always done. But her next one or two million years would be spent in quiet convalescence. Her transition into the process would include divesting herself of humanity, and rightfully so. For hundreds of centuries, the humans, nurtured in her selfless generosity, thrived upon her bounty, secure in the knowledge she would continue to provide all they needed. The day came when they betrayed her, defiled her beyond description, realizing too late the cost of the devastation they had wrought. Humans faced the demise they brought about, and no matter where they looked, they could see no chance of escape.

From the darkness, some of the more gifted devised a plan, which gave them only the slimmest of chances; to improve their world from the past. Devoid of any other options, they would take tremendous chances. As the project proceeded, there were instances when time itself soundly rebuffed their efforts, responding with something as overt as sending a runaway car to finish the job they'd interrupted.

Anytime something like that occurred, they showed enough good sense to take heed, and back away respectfully.

Jeff stretched. "Oooh … ergg … aaaggh. *Man,* am I tired. How long have we been at it today?" he asked, yawning.

Rose yawned and slapped his shoulder, and said, "Don't *do* that, it's catching. Now you've got me started." She looked at the clock on the wall. "Five more minutes, and it'll be fourteen hours. There are no more hops expected tonight. How about we go home and get some rest?"

"Sure, my place or yours?"

"Big talk for a guy who can't keep his eyes open. C'mon, you can be designated drinker, since I drove you here this morning, anyway."

"Oh, yeah. I forgot. Wait, oh, *man.* Have you been waiting for me to finish?"

"I didn't want to disturb you. I didn't have anything going on, anyway," she said, shrugging it off.

He dropped his head and shook it. "I'm an idiot. I've been dubbing around here, waiting for *you* to finish up. I clean forgot that you drove me in today. Sorry, Rose."

"Nah, don't worry about it. You've got a lot on your mind. Besides, it's not like it's the first time I've had to babysit you," she teased, "and I doubt it'll be the last."

"I hate when you say stuff that sounds so much like me," he said, with a grin.

She acknowledged by saying, "I think we need to go out scrounging for some more parts for that piece-of-shit chair you're rattling around in. There must be a better wheelchair around somewhere. That thing looks like it's on its last legs—if you'll pardon the pun," she said, and held the door as he rolled and rattled past her on his way into the corridor.

"What, are you talking about my baby here?" he asked, with an exaggerated look of surprise on his face. "This chair is a classic, built in 2013, it's practically brand new. Barely eighty-five years old this year," he quipped as he enthusiastically squeaked and wobbled down the hallway. "Plenty of life left in her."

She looked on in wry amusement. *Nothing ever really seems to get to Jeff. Look at that wheelchair of his, literally held together with baling wire and odd bits of this and that.* She worried sometimes. Occasionally, something gave out, as often as not dumping Jeff unceremoniously onto the floor, where he laughed and joked good-naturedly; waiting patiently while they scraped together enough new bits and pieces and baling wire to make him mobile again. Of everyone she knew, he was the most full of life, and his yawns weren't the only contagious thing about him. His smile was infectious, as was his zest for life. And though she chided herself for thinking it, she thought that maybe—just maybe—she saw something more when he looked at her and smiled.

*Is it me? Or does he sometimes look at me just a little longer than he probably should?* She knew they were close, of course, but now and again it seemed to her that they stayed connected for an extra moment, however fleeting. She dismissed the lingering thought. *Don't be ridiculous. You're just seeing what you want to see.*

There was plenty of truth to that. When he looked at her, she *did* want to see that. He wasn't macho or conceited, like so many other men. Like her, he was kind of a geek, but his mind worked in wonderful ways that she found stimulating, and yes, even exciting. In a world where so little remained that their only hope lay in the past, their two minds worked together in a way that was nothing short of magical when it came to innovations and problem resolution. The present Ops facility became operational twelve years ago. They worked together upon occasion during the initial phases of first-year operations. By the end of the first year, she found some excuse to end up in the same room as him every day, if only for a moment or two. She soon sought a transfer to the Ops team, and for more than eleven years, they'd worked closely together.

Finding the words to say how they truly felt about one another wasn't easy. It was no easy world to live and love in, and trust was among the scarcest of commodities. Each regarded working so closely together as a gift, yet both refused to take that subsequent small step, to chance rocking the boat, to risk losing the closest thing to love they'd ever known. They were more than the best of friends; they were inseparable. In time, each knew most everything there was to know about the other. Together, they attended gatherings with their friends and co-workers, and spent many hours with each other in their small, lonely apartments, cloistered away from the remnants of the world outside their doors, beyond the compound walls.

Over time, a relaxed, symbiotic relationship formed without much thought going into it; she washed and folded his laundry, and often cooked for him. Just as readily, he unclogged drains and laid claim to any handyman work below the five-foot mark. Late in the chill of the winter evenings, he would slide from his wheelchair onto the sofa, where the two huddled close together, and said nothing. Not because there was nothing to say, rather because the everyday things one might ordinarily say didn't need to be said in the welcome silence. The few not-so-ordinary things that one might say were imagined in the warmth and close proximity of the other.

Deep inside, each of them worried that their relationship must certainly come with an expiration date. With that fear, unspoken but looming and ever-present, Jeff and Rose silently stored every day and night in the backs of their minds as personal treasures, something precious and heartening to cling to when the inevitable happened. She wondered if she was poisoning her present through her fears of the possible future.

He remembered Spud, a small dog he had as a boy, and often thought of how he kept a certain distance between himself and the sweet little mutt, though it followed him everywhere, and gave love so unconditionally. Years passed, and when the little mongrel died, Jeff was inconsolable and grieved for Spud, and for the many lost opportunities to give and get love.

As for Jeff and Rose, it spoke volumes about the world around them that, even with such reservations and vivid life-lessons so clear in their minds, they remained afraid to venture beyond the lines they'd drawn in the sand, too hesitant and uncertain to take even the smallest of chances.

Their relationship neither surged forward nor fell back. Year to year, it maintained the same safe, glacial pace.

# 7

*Operations Command Center*

Jeff looked at Rose. "You're serious. They okayed both of us going out at the same time? Not a chance."

She shrugged. "It wasn't that big a deal. I told them you need a new wheelchair in the worst way. You've ended up flat on your ass twice this week already, and it's time to take care of that. Besides, it's not like you can go out searching for it alone. It's dangerous out there."

"I can take care of myself, Rose."

She squinted at him, and said, "I can take care of myself, too, but I wouldn't go out there alone. That's suicide."

"But where? We've been through the local hospitals, and I bet we've gone through every old house and structure within fifty miles. There's not a chair left anywhere."

"Bangor. Portland, if we have to. You need that chair, Jeff, and we need supplies. The fortress here at Loring is safe, but if there's one problem we constantly have to contend with, it's getting supplied. And that's just normal supplies; never mind something as specialized as wheelchair parts. Sometimes we have to venture out a ways. It's worth the trade-off."

"So, there's a detail going out for supplies anyway?"

"Yes. Well, actually, we volunteered to *be* that detail."

"You mean, *you* volunteered *us* to be that detail."

"Isn't that what I just said?" she asked, with a grin.

*   *   *

Maine's Loring Air Force Base, decommissioned in 1994, was located in the remote northern end of Aroostook County, outside of a small town once nestled among some of the largest, richest potato fields in the world, a town which carried the picturesque name of Caribou.

In its day, the base was a small but bustling self-contained city, well suited for the northern clime and the remote location.

For miles and miles around it, fertile potato fields and forests of mixed hardwoods and conifers stretched as far as the eye could see, long since abandoned by all but the hardiest of souls; dyed-in-the-wool Mainers who took in stride all the hardships, frigid winters, and deep snows that accompanied Maine winters.

The rugged geography and weather patterns of the location alone made it the perfect choice for the fortress. But there was more. Spared by the ICBMs for the simple fact that the military decommissioned Loring twenty-one years before the nuclear exchange, its retired SAC runways were long enough to land any plane in the world. As one of the coldest areas in North America, this part of Maine was sparsely populated, due to the lack of heating oil and other amenities that civilized people preferred. Surviving in the far north was difficult. Most of those prone to robbing others and seeking targets of opportunity found it easier just to move south. Only a well-armed, disciplined, and determined force stood any chance of breaching the compound.

The cold itself preserved the massive concrete structures, which remained perfect for filling the many and varied requirements for constructing a time travel facility.

More than that, the military—or what remained of it—was able to locate the diagrams and specs for every building, every piece of city-support equipment, every pump in the fuel-storage facility; in short, every inch of infrastructure. The reorganized government reoccupied and began the resurrection of Loring in 2029. Subsequent to that, a fifty-foot concrete wall was poured all the way around it. The towering wall, backed by a huge earth berm, was designed to stop anybody who might have ideas of burrowing through unnoticed. To do so would take dynamite, bulldozers, backhoes, and a week of work.

Over the years, some tried, of course, though not many. There were, of course, a select few who had to make the attempt, desperate to get to the food, shelter, or heat beyond those walls. Those few became examples when they met with violent ends, learning too late that Apache attack helicopters from within the compound would flank attackers and put an end to their miserable existence within minutes.

Sadly, had they simply come to the gates as citizens in need, they would have been brought inside, given shelter until the end of the storm, cold snap, or blizzard, and sent on their way, with a full belly, rested, warmed up, and maybe with a little food.

The wall was patrolled every minute, day and night. Loring was dubbed "The Great Northeastern Fortress," upon its completion, when it became the military headquarters for the northeastern U.S. territories.

"What are we taking out there?" Jeff asked.

"Blackhawk."

"Yeah!" Jeff said enthusiastically, "I love flying. Are we taking a big crew?"

"We're taking six grunts along for a show of force. I told them to bring empty backpacks, because like it or not, they're helping me shop. You ready for this?"

"I was born ready," he said, unable to repress his excitement.

"Glad *you* were. If I didn't have to go outside of these compound walls, I'd stay tucked away inside."

"It's not that bad out there," he said, "I go up on the wall sometimes and look out from there. It's kind of peaceful. This far north, there's some pretty countryside out there."

The beauty of the land surrounding the fortress contradicted the ravaged world beyond those fields. Those potato fields provided them with a great deal of their sustenance, and that, combined with the military's ability to access food stores around the country, assured that nobody within the walls of the fortress went hungry.

But the earth was dying. In the eighty-three years since the bombs fell, the decline of the planet was evident anywhere one cared to look. The skies, darkened permanently by the effects of the bombs, offered more clouds, and less sunlight. The light that did reach them was not the warming, benevolent sunlight enjoyed by those several generations ago. With the ozone layer ripped away, the sun seared and burned. The bombs were only the first domino that fell. The water everywhere was ruined, and small towns battled one another over single wells that provided barely drinkable water.

The ravaged skies, radiation, and brutal sunlight affected plant life the world over. Plant life meant food sources, and year by year, those lessened as well. It was felt all the way up to the fortress, where the local potato farmers offered up their seed potatoes to the ground each year, only to harvest less than they did the prior year. The decimation of the plant life meant that the planet was dying a slow death, and if nothing else backed up such a diagnosis, the foul air carried enough weight to settle the argument. Without the trees—which were nearly gone, unable to survive the murky skies—the diminishing plant life struggled to regenerate the oxygen, and the air quality worsened every month.

Ironically, the successive generations of humans showed a higher resistance to the radiation, and every person that remained on the planet showed no ill effects from the high levels of radioactivity, levels that past generations would have found alarming. Whether they had evolved successfully and rapidly or not, one thing was certain. Without oxygen, humanity would not survive.

"It is beautiful, she said. "Of course, this far north, all we have out there are the die-hard potato farmers who make a living supplying us. We're going down to *the world* today," and her emphasis on *the world* left no doubt that she dreaded going there.

"I know, Rose. I grew up there," he said, and upon saying it, the carefree, cheerful demeanor disappeared. "I'll be watching your back every second." He lifted his jacket slightly so Rose could see the semiautomatic pistol holstered underneath.

One of the things Rose most loved about Jeff was his relaxed manner. But he came from those killing streets, and she knew that was what had put him in the wheelchair. Anytime she saw him like this, it saddened her. If she had things her way, he'd never have to step outside of his normal persona. When she saw him strapped-up like this; looking dead-serious, she found herself wondering which persona was Jeff, and which was the façade. Though not yet outside in the cold, a shiver ran through her body.

She pulled her jacket closer around her.

# 8

"Isn't this great?" Jeff shouted, leaning close to Rose to make his voice heard over the turbine noise of the Blackhawk helicopter. "I'd do this every day if I could." He watched the rugged terrain pass below them, his face glued to the window like an eager child.

"I'm glad you're happy," Rose replied, and gave him a thumbs-up and attempted a half-hearted smile that didn't at all match the look on her face. Though a hop machine was far more dangerous than a helicopter, she preferred it—indeed, preferred almost anything—to being dangled over the countryside in a Blackhawk.

Jeff turned to her. "I've given the Hop 206 crash a lot of thought. You're well-read on the Roswell crash, right?"

"Sure, everyone in Ops is. Why?"

"What do we know about it? We figured out a few years back that what people were calling UFO sightings were actually sightings of our hop machines in transit, or eluding their aircraft. I don't know why we didn't put some of this together sooner. It was right in front of us. We know there were rumors of a cover-up; that there were purportedly alien bodies in the crash. We now know that it was Hop 206, so the question has to be asked; how could they mistake humans

37

for aliens? They couldn't, could they? I've been racking my brains, trying to figure it out. Once I started analyzing the crash, it began to come together. First I took into account the velocity at which they crashed. Their restraints would have almost certainly failed under such stresses. The next step is what happens after the restraints fail."

"She said, "They'd be thrown … violently.""

He nodded in agreement. "They'd be thrown about violently, and once the inertial dampers failed, the cage wouldn't be strong enough to hold them. The cages are just passive restraints to prevent accidental contact with the fields. At that velocity, they'd be ejected."

Realizing the direction the conversation was taking, she put her hands to her mouth in anticipated horror. "Oh, no. Do I really want to hear this? I'm going to be sorry, aren't I?"

"Maybe. You know what happens when human anatomy meets with a generated singularity field. I'd say it's reasonable to assume that upon impact at that velocity, the crew members were ejected, passing through the field in an instant. Normally, living matter would simply disintegrate upon touching a field, but let's say—hypothetically—that they passed through it at such velocity that it didn't have sufficient time to disassemble their atoms."

"Agreed."

"We ran tests on such situations, and as I recall, the living matter that doesn't disintegrate during a high-speed pass through a field is altered profoundly, at the DNA level. Water content is forced from the tissues. Clothing, of course, turns to ash, as do hair and fingernails. The eyes would bloat with blood from the internal pressure, which would turn black at any exterior points as it desiccates with the rest of the body. With the exception of the skull, the bones would shrink to some degree. The brain couldn't desiccate that quickly through the skull. Due to the internal pressure, the skull would be unable to shrink, and then, of course, it would look too large for the body. They'd be nearly skeletal. But you know all this. It's textbook stuff, quantum singularity field science one-oh-one."

As the repressed picture formed fully in her mind, Rose's eyes opened wide, and she grimaced, recoiling in horror. "Ewww, Jeff, that's horrible! You're saying they never found aliens? The big heads, the huge black eyes, the skinny little limbs. That was our hop crew?"

"I'm afraid so. It had to be. And if the rumors were based on any truth at all, it gets worse," Jeff said. "I know I said that the crash would not be survivable. And I know that we were told that it can't happen, that nothing living can survive passing through a field. But we can't ignore the stories about the one that was found alive and walking around. If that was true, one of them somehow survived his pass through the field. I can't imagine how profound the physical damage would be. His higher brain functions would be devastated. He would be blind. It would be excruciating. I can hardly stand to think about it." It was his turn to grimace, and he shuddered violently, as though somebody walked over his grave.

Rose laid her hand on his shoulder. "Oh, God, Jeff," she said.

"Yeah," he said, disturbed by the knowledge that his assumptions were probably correct, or very close to it. He didn't know how to deal with the incredible grief he felt for their lost crewmen. Turning away, he looked out the window again, at a complete loss for words.

"Two minutes, Lieutenant," the copilot said.

The team leader, Lieutenant Morse, spoke up. "We're over Portland. Our plan is to land on the roof of Maine Medical Center." He pointed to the men. "Rockman, Griff, you two remain here with the pilot to guard the heli, and the rest of us will accompany Mr. Waldron and Ms. Rios inside, where we can hopefully locate some wheelchairs or wheelchair parts. If anything forces the Blackhawk to leave, SOP is that they will attempt to return every two hours. If they don't spot us here, they'll search the local rooftops for us, just in case we can't access this one for any reason."

"We're on approach. One minute. Be ready," the copilot counted down.

"Ahh, Lieutenant?" Jeff asked. "I'm not so good with climbing onto rooftops. How about if they have to come back, they search the local parking lots where the Blackhawk can fit?"

Morse had to agree with him. He turned to the pilot, who gave Jeff's suggestion the nod. "Okay, our alternate plan is changed. Local parking lots are our alternate evacuation points. Good call. Any questions? Then, let's move out!"

The Blackhawk touched down onto the helipad on the roof of the medical center, the door slid quickly back, and the soldiers exited. Seconds later, Jeff's chair was rolling on solid ground. Two men remained, guarding the Blackhawk, while the rest headed for the entrance.

"L.T., I can get *down* stairs, but I'm going to need help on the way back up," Jeff said.

The lieutenant gave a quick nod. "Understood. Shouldn't be a problem."

As Jeff deftly balanced his chair and lowered it step by step at a good pace, they started down the stairwell, where they met with no resistance. Anyone on the street who wanted to get to them faced a long climb to the top of the building. But there was always a chance that some unsavory types were already inside, in which case things could get dicey in a hurry. With a little luck, they would quickly be able to find some wheelchairs on the upper floors, and depart without incident.

It was a crisp winter day, and the sky was relatively clear, as their skies went. Upon exiting the stairwell to the tenth floor, they found a well-lit hallway, with light filtering in through the room windows. The rooms were empty, except for bits and pieces of equipment long since functional, and none of the doorframes had doors.

"This looks good," Morse said, "we're able to see what we're doing. Thatch, watch the stairwell, listen for anybody who might want to 'greet' us."

"Yes, sir," Thatcher said, and stepped back into the stairwell.

The rest of them advanced down the hall, Jeff taking one side, and Rose taking the other. Rose held her pistol at the ready, and Jeff kept his holster unsnapped, while he used his hands and arms to push his chair.

He whispered loud enough for the others to hear. "You know, empty buildings are enough to make most people uneasy. Waiting for someone to leap out and start shooting at you adds substantially to the level of tension, don't you agree?"

Rose grinned as she turned to him and mouthed the words, "Shut up!"

While Jeff checked out a room, Morse looked out the window. The medical center was located on the highest hill in the city. From the top floor, he could see across the seemingly dead city, out over the bay and inlets, and across the countryside. His gaze lowered to the empty streets below, and he saw nobody moving about. He didn't expect to. Streets had long ago ceased being paths for travel. To venture onto an open roadway or street exposed one to attack from any direction. His senses told him what the empty streets below did not. Invisible eyes followed his every move; watching him, probing him, looking for any weakness. His attitude wasn't fatalistic, but he wasn't frightened by it, either.

For better or worse, this post-apocalyptic world was his; he had never known anything else, and he accepted, with neither joy nor anguish, that in this world, a window with a view made you a target. He never stood too long in one place; an unconscious protective measure which time and his military experience had engrained into his movements. When Jeff moved on to the next room, the lieutenant backed away from the window and turned to rejoin the search.

He walked alongside Jeff as they searched. In low, restrained tones, he asked, "Where are you from, Mr. Waldron?"

"Call me Jeff. I'm from right here in Portland."

"Is this city a rough place?"

He nodded. "Rough enough. I belonged to a small community of families that lived in what used to be the library. We used to go out and about only in groups, so we had it better than most. I worked down at the port. Have you ever been to the Old Port area?"

"No," Morse responded. "I've heard about it, though. What did you do there?"

"I worked in security, mostly. Lots of turnover in the ranks there, so that was one of the few jobs a man could get. Mostly, our job was to keep people from the city out. But, on more than a few occasions, we'd be called upon to help them repel a pirate attack from the harbor. When I was eighteen, I started riding shotgun on the trucks making runs out into the countryside. Those were tough times to work security. If bandits wanted to stop a truck full of food and supplies, all it took was to shoot the driver. Then, they'd either convince the security detail to run away, or shoot them.

"I'd thought about it a million times. You know; what would I do if somebody sniped the driver; that sort of stuff. One day, riding shotgun in the back, my number came up. A single rifle shot rang out, and I felt the truck slowing down. You think you will be, but you're never really ready for it when it happens. I jumped up and ran toward the back, but never made it. They planned it perfectly. The truck rolled straight off the curve in the road, and flipped down the embankment. I was thrown about like a rag doll, pummeled and crushed by the shifting cargo. I woke to people stepping over me, carting the load away. My legs wouldn't move. I asked them for help, but they just ignored me and went about stripping the load."

"That wasn't your lucky day, was it?"

"In a way, I *was* lucky. Bullets were as precious then as they are now. They used one on the driver, but a man with a broken back was no threat to them. My gun was gone, along with the two dozen rounds I carried, and my knife and money. The last man came through to do a final sweep, and he surprised me with an act of kindness. On his way out, he reached into his pockets, pulled out two potatoes, and handed them to me.

"For three days I lay there, half-frozen in the wreckage. Some good folks found me, and pulled me out. They got me back home, but there was nothing anybody could do about my back. I've been in this chair ever since."

Morse asked, "What was a guy with your education doing working the docks, anyway?"

"I only had a basic education then. After my injury, I spent several years inside, and since we lived in the old library, the next step was reading the books, or more precisely, whatever books were left. One of the library's residents, our neighbor, Mr. Salls, had been my teacher when I was younger, and he worked with me to find what possibilities there were for me. Turned out, I had a knack for the sciences, and one day my former boss from the port mentioned me to a military officer. They came to see me, and offered to complete my formal education. I accepted, and I've been working with them ever since. Here I am," he said, opening his arms.

"Well, it was lucky for us," the lieutenant said.

"Speak for yourself," Rose said.

"Will you look at that," Jeff said with surprise, pointing to a pile of rubbish. Several wheelchairs protruded from the pile, mostly buried, but just enough remained visible for a pair of keen eyes to spot.

Rose holstered her weapon and climbed into the pile with two of the men, and minutes later, the extracted chairs were laid in front of Jeff for inspection. "Nice. There's enough here to make a real nice chair, with some spare parts to boot," he said, delighted at the find.

"Take the wheelchairs up to our ride," the lieutenant said to two of the men with him.

Once the men reported from the Blackhawk that the wheelchairs were secure, he said, "Looks like we're finished here. Anything else? Okay. We should make tracks. Let's get back to the—"

Shots rang out from behind, and since they now faced the stairwell, they were momentarily unprotected from that direction. Lieutenant Morse wheeled and raised his weapon toward the shooters. Just then, two bullets impacted him. He went down hard, with a grunt. The remaining soldier dove to the ground behind an old gurney, and returned fire while he called for backup.

Though many years had passed since he'd lived in the remnants of this city, Jeff's survival instincts remained strong. Reversing his chair into Rose, he simultaneously threw his head back into her and bumped her hard, forcing her back through a doorway into a room, out of the path of the gunfire. Then he pushed forward again, across the hall. Like angry hornets, bullets whizzed past him in both directions.

In the frenzied crossfire, he should have been hit, but somehow managed to launch himself from his chair and roll forward through the doorway in front of him, coming to rest with his legs inside the room, and his head in the doorway. Rather than complete his retreat inside, he pulled himself back out, far enough to reach the felled lieutenant, who he could see was bleeding badly. He saw Rose across the hall, pinned down by the fire and looking on helplessly and in horror while he scrambled to reach the man in time.

Reaching inside his vest, he pulled out his pistol with one hand and sprayed as many bullets as he could toward the other end of the hallway. All he needed was a few precious seconds to reach out, locate, and grab the straps on the back of Morse's flak vest with the other hand. Thatch took advantage of the opening, and made his way down the hall toward them from the stairwell, returning fire as he approached.

With Thatch keeping them busy, and his own weapon now empty, Jeff dropped the pistol and grabbed the door frame for leverage. Everything he needed to do, he had only his arms to do it with. He yanked, pulled and rolled, struggling with all his strength until both he and the lieutenant were safe—at least for the moment—within the walls of the room. He looked across at Rose, and gave her the thumbs-up signal to indicate that he was okay. Now recovered from the initial shock, she returned fire as she could from her doorway, and gamely gave the thumbs-up gesture, accompanied by a look of barely restrained terror.

Thatch and Miller moved past them, toward the gunfire into two opposite rooms, where they were able to defend the hallway from the encroachers with crossing fire. The Blackhawk could be heard taking off a moment later. But it didn't leave. The *fwop-fwop-fwop* of its heavy blades grew more intense as the sound grew louder and closer, until it seemed they could feel each beat of each blade inside their heads.

Griff and two more soldiers stormed down the stairwell. One stayed to hold the stairwell and the other two pounded toward them up the corridor, braving the hail of fire, reporting back to the Blackhawk as they ran.

Bursting into the rooms occupied by Rose, Jeff, and the

lieutenant, they yelled, "Stay down!" and dove protectively on top of them. It was then that time seemed to slow down, and Jeff saw and heard everything in a sort of slow-motion. From farther down the hall came the sounds of glass breaking, bullets ricocheting, and muffled screams.

Based on the slow, steady pulse of the repeating gun, Jeff surmised that Rockman, the Blackhawk's door gunner, had opened up his 50-caliber gun on the attackers, and knew the hospital's cinder-block walls would offer them little protection. The machine gun paused and the Blackhawk backed away from the building.

Small arms fire erupted once again from the same location down the hall.

The grunt on top of him yelled something, but the words were slow and dragged out. His gestures seemed to indicate that he wanted Jeff and the lieutenant to stay down, which suited them both just fine.

Lucky enough to survive the machine gun, several attackers down the hall had chosen not to retreat and fight another day, and had instead elected to continue the fight against the Blackhawk. It was a poor choice, and one they would not live to regret. Down the hallway, there came a deafening roar, and the floor below the away team heaved, tossing them all a few inches into the air. Fire consumed the air around them, while debris flew everywhere, followed by billowing clouds of smoke and dust. He felt the increasing weight as they were literally buried in concrete, glass, and debris.

The gunfire stopped altogether, although it was doubtful that they could have heard it through the ringing in their ears. Blasts of cold wind entered the building, pushed by the thumping blades of the Blackhawk. The wind swirled through the hallway, pushing much of the dense, acrid clouds of dust and smoke from the air around them.

As the air cleared, they heard and felt the ominous pounding of the Blackhawk's rotors as it faded back from its attack position and turned to patrol the rest of the building's exterior; no longer tentative, now transformed, fully manifested as a menacing presence, *daring* other interlopers to try the same again.

Moments later, many hands scooped up Lieutenant Morse, and then Jeff, who, though dazed, saw that Rose was ambulatory and walking ahead with Thatch and Miller. As they entered the hallway, his eye fell upon some twisted, compressed bits of broken steel and tubing, which he recognized as the remnants of his trusty old chair. Feeling the cold wind, he looked back down the hall. The hallway now ended just forty feet from them, and didn't begin again until eighty feet away, the result of the air-to-ground missile fired from the Blackhawk.

It was time to leave. Wrapping Jeff's arms over the shoulders of a man on either side of him, the soldiers made short work of evacuating him and the others to the roof, where the Blackhawk landed briefly.

Moments later, high above the trees, they moved quickly to the north.

Some minutes later, when her breathing and crazy-fast heartbeat slowed, Rose found herself hugging Jeff tightly. It occurred to her that this was the first time she'd ever been delighted to be inside of a helicopter, safe and sound. An ironic thought worked its way forward into her conscious mind. *Perspective really is everything, isn't it?*

The lieutenant sat upright and alert, as Griff worked to staunch the blood flow from his wounded arm.

Rockman continued to man the door gun and scan the area for a short time, but finally he closed the hatch and allowed himself to relax. "L.T., how bad is it?" he asked.

Morse shrugged it off. "One went through my arm. The other one hit me in the vest, knocked the wind out of me. I'll be fine."

"If I can get this leak in your oil pan stopped, maybe you'll make it," Griff said, concentrating on the wound.

"You'll get it, Griff," Morse said. "Keep at it. That's an order."

"Yes, sir," the medic said, and wrapped the bandage tight enough to make Morse wince.

The officer grimaced, gave Griff a dirty look, and then grinned. He turned to Jeff and said, "I didn't get a chance to thank you for pulling me out of that shooting gallery back there. That was a brave thing you did."

Jeff waved it off. "You'd have done the same for me."

The lieutenant looked at the others, and then back at him with an amused look, and said, "Wanna bet? They were *shooting* at us in there!" Laughter erupted from the whole group. Jeff and the L.T. knew that any man in the group would do the same for any other man in their group, but the same was not expected of him.

The men knew what kind of a man it took, the level of valor required to maintain the cool to pull the lieutenant from that hallway under live fire.

# 9

"There appear to be three bodies in the wreckage," Major Marcel said to Mack Brazel and Sheriff Wilcox, "at least two of them were underneath it, as though they were ejected before it came to rest against the outcropping. No telling how badly they were thrown about during a crash like that."

"Is this one of your aircraft?" Wilcox asked the major.

"No. I don't see anything I recognize as ours. And I sure as hell don't know what those bodies are in the wreckage. I've never seen anything like them."

A shout echoed from the far side of the rock outcropping, followed by several more. A soldier ran around the outcropping and toward them.

"Major! Some of the men just found something. You've got to see this," he said, and ran back in the direction from which he'd come.

"You two. Come with me," Marcel called out, to the two men working the wreckage with safety gear, which in 1947 consisted of a pair of goggles, a gas mask, and a pair of heavy leather gloves. For that time, it showed how seriously they regarded the situation.

Standard safety gear used in the Manhattan Project's recent nuclear tests consisted of a pair of goggles. Period.

Mack and Wilcox followed the major around the far end of the rock, and nearly ran into him from behind when he stopped short. His men had surrounded a small being. It stood upright, no taller than four feet two inches, with hands raised defensively in front of it, and it appeared to be agitated, moving about as though unaware of the soldiers around it and walking alongside it, as it staggered and tripped over rocks. It emitted a keening sound, as though it were frightened, confused, or in pain. Perhaps all three.

"We found it crouched over against those rocks, Major," one of the men said, "I touched it, and it got up and started moving around just like this. There may be something wrong with it. It doesn't seem to be able to see or hear us."

The major rolled his eyes upward. "You—you *touched* it? Why do we even bother setting protocols, when you men think it's okay to *touch* everything you see?"

To the two men in the safety gear, he said, "You two. Take hold of its arms, and let's take it back to base with us. Easy. Be careful with it."

The men stepped forward and gently took the small being by its arms. For a second or two, it struggled to escape their grasp, but then calmed, and a second later, crumpled. The only thing holding it upright was the two men. The men briefly discussed it, and decided it would work best if they carried it. They lifted it gently, and held it between them. It weighed so little that it required almost no effort. The keening faded to a soft groan, and a few seconds later, the small being stopped making noise altogether.

"Is he still breathing?" the major asked.

The men stopped and studied the creature's breathing, and one said, "I don't know if it's a he or a she, but yes, sir, it's still breathing, though the respirations are shallow. It seems to be unconscious. I'm afraid it's in pretty bad shape, sir, though I couldn't say for sure."

Marcel leaned forward and looked briefly at the inert being, stepped back, and said, "I'd have to agree with your assessment,

Sergeant. Go on. Get it back to base, and let's see if anything can be done for it. Let's move."

He turned back toward the vehicles, and found Mack Brazel and Sheriff Wilcox standing there, both with stunned looks on their faces.

"Major, is that what we think it is?" Wilcox asked.

Marcel said, "Gentlemen, I think it's safe to say that we have a flying saucer crash here. We have proof here of something about which people have only speculated."

*   *   *

Later, back on base, Marcel held up a paper. "Lieutenant Haut, here are the details for the press release."

Haut picked up the paper and studied it, then looked at the major. "Sir? You're going public with this?"

Marcel said, "Not me. Orders from Colonel Blanchard. We're only reporting the crash and the wreckage. We're not acknowledging the occupants yet. We have the first real proof that there's something more out there. Somebody besides us. He feels people should know about it. We're the first to have proof. That's a real feather in our cap. Besides, there were too many people involved in this, too many to keep it a secret. This way, we can control the release of information. Make sure you get that into town right away, and get it on the wires." He looked at Haut. "You've seen them, what do you think?"

"I've never seen anything like it. Not on this planet."

"Yeah? How many planets have you been on?"

Haut laughed. "Good point," he said, holding up the paper. "I'll get on this release," and left the major's office.

Marcel, normally tight-lipped about everything that happened around the base, was excited. The Manhattan Project was hush-hush, and though the public knew of its existence, no information related to Manhattan was allowed to leak from the base. But they were under no such constraints regarding UFOs. In fact, there *was* no precedent for such an event here on this base, or any other base, for that matter.

Beyond the Manhattan Project, they had no orders related to anything outside of their military aircraft and prototypes.

Certainly, none for UFOs.

# 10

Jeff continued to track the movements of the Roswell wreckage in whatever ways he could, which meant he spent a lot of his time online, pretending to be John Titor.

"How's that new wheelchair?" Rose asked, bringing him a drink, and sipping her tea.

"Those chairs we found made one nice chair. I'm feeling pretty stylish."

"I'm glad to hear that," she said. "Anything new going on here?"

"I've been making a few dire predictions, feeding the fire with some of that era's elements. Last week, I predicted that in 2012, the Spanish Flu would break out again, and spread worldwide, unchecked for a time. I've got a number of them sending me Personal Messages, some are calling me crackpot, some actually believe it, and some are just asking a lot of questions. There are a few who want to help me, and with those I've casually brought up the Roswell incident. Imagine my surprise when one of them volunteered that he has first-hand knowledge of the Roswell incident. Not only that, but he says he knows quite a bit about what was done with the wreckage. He says he knows what happened with the bodies as well."

"Really? Okay, I'm listening," Rose said, sitting down. "Shoot."

"Well, you know about Area 51, right? Sure, everybody does. But have you ever heard of Warehouse 15? Apparently, it's in the Black Hills, underneath Mt. Rushmore. According to him, Mt. Rushmore was built simply to create a cover for the road system they created for Warehouse 15. Beyond that, Rushmore provided a place to easily dispose of the excavated rock in plain sight, without moving it long distances. After Rushmore carving crews left for the weekends, the cavern excavators ran conveyor belt feeders up and over the top, to dispose of the rock they'd excavated. The feeders were routed through something called the Hall of Records; an unfinished, discontinued part of the monument. They said the word was that the monument project was shut down due to loss of funding, but that wasn't the reason. They'd finished creating the cavern for Warehouse 15, and the monument was complete enough by then. According to my guy, if anybody actually took the time to accurately survey the rock at the base of the monument, they'd find the volume of rock there to be exponentially more than the amount required to sculpt the four presidents' faces."

Rose felt her eyes begin to glaze over, and held up her hand to stop him. "As mesmerizing as this fact session is, I still have to ask; what does it have to do with our job here?"

"The wreckage was not taken directly to Area 51. It started out at Wright Army Air Field in a secure building, until they secured Area 51, when it was moved there. Then, at some point, it was secretly moved to Warehouse 15, where they could work on it without the prying eyes of the public scrutinizing their every move."

She asked, "How does he claim to have come by so much sensitive information?"

"He says he was a warrant officer involved with it from the start and assigned to the project. His father was involved in the Warehouse 15 project when he was very young, so our man learned about keeping government secrets long before he ever entered the military. He's promising more information will be forthcoming."

Rose looked puzzled. "From everything I've ever read, an

inordinate amount of secrecy surrounded the Roswell crash. Why would he volunteer this information?"

"He was sworn to secrecy with the threat of dire repercussions, but that was at the time of the Roswell crash. Fifty-three years have passed at the time we're communicating with him. At about eighty years old, it happened so long ago for him that I don't suppose he fears much from anybody. He's lived a long time, so it's a pretty good bet that after years of living under such threats, dying doesn't hold the same fear for him."

# 11

The pounding at the door grew louder. Whoever it was, they weren't going away.

"Hold your horses, I'm coming!" the man inside yelled, reluctantly leaving the comfort of his armchair to do something about the incessant noise. "Now, what the hell is so God-damned important—" he started to yell as he opened the door.

A large, uniformed man filled the doorframe, flanked by four soldiers armed with rifles. The man addressed him. "Mr. George Dunbrook?"

"Uh, Yes? What do you want? Why do you have guns?"

"Mr. Dunbrook, do you own a 1946 Ford truck? Maroon?"

"Yes, I do."

"You'll need to come with us, sir."

"Why do you want to know about my truck?"

"Sir, we already have your truck. We'll need you to—"

"The *hell* you do. My truck is right out back. Come on, I'll show you."

He showed them through the house and out the back door. There, parked in his back yard, was a new maroon Ford pickup truck,

57

obviously well cared for, sparkling clean and polished to a bright shine.

"You mean *this* truck?" he asked.

One of the men opened the engine cover and checked the numbers of the truck, then rechecked them. Looking confused, he directed another one of the men to climb underneath the bed and read out more numbers. As he listened, he wrote the numbers. Comparing them, his eyebrows rose, and looking over his sunglasses, he turned to his superior, who stood on the rear porch with Mr. Dunbrook. "The numbers check out, sir. *All* of them. Even the license plates match."

\*    \*    \*

*Eighth Air Force Headquarters*
*Forth Worth Army Air Field*
*July 8ᵗʰ, 1947*

Roger A. Ramey, Commanding General of the Eighth Air Force, surveyed the wreckage arrayed across the hangar floor before him. Having ordered the wreckage to be brought to the Fort Worth Army Air Field, it was his responsibility to determine just what they had there. Once the autopsies were completed, the 'occupants' would follow. One specimen remained alive, and the doctors there in Fort Worth were working hard to keep it alive. Verbal reports thus far indicated they were losing the battle.

"Christ, what a mess," he said, "Report, Captain. Has the owner of the truck been found yet?"

The captain said, "Yes—and no, sir. We're having trouble identifying where it really came from. According to the plates and the factory identification numbers, it's from Arizona and belongs to a man there, a Mr., uh …" he consulted his notes. "Dunbrook, George Dunbrook. At first glance, *he* appears to be the owner of the truck. He owns a truck that's the same year, same color, the same manufacturer's numbers and plate numbers. But there's a problem. He *has* the exact same make, model, and color truck with those same correct numbers, and it's sitting right there in his yard. The local sheriff brought our people there, and they just confirmed it.

"There appears to be no tampering with any of the numbers on the truck in our possession. We consulted the factory, and they appear to be genuine. The crew we sent to Arizona has done the same. All the numbers on *that* truck appear to be genuine as well. The factory confirmed all of our numbers, on all the components. Twice. It's like the same truck was built twice, right down to the numbers, and the Ford factory says that just can't happen. At least, not without them knowing all about it. And in anticipation of your orders, I've taken the liberty of dispatching a detail and truck to Arizona to pick up Mr. Dunbrook's truck."

"Yeah, that's fine. We need to get to the bottom of this. What's the rest of this?"

"The silver-colored metal pieces appear to be some sort of alloy, but it's so broken-up, we can't determine how it was configured. As near as we can determine, the girders formed some sort of lightweight, interlocked frame assembly, so they could fold up, or bend. Maybe they were part of a cage of some sort. But it's a real mess. No telling how long it will take to sort out."

"I expect you to sort it out, Captain, and soon."

"Yes, sir. Understood."

A company clerk approached the general, out of breath, and handed him some papers, with a brief explanation. After reading them, the general handed them back to the clerk and said, "Get Warrant Officer Newton. I want him in my office in ten minutes."

After the clerk ran off, Ramey said to the captain, "This whole situation is starting to fall apart, Captain. As of right now, nobody is to have access without top-level clearance, is that clear?"

"Clear as a bell, General. I'll seal this place up airtight."

"Christ," Ramey said to nobody in particular, shaking his head as he hurried off.

*   *   *

"Newton. You're aware of what's going on around here?"

"Yes, sir. Painfully aware. The colonel's been in touch with Washington, and he filled me in. They're sending somebody down to address the situation. There's a suit waiting outside, civilian—plainclothes. I think it might be him."

"That's just who it is. Before he comes in, can you give me some sort of indication as to where we are, and what's expected? The short version, of course."

"Yes, sir. The brass in Washington has expressed concerns over individuals acting without orders and releasing information to the public without their authorization. One of their own people was dispatched to contain the situation, to make it go away—whatever that means. They don't want their names brought into this, whatever it takes. It seems that, since all of the people involved are under your command, sir, the colonel feels it's *our* heads that should be offered up for the chopping block, and that it falls upon *you* to handle this matter as expeditiously as possible. I probably don't need to say this, but he stressed that any other outcome is unacceptable."

"Jesus. I'm being handed my own personal hornet's nest, and they already shook it," he muttered. "Very well. Show their man in."

The man who walked through the door was as neat as a pin, of medium height and build, with unremarkable features. Ramey's first impression of the man was that he almost appeared to be purposely forgettable in nearly every detail. Probably with good reason.

The man extended his hand. "General Ramey. I'm William Wren. I assume you have some idea why I'm here."

"Yes, Mr. Wren, I do. Washington sent you here to tell me they want the cat put back in the bag. How am I doing so far?"

"You have a succinct way with words, General, a knack for summing things up."

"Since you enjoyed that so much, I have another one for you. What's done is done. It's already in the news, for Christ's sake, everybody's talking about it. We can't just pretend it never happened.

How do you expect to undo something of this magnitude?"

"Washington feels the best way to proceed is to show a unified front, and to claim a mistake was made. We need to come up with a plausible story the public will accept, and convince some people to change their position—to adopt the story we give, and to say they were wrong, or that they simply didn't know what they were looking at. Give them a reasonable, face-saving way out. Beyond that, steps should be taken to discredit or silence those who won't go along."

"What do you mean, '*silence*'?"

Wren adjusted his tie, cleared his throat, and said, "Please understand, General, this isn't my idea. This comes straight from the Pentagon, and I'm just the messenger. They want you to contain the situation, whatever it takes. And they want you to do it quickly. They sent me to help with that."

"We're talking about a substantial number of civilians here. I can't just tell them what they saw, and expect them to just follow along."

"But you can discredit them, even if you have to invent evidence."

Ramey was astounded. "You're talking to a general here. You can't possibly expect me to go along with inventing evidence and lying to the public."

Wren looked uncomfortable, but to his credit, he did not shift in his seat. "General, need I remind you that you serve at the pleasure of the President of these United States, as a senior member of one branch of his military forces? Military secrets are military secrets, and you are expected to protect them using whatever measures the situation may require, even if those measures are, shall we say, extraordinary."

And with that statement, Wren revealed beyond any shadow of a doubt that he was much more than just the messenger, far more than a disinterested workaday bureaucrat, and that he was acting under iron-clad orders issued by those who breathed the thin air at the top—orders which Ramey sensed he was more than capable of carrying out.

He tempered his response accordingly, and though he was angry, he said, "I guess I can live with it, but I don't have to like it. I don't want anybody hurt. Am I being perfectly clear, Mr. Wren?"

"Yes, General, but so is Washington. There's a lot riding on this—like the careers of certain individuals on this base—and we don't have the luxury of time to deal with this."

Ramey ignored the veiled threat, and countered by highlighting the obvious complexity of the situation. "Well, then, Mr. Wren, since you're so adamant about this, what course of action do you suggest we follow with those who won't say they didn't see what they're sure they saw?"

Wren didn't hesitate either. "Families. Loved ones. Careers. Ninety-nine percent of those people feel their homes and the safety of their loved ones is more important than the truth. We'll just have to remind them of that."

The general leaned forward, his face flushed. "We're going to *threaten them*? Is *that* what you're telling me?" His volume escalated as he went on. "We're going to threaten and hold hostage the lives of the very people we're sworn to *protect*? Our reason for being here? The people the president charges me with protecting, even if it takes my own life to do so? That's your *plan*? God *DAMN* it!" he bellowed, snatching up the heavy ashtray he'd kept on his desk for twenty years, heaving it against the wall with such force that it smashed into a dozen pieces.

Wren—or more precisely, the people who sent Wren from Washington—had placed the general squarely in the hot seat. Their orders were to be carried out, and the general's ass would be the one on the line if—and very likely *when*—it all hit the fan. Furious, he stood, and paced around the office, stomping, swearing under his breath, and working off angry energy that permeated every pore of his body. A full minute passed before he felt calm enough to return to his desk.

Lowering himself slowly into his seat, his eyes locked on the silent Wren, who, from the moment the large ashtray sailed past his head, wisely chose to say nothing and remain as unobtrusive and un-target-like as possible.

"Son-of-a-*BITCH!*" Ramey sputtered. "The reason I'm so angry, Mr. Wren, is because *you* people are putting me in an impossible position. My moral values leave me no choice but to resign my commission."

He continued to look straight at Wren with a stare that would wilt most men. "But that won't stop *them,* will it? Once I stepped aside, there would be nothing between these innocent civilians and your people but a bunch of career-oriented cutthroats who don't know any better than to take their orders literally, who will implement blanket orders to silence noncompliance at all costs. Hell, I'd just end up as one more they'd have to silence, wouldn't I? Well, that's not going to happen. My job is to protect America, and Americans, from all enemies, foreign and domestic. I won't say out loud which of those I believe *you* to be, but believe you me, I am *not* stepping aside."

He rose, and looked down upon the seated Wren from above. "Here's what is going to happen, and you'd better write this down, because I mean every word. We have no choice but to proceed with this, and I know that people are going to be threatened. I know that people are going to be coerced. Now, you know *this,* and you'd better make damn sure your people know this too. If anyone is killed or injured, I promise you there *will* be a full investigation. There will be repercussions. I *will* find out who is responsible, and I *will* end their career, whatever it takes, no matter how long it takes."

He turned away, and gazed out the window, and said, "Go ahead, use my name to contain the situation. But you make *damn* sure that every military individual you involve knows that they are sworn first to protect the citizens of this country, and never more so than now. Don't let me hear otherwise."

"But, General—"

"Find a way, Mr. Wren. Dismissed."

"But, General, there are—"

Ramey wheeled and slammed both hands down on the desk, and snarled, *"DISMISSED!"*

Wren left the office in a hurry, with his feathers good and ruffled, which Ramey thought was probably not an easy thing to do. At least he could derive that small amount of satisfaction from the conversation with the objectionable man.

He called out, "Mr. Newton, did you hear any of that?"

Newton came in to the office. "Yes, sir. All of it."

"Good. With my apologies in advance for this, I'd like you to work with that weasel, help him come up with some sort of cover story for us to release to the news. If you can, try and make it something that will mitigate the amount of damage he and his people will cause."

"I had a thought about that already, General. I've had occasion to work around some of those weather balloons that were set up with radar and listening gear. It's a fairly sizable setup, and civilians have found them before. I could go on record identifying it as one of those. The color of the gear is right, more or less, close enough to match what we found."

"You think it would provide a plausible story?"

"As plausible as any, General. So many people are involved right now, and so much water is under the bridge; I don't know if we'll be successful. No story is going to stand up to any real scrutiny. I think this as close as we'll be able to come to a truly plausible explanation, considering the fact that we've been given zero time to come up with anything else."

"It sounds pretty good to me. Okay. If anybody asks, you've become our 'expert.' Do me one favor, stick with this character as much as you can as long as he's around, and keep an eye on him for me, will you? I want somebody from our camp to have eyes on this situation whenever possible, for as long as possible. You'll report directly to me. I'll notify the colonel. See him, and he'll give you what you need. Dismissed."

Newton walked away, and with a sense of growing dread, he recalled a line he'd read long ago in high school. It was Shakespeare, or maybe Sherlock Holmes. Maybe both.

*The game is afoot...*

# 12

"Mr. Waldron, report. Re-entry status?"

"I've got them sir, good telemetry. Window is open and we're still receiving strong signal. They're already vectoring for the Dakotas, on-time and on-track. But the window is beginning to close, and we've got no maneuv— wait, here it is. Maneuvering telemetry's coming through. They're in good shape, and manually in control of the hop, sir. Ahh ... that's it. The window's closed."

The portal generated by the hop machine as it traveled to its intended point of arrival provided a momentary window, enabling the Ops Center to receive telemetry. The dwindling portal couldn't accommodate a second vehicle, but, for a brief period, it could maintain enough integrity to transmit the data for Ops to know where and when the hop arrived.

He turned to Colonel Clayton, and said, "Textbook mission so far, sir."

Clayton said, "That's what I like to hear. Now, we'll have to wait and see what they find when they get there. There's no telling if the facility under the mountain is still intact. Hopefully, they can find

65

it."

Jeff said, "We have no definitive proof there even is a facility there, though our satellite file photos do show the volume of the rock pile at the base of the mountain to be millions of cubic yards more than the carving of Mount Rushmore would have produced. All of that excavated rock had to come from somewhere."

From her station next to Jeff's, Rose asked, "Do you believe your source?"

"I've been over everything he's told me. I think he's being honest. He has no reason to lie at his age—assuming, of course, that he *is* that age."

\* \* \*

Rick Savage and his hop crew surveyed the Black Hills below them. As they neared their target area, they looked with a sense of loss and some sadness as the first rays of the sun played across the time-ravaged stone faces of the four American presidents who gazed out and over the land from the mountain above them—four symbols of what was once the most peace-loving country in the world, and the people who treasured that peace. In the shadow of something once so majestic and meaningful, one could not help but wonder what could have transpired to take it all away.

"Is that what I think it is?" one of the men asked, pointing to something on the ground below them. A large, white tube seemed to have driven straight off a curve in the road. Uprooted trees marked its path where it had carved its way into the woods.

Savage said, "It is, if you think it's an airliner. They probably tried to land on that highway after the bombs went off. There are thousands of them dotting the countryside. Any within thirty to fifty miles of a detonation lost all power from the EMPs, and dove straight in. Those were the lucky ones. Others were unaffected or only lost partial power, and looked for emergency runways to land on. The lucky ones crashed. Those who landed safely were left out in the open, unprotected, with bombs detonated all around them, and dense radioactive fallout. Nowhere to go, nobody to rescue them. Those poor sons of bitches, they died slow, and hard. I think we're here. Land over there. See that spot?"

After the hop set down, they checked their charts, while the men stomped their feet on the ground, and rubbed their hands briskly together in the frigid morning air.

"We aced the landing, sir. This is the main parking lot of the tourism facility for Rushmore."

Savage looked at the map. "Excellent. We'll follow the main road north and west out of here, until we reach the rear of the monument. We should find the facility there. Waldron's contact told us what to look for, and he told him twenty-seven years before the time we're occupying right now. After that, the facility should have been active for fifteen years, until the nuclear exchange."

"Why didn't we come here in our time, sir?"

"Good question. When the satellite photos were taken in 2098, they showed a lot of changes. It appears that a large section of the mountain collapsed behind the monument, as well as part of the monument. Washington's face is gone. The point is; the cavern that houses the facility we're searching for collapsed between this time and ours, partially, at least. In this time, the facility was active fairly recently—just twelve years ago—and theoretically still in good shape—so the odds are better that we'll be able to get in and find what we're searching for. We'll need lights, if this place is as big as they say. The biggest potential benefit of this time period is that, should we find functional generators, the fuel may still be good."

Back on the hop machine, they fired up the generators. A moment later, a bubble encased them, comprised of the fields generated by the active time machine. If they chose, they could now enter coordinates for another time. But since they had just arrived in this time, their needs were different. Since they were quite alone, they could utilize the hop machine for 'ground' transportation. Had it been warm, they could have lowered the shields to allow air flow for local forays. Or, if for some reason they needed to work in a populated area, they could land, retract the framework into the bed of the truck, climb into the cab, and drive the truck away.

In the air, hop machines could travel the globe at speeds that boggled the mind. They could be in Tokyo in twenty minutes. A hop machine was much more than just a time travel device. Its speed and maneuverability far surpassed anything else man had ever created. If, for some reason, they found themselves in the vicinity of aircraft, or a military fighter challenged them, the hop pilot could simply allow the machine to auto-evade, and the machine would instantly calculate and execute the necessary maneuvers, taking them away from the danger at incredible speeds. Astounded aircraft pilots were treated to spectacular displays of maneuverability; incredible twists, impossible right-angle turns, and speeds reaching thousands of miles per hour within a few seconds. Pilots witnessing this phenomenon were invariably left far behind, incapable of achieving, or even approaching, such speeds. UFO reports from all over the world chronicled hundreds of such encounters during the second half of the twentieth century.

In the quiet, crisp, South Dakota countryside of 2027, it was doubtful that Captain Rick Savage and his people would meet any living souls, with or without aircraft. The need for evasion on this mission was minimal; unlikely, in fact.

Guiding the hop machine north over the roadway a hundred feet below them, they searched the roadsides, seeking the rock formations their informant had described. They passed the monument on their right, and a moment later, they spotted the rock formations just as described. They set down in a long, protected, carved-out area, behind the formations that ran alongside the road, and found the area was visually isolated from the main road. The formation acted as a secret entrance gate, perfectly camouflaged; indistinguishable in color and texture from the rock surrounding it.

The area where they set down was as long as a football field, and half as wide. A fleet of tractor-trailers could be parked there with room to spare, with no fear of being spotted from the road. The rock overhang carved into the mountainside offered some protection from satellites which might pass overhead. They'd made their way successfully past the gates, but, from all appearances, to no avail. Every surface in sight was solid rock.

Savage looked around, and asked, "Anybody see a way in?"

Parsons said, "Judging from the gates out there, I'd say we should look for a camouflaged entrance. This was a roadway. I'm going to follow it to that rock wall and look for some sort of an entrance device."

Savage waved the others on. "Go with him; see what you can find."

The men scrutinized the wall ahead. It didn't take long. "Captain, you might want to see this," Parsons called out, and popped what appeared to be a panel from its wall-mount.

Closer inspection confirmed it to be the control panel they sought, but they had a problem or two yet to overcome. Like the massive, nearly invisible doors themselves, the control panel blended perfectly with the surrounding rock. Though various buttons could be identified, there were no markings to indicate what controlled what, nor did the exposed wires give anything away. And of course, even if they could have identified them, there was no power to the panel, nor had there been for over ten years.

"Try and figure out the panel and determine what kind of power you need. I'm going to fire up a single generator on the hop and run a cable from the converter," Savage said. "Does the main power for the doors run through this?"

Parsons nodded, "I think actuation wires for a heavier relay run through here, Captain. Right now, we need to actuate the main lock. Once that's unlocked, I think we can manually move the doors enough to get in."

"What are the doors made of?"

Parsons shrugged and said, "We'll know once we get them open, but the exteriors seem to be made from the original rock face. The façade is remarkable. Just try and find the seams. The craftsmanship that went into this wall alone is amazing. I can't even imagine the cost that went into building it."

"I get the feeling that cost wasn't an issue here."

Twenty minutes later, after some experimentation, the bolts in the doorway retracted with a heavy *thump*. The massive doors, unlocked, shifted just enough to allow them to gain a handhold and pull. With some grunting, shoving, and some swearing, they opened the doors enough to enter. Grabbing their headlamps and backpacks from the hop, they walked into the dark entrance chamber.

Across the wall, twenty-five feet above them, the number 15 stood alone, painted in letters eight feet tall. "Warehouse Fifteen," Savage said, "just like the man said. If he's true to his word—and so far, he's been spot-on—we'll find the Hop 206 wreckage stored in here. Let's go."

Eschewing this second massive set of doors, they instead chose the standard entry door off to the side. They made short work of it with the judicious application of their crowbar, and the passage opened into a pitch-black, massive cavern, two, maybe three times the size of the largest aircraft hangar at Loring. The light from their flashlights dissipated in the distance, without illuminating anything.

One of the men said, "He wasn't kidding when he said this place was big. It's huge. This'll take days."

Parsons said, "Captain, there must be an office around here somewhere. If we can find a diagram of the place, it should cut down our search time looking for the generator room and the restricted area."

Savage nodded. "Good idea. Go ahead with that. I'll take Thibodeau and we'll search for a generator. If you see a generator room on the diagram, let me know. The rest of you; let's make getting lights on in here a priority."

Thibodeau spoke up, "If they used any sense at all putting this place together, the generators shouldn't be too far in, probably down this wall here, along the front—I'm assuming this *is* the front—and I can't even be sure of *that* until we get some lights on."

Savage said, "Lead on, Thib." For lack of any better direction, they followed Thibodeau's hunch, and five minutes later, they found a large generator room, as long as a football field, and just as wide. As big as a large truck, the main generator was by far the largest. Moving across the room, the generators grew smaller as they progressed. Against the wall, Thibodeau poked around until he found a long rod with graduated markings, and started plumbing the depths of the fuel tanks. "Let's say they left in a big hurry, and left everything running. All the fuel will be gone, and we'll be out of luck. But maybe, with a little luck, they'll have shut one or two down before they left. We might find some fuel in some of those tanks."

Scaling the tank next to the largest generator, he plunged the rod in, lifted it, and inspected it. He glanced at Savage and shook his head in disappointment. "Empty. Too much to hope for with this one. Let's check the standby generators. They'll have their own tanks."

They split up, banging on fuel tanks and checking anything that sounded like it might have some left, until Thibodeau gave a shout. "Captain! Over here. I found a full tank on this one. Let's see if we can get it running."

Savage returned, and found Thibodeau already at work checking the generator for signs of life. "This is a pony motor, Captain. It's an eighteen-horse motor, and it starts by battery, or by hand. Once it's running, it can provide enough juice to turn over the bigger generator. We're now down to the third level of generator redundancy. Well, more like standby for the third level. It's not tied into the automatic redundancy system or the main grid. It was used to power non-critical systems, and it's tucked away from the big generators, way over here in the corner. If anybody was here at the end, my guess is that none of them knew enough about the system to know they could use this to reroute the electricity into the mains. From what I can tell, everything looks good. I'm going to give it a shot."

He pushed the button. The small pony motor moaned, made a feeble attempt at turning over, but it barely turned before the solenoid started clicking rapidly. The battery was depleted. Too many years had passed since it had held a charge. "Okay. On to Plan B," he said, giving the pull-start a yank. He stopped, rechecked the choke setting, turned off the breakers on the electrical box, and gave it another. When he pulled, it turned over a few times, but still showed no inclination to start. He worked the primer lever a few more times. A few more good pulls, and the motor gave a muffled pop. Some more tinkering, and several more pulls, and the motor started. With a few adjustments, he had it running strong.

"That's just the pony motor," he shouted, over the noise, "Now we'll see if we can get the generator motor running and reroute this juice to the main grid."

A few more checks of the generator motor, and Thibodeau looked at Savage, raising his eyebrows apprehensively. It was anybody's guess whether it would start or not. "Here we go, Captain," he said, and pushed the start button. The big motor began to slowly turn over, but the pony motor began to bog down under the strain. As it bogged down further, he released the button. "Let's give her a minute!" he yelled, and sat down to watch. Another two minutes went by, and he pushed the button again. It turned over faster than before, but the pony began to struggle again. Another wait. Another try.

On the fifth try, the generator came to life. Though it was one of the smaller power generators in the room, it was large enough that they felt the engine vibrations through the concrete floor. Rerouting the power through it a single breaker at a time, Thibodeau carefully switched them on, monitoring the amperage draw on the power panels. Savage watched from the doorway, calling out the results to Thibodeau as, line-by-line, lights came on across the high, vaulted ceiling, and stretched endlessly back into the cavern.

Thibodeau stepped out of the room, inspecting the results. "I think we're putting about as much strain on the backup generator as it can stand, sir, especially if we take into account that we'll probably need some extra power for lights in other areas, and opening doors."

Satisfied, Savage said, "Well done, Thib," and slapped him on the back. They left the chamber to return to the rally point, and met up with the others a few minutes later.

Parsons reported that he had located a diagram showing several restricted areas.

The crew walked a quarter of a mile before they came upon a pair of massive, ominous-looking doors off to one side. They were tightly sealed, with bright yellow-and-black safety stripes and warning signs. With power now coursing through the conduits, Parsons and Thibodeau easily bypassed the codes and unlocked the doors in a matter of just minutes. Upon entering, they found themselves in a large lab. It didn't take them long to find what they were looking for. Four large, clear, vertical tubes, each perhaps thirty inches wide, all filled with some sort of clear blue liquid, and inside them, on display, were the "aliens." The tortured, twisted, flayed-open bodies of the crew of Hop 206 showed obvious signs of extensive autopsies. For two minutes—which seemed like an hour—they all stared, mute and horrified at the manner in which the bodies of their fellow crewmates were exhibited, appalled at the utter disregard for their human remains.

Human remains. That was the problem, of course. Nobody in 1947—or in 2010, or 2015, for that matter—*knew* that these remains were human. Twisted and shrunken, their DNA mutated beyond anything remotely recognizable as human when they passed through the hop's micro-singularity fields during the crash, they were viewed as alien by those who originally found them, and by all who viewed them since. It didn't help that every single human being that lived in 2098 carried a measurable base level of radioactivity many times higher than any living being from the twentieth century, all thanks to the holocaust of 2015.

Mercifully, by all reports, three of the four had died instantly. But there were the rumors about the last "alien," the one that lived; no one knew for how long, or what tests they performed on it while it was still alive.

Savage broke the terrible silence. "I don't give a shit what it takes to get it done. Get our people out of there. Find some caskets, or canisters, or sealed shipping crates. Before we do one single thing else, we're taking them home. Am I clear?

"Yes, sir," they said in unison, and got to work.

*    *    *

Clayton was waiting when Savage walked into Ops. "Rick," he said, offering a hand, "did you find it?"

"Yes, sir," he said, "I found all of it."

"Our people?" Clayton asked.

"We recovered the remains of all four. We brought them home and buried them in that time. I have the coordinates for the graves. They've been back home for seventy years, out behind Hangar 5, two years before the fortress was reoccupied."

"Good work, Rick. Get a detail on that, would you? I'm looking forward to your report on the wreckage and whatever you gathered on it."

"The crew took a lot of photos, and grabbed whatever files we could find that we thought might be of immediate use to us. I think we got a good start on it. We'll need to make several return trips. The warehouse is all locked up again, but now that the batteries are charged, it won't take a lot of effort to fire up the generator when we return."

# 13

The wrench clanged to the floor, and a stream of expletives followed. Jeff had just entered when he heard the voice, and rolled his chair around the shelves, navigating scattered, orphaned hop machine parts in his effort to locate the source of all the noise. He came upon a pair of overall-clad legs protruding from under one of the first-generation time travel machines. There was a fresh, loud clang accompanied by a second barrage of obscenities, and he found it intriguing each time the legs kicked up in the air, conveying angry emotions as the burrowed-in individual hammered the offending item.

From what Jeff could gather by listening, he was a witness to the aftermath of a terrorist act committed upon the unfortunate supine man, an unprovoked attack which was carried out by a stubborn and particularly vicious part of the machine; a machine which—according to the man's accusations—was of questionable parentage.

"Who's winning?" Jeff asked.

Roused from his personal vendetta, the embattled man ceased his hammering and poked his head out. "Me, who else? You don't think

75

I'm gonna let a god-damned *machine* beat me, do you?"

Jeff shrugged and said, "I don't know, Ephraim. Sounded touch-and-go for a minute, if you ask me."

"Bah," the man said, waving aside the negative comments. "I was just lulling it into complacency. Had it right where I wanted it. You came in too early. I was just about to pounce on it and teach it a lesson."

"Well, you sure fooled me. I thought for *sure* you were going to use the word 'trounce' in there somewhere."

"That'll teach you to stick your nose in where it doesn't belong."

Ephraim Caine was a mass of contradictions. Anyone looking at him, covered in grease, his hair on the long side, and always a bit wild-eyed, might have dismissed him as a heavy drinker, or, just as likely, somebody a few marbles short of a full pouch. And perhaps, some aspects of those assumptions might have proven true. For instance, he was known to consume impressive quantities of alcohol upon occasion. Admittedly, more than a few of his escapades fell under the classification of crazy, wild, and yes, sometimes insane. Ask him, and he'd say, "All true, all true," without blinking an eye.

Visually, one might never suspect he was a quantum physicist of almost immeasurable brilliance, a man who could crack time travel theory as easily as the average college graduate cracked the *Sunday Times* crossword puzzle (were there still such a thing as a newspaper).

It was also true that he refused to subscribe to many of society's more pedestrian expectations. He was not a bad person, and would never harm a soul. Not physically, anyway. With a penchant for unfailing abrasive commentary and colorful language, he'd meticulously cultivated an almost universal ability to offend those around him. Examples of those traits at work were documented in any number of base personnel incident reports.

But, the program couldn't have advanced as it did without him. No one denied that; least of all Jeff and Rose, who based everything they did upon Ephraim's ever-expanding, rock-solid breakthroughs in time-travel theory.

Anyone describing Ephraim would be honor-bound to first

reference his more extraordinary characteristics. Conversely, they would feel the need to balance their statement by pointing out that he was usually—with good reason—assigned to remote portions of the base where his personality and sunny disposition were less likely to piss others off. Most days he could be found spending his time in the Research and Development lab.

The one person within the great northeastern fortress Ephraim had never once managed to piss off was Jeff Waldron. Contrary to all expectations, the two had formed a concrete friendship that, so far, had stood the test of time, seemingly impervious to Ephraim's best efforts.

He asked Jeff, "Want a beer?"

"Sure. Where did you get beer?"

"I brew it myself. Got some potato whiskey if you'd like, too. It's better than the beer."

Jeff thought a moment. "I'll go for the beer, and how about a shot of that whiskey on the side?"

"One boilermaker, a beer and a bump, coming up, son," Ephraim said, though he wasn't much older than Jeff. As he served Jeff, he asked, "Is Rose still ticked off at me?"

"What do *you* think, you moron, after you said something like that to her?"

Ephraim thought about it for a second, then said, "Well, I was *right*, wasn't I?"

"Not when you said it the way you said it. You weren't right at all, Eph. You know, for a smart guy, you don't have enough brains to filter what leaves your mouth sometimes. It would seem to me that being around a lady would be the first place you'd know to do that."

"I s'pose."

"You s'pose. Do you s'pose you could learn to take your ass off your shoulders and just get along with people a little more? You're a nice guy, and you know it, and I know it. Thousands of people on this base could know it, too, if you weren't always so busy reminding them just how smart you are."

Ephraim gave him an evil squint, and said, "Be nice to me. I'm buying the drinks."

Jeff stared back at him, not the least amused. "You *know* what I mean."

Ephraim dropped the squint, and lost the staring contest. He mumbled, "Yeah. I know what you mean. Tell Rose I'm sorry I spoke to her like that. Maybe you could explain to her that I'm emotionally stunted."

"She already *knows* you're an asshole. She wants to know when you're gonna grow up."

"Hmpph," Ephraim said, and stood up. "I'm gonna … have another. Want one? Want to see what I'm working on here?"

The man had reached his limit of endurance for polite dialogue. Discussion over; he was moving on. Such was Ephraim Caine. Perhaps he'd relent someday, but short of a miracle, the best Jeff would ever be able to manage was the baby steps of one small issue, one small bit of improvement at a time.

Jeff said, "Sure, I'll have another. Whatcha got?"

Ephraim walked over to the antique time travel craft, which appeared to be the same version as the one in the photos Jeff uploaded while posing as John Titor. Perhaps even the same machine. This machine could travel through time, though it would always be inconsistent and unpredictable. The reasons for the issues were unknown at the time of its inception, and once those reasons were known, all of the first generation hop machines were mothballed. This model was not designed—nor intended—to travel beyond the earth's atmosphere.

That in itself wasn't a problem, but it took Ephraim Caine to determine that without leaving and re-entering the atmosphere, a time machine couldn't establish a dependable point of arrival, or, for that matter, return. These old hop machines were designed for an absolute maximum of a forty- to fifty-year hop. *That* was a problem. Ephraim's algorithms established the critical need to leave the atmosphere at escape velocity speed and re-enter at another point in order to dependably plot a hop. At speed, the shortest reliable outbound and re-entry arc consumed sixty-eight point seven years each way, both outgoing and returning to base. The math proved that accurate time travel was possible, but only to destinations sixty-nine or more years away.

Accordingly, a safe minimum of seventy years of travel was established as a rule. The new hop machines were all equipped with a lockout which prevented any hops shorter than that. A seventy-year arc required power levels the first-generation models couldn't hope to achieve on their best days.

By comparison, the early attempts with the first hop machines were archaic, and highly experimental. In those days, hop crews consisted of one man, the pilot. One by one, those pilots were irretrievably lost in the dark folds of time past, the holes and cracks of times gone by. Hop machines were simply parked ten, twenty, or fifty years in the past. Pilots and machines disappeared, often without a trace. Over time, some of the machines were located by metal scrappers who dismantled them and sold the metal. If the Board could have been sure all the older machines would meet the same fate, they wouldn't have worried. Their concern was that somebody might find one and somehow fire it up, a situation which literally made any of the lost crafts a paradox waiting to happen.

Of the original twelve machines, four had survived and returned home. Those few pilots had the presence of mind to hop *again* into the past, to a point where, eventually, a hop crew with a newer machine located and picked up the pilot and machine, and brought them home. One famous pilot, Charlie Troyer, had hopped three times, then had carefully hidden his hop machine and lived through the 1980s, until Flash located him in the mid-1990s and brought him home.

Unable to accurately establish hop parameters for outbound and return missions, the scientists running the first program gave up, and declared practical time travel an impossibility. The Hop Ops program was mothballed for fifty years. Charlie was marooned in the past, where he lived for over fifteen years, abandoned and—they could only assume—desperate.

The first machine was recovered by sheer luck, only because it returned to a time only two weeks before the program was mothballed.

The original hop machines were designed to generate enough power for two hops—theoretically—one outbound, one return. But they were notoriously unpredictable, and the first hop might deplete the power after far-overshooting the destination year. On the other hand, it might last for three hops, as in the case of Charlie Troyer, who tried to return and instead ended up late in the summer of 2015, the year of the nuclear war.

Knowing what fate awaited him just weeks later, he tried another hop, and set the controls to hop to as far in the past as it could. He had no idea if it would kill him, or drop him from fifty thousand feet, but he had nothing to lose by trying. Fortunate enough to arrive safely in 1982, he hid the machine, found a job, rented a place where he could stash the craft long-term, and set himself up to live out his existence in that beautiful, vital, living world; a world his people hadn't seen in many years, and would never see again.

The program, fresh out of mothballs some fifty years after Charlie was lost, was revitalized through Ephraim's leaps in time travel theory. Finding the older machines to prevent the possibility of paradoxes went to the top of the list, and became their first and highest priority. The "R" in T.I.T.O.R. stood for *recovery,* and some of the older hop machines were the first items to be successfully recovered. Charlie was the first pilot successfully recovered, and the only pilot recovered with his hop machine intact. It should be noted that he was recovered literally kicking and screaming, refusing to come along quietly back to 2095. He openly lamented being forced to return with his machine to another time also not his own. Now, fifty years in his own future, he was an expert on the 1980s and 1990s, and he reckoned—from the condition of his new home, the bleak world of 2096—far worse off than he ever was in the twentieth century. He asked any number of times to be sent back to the day they removed him. He tried everything. Formal requests. Informal requests. Pleading.

"You represent a potential threat of paradox," they said.

They remained obtuse, and completely ignored the fact that he had lived there in bliss for over fifteen years without incident, and now that the hop machine was recovered, what threat remained? He represented little—if any—threat of paradox.

The Board came back with its answer each time: Permission denied.

As if that wasn't enough, he was left with no choice but to endure a unique, agonizing forced-paradox, where his body alternately went through bouts of intense aging, then grew younger. There was a difference between returning to one's own time in the future, and traveling *beyond* one's own time.

Time travel was technologically advanced, but one thing never changed. If one traveled back and stayed three days in another time, they aged with each day, and, using the same hop machine, could only return home those same three days later. No matter what point in time a hop crew traveled to, time in the present continued to pass at the same rate. It was one of time travel's insidious and enigmatic conundrums; another of its unchangeable, pound-of-flesh rules: Your life was your life, and wherever—and *when*ever you were, that unchangeable cycle marched forward, day after day, inexorably, toward its completion. And thus far, nobody had found a way around it.

The situation took on an altogether different outlook and compounded the situation drastically when one traveled *past* their own time, and into the future. This could only be achieved by that individual riding in a hop machine which came from their own future, since no hop machine (thus far) was capable of traveling forward beyond its own time. "Its own time" being no farther into the future than the number of days they spent in the past, added to the day they departed; the unchangeable rule.

One can imagine Charlie Troyer's dilemma, having lived to the age of twenty-five in 2050, and then, having lived fifteen years through the 1980s and 1990s, being taken from 1997 to 2095 at forty years old, where he was forced to remain and suffer through an age transition paradox.

Even Ephraim couldn't generate an algorithm complex enough to predict how the many conflicting factors might ultimately affect Charlie, whose ultimate fear was of aging fifty years in reverse, since he had but forty years of existence to offer up. Much to his relief, his transitional 'growing pains' subsided by the time three years passed, and by then he estimated he'd lost five to seven years from his physical age. Not altogether a bad place to end up age-wise, he reasoned. It was painful, but could have been worse.

If only he hadn't been delivered back into Hell.

Now, Charlie's old hop machine stood before them. Ephraim had a soft spot for it, since it had performed better than many of the others, though just as unpredictably. Ephraim was often found underneath it, tinkering on something, and the ancient power couplings gave him endless fodder for swearing. He loved it. As the only civilian on base authorized to establish a field on a first-gen hop machine, he often did so just to run around the base and have some fun. In the previous century, a man might have enjoyed a sports car with a drop-top, driving the back roads to revisit his youth. In 2099, Ephraim's version of that was to travel the six miles across the base in about eight seconds and stop just short of the wall berm, and do it all at twenty to thirty feet above the ground.

Jeff said, "I've been meaning to ask you something. How did you discover the breakthrough that made the time travel viable?"

Ephraim said, "You know, nobody has ever asked me that before. Doesn't that just blow your mind?"

"I guess so," Jeff answered, not quite sure what that meant.

"I was going through some old data one day, and I learned that NASA had to account for discrepancies between their clocks and those in space. Time doesn't pass the same in space as it does down here, did you know that?"

"Really? No, I didn't know that."

"Wild, eh? So it got me thinking, I wondered if that's something that needs to be factored into the time travel. You know, not just moving through *time,* but having to move through *space* as well. *Outer* space, I mean. Once I determined that speed was a big factor, and thought about the friction that kind of speed would create inside our atmosphere, suddenly there it was, inside my head—everything I needed. I still had to sort it out, apply the math, calculate trajectories and escape velocities, factor in the Earth's rotation, and how to best use it to facilitate forward or backward travel."

Jeff considered what a crazy ride it must be to live inside a perpetually moving mind like Ephraim's. "That is *wild*. Have you ever crewed on a hop? You must have."

Ephraim turned to him with a solemn look. "No. You've known me for years. Have you ever seen me go out?"

Jeff looked surprised. "No, now that you mention it. But why not? You're the guy who made it all happen. And unlike me, you can pass the physical. It's not like you don't know how to run the damn things. You built them."

Staring at the ground, somewhat drunk and brooding, Ephraim said in a derisive, nasal imitation of his superiors, "I'm too *valuable*," and waved his hand, disgusted. "They can't risk me going. They said it could create a paradox if anybody else got their hands on me."

He threw the rag he held at the floor, and said, "As though I'd tell anybody what I do. I know it's not a toy. I know this isn't a game. Who wouldn't resent creating all of this, just to be denied the use of it? Nobody wants to go on a hop more than I do."

"Except … except maybe me."

"Yeah. Except maybe you. Maybe."

They sipped away at a few more beers, and maybe another shot, or two; probably no more than three or four, and absolutely no more than five, discussing the patent unfairness of the situation. Two men who labored so long and hard on a mutual dream, bringing so much to the revitalization of the once-dead program, now wallowed in the disappointment and burning resentment of being rubber-stamped 'unsuitable.'

Jeff had fallen behind, as usual, but still felt the effects of the whiskey. He said, "Sucks, don't it?"

Ephraim struggled, pushed, and pulled his way to his feet, where he stood more or less upright, and none too steadily, he said, "Oh, yeah. I was gonna show you thish. C'mere, Jeff. C'mere," he slurred affectionately, waving his friend over toward the hop machine, indicating that Jeff should expend the considerable effort and coordination required to roll his chair over there.

Though his hands didn't work well, he finally rolled his chair across the floor. In an expectant tone, he said, "Okey-dokey, I'm here, bud. Whatcha got?" He was in the mood to be impressed, and impaired enough that he probably would be, no matter how good or bad it was.

"Feets yer eyes on thish, misser," Ephraim said, and hit the power-up button on the remote startup unit, establishing a field around the machine.

Drunk or not, Jeff's mouth dropped open, and he grabbed the arms of his chair to sit himself up straight.

A shimmering, silvery field rose around the machine, the same fields they saw every day on the hop machines. Viewed from the top or bottom, the field resembled a huge stainless steel saucer. From the sides, it resembled a flattened oval with pointed ends.

There was just one small problem with that.

"Jesus, Eph. That's not yellow. It's *silver!* What the hell did you do?"

"Yer damn sp-sp-spippy it ish. This ain' no an-tique firs-gen wannabee hop. Dual quadratic i-shometrics with fully innagrated high outpush genertators, and brandy-new power couplingsh all 'round. Thish baby's runnin' on all eight, buddy. Ashholes think they run me. Nobody ru— no— nobody runsh me. Whadya think?"

"Christ, Eph, if they find out, I think there'll be hell to pay," Jeff said, clarity rapidly returning to him as adrenaline pumped through his veins, counteracting the effects of the alcohol.

Having a rogue time machine was tantamount to treason; a parallel could be drawn to a civilian defense contractor on a base, building a nuclear weapon in his garage. This machine in the wrong hands could literally equate to Hell on earth. Or Hell on what was left of the earth.

"Then ya prolly shouldn't tell 'em, eh?" Ephraim said, with an expectant—and somewhat defiant—look.

Caught off guard, and panicked like a deer in the headlights, Jeff's thoughts raced. He knew that Ephraim wanted to crew on the hops, and nobody understood that burning desire more than he, who had helped Ephraim take the second generation machines from ideas on paper to fully functional time travel machines that worked beautifully. In his heart, he believed that Ephraim would never take this or any hop machine through time without permission and proper authorization.

But this by itself went far beyond even Ephraim's usual artificial expansion of boundaries. This was no flight of fancy. He'd taken an antique hop machine, and installed the new-style quadratic/isometric field generators, right down to a complete set of the newest, most advanced power couplings. Couplings the *other* second-gens didn't even have installed yet. It no longer generated the weak, low-powered yellow fields that easily identified the antique models. But it wasn't the same as the new versions either. This hybrid hop machine was *more powerful* than the new ones. It was truly "hopped-up," and from what he saw before him, Jeff estimated it could travel at thirty to forty thousand miles per hour without breaking a sweat.

Ephraim had built this suped-up version just to blow off steam. Jeff understood that. They were like brothers, though they didn't spend as much time together as they would have liked. He felt protective of Ephraim, and because *he* understood the man, he felt that others mostly misunderstood him. One thing he knew for certain.

They wouldn't understand *this*.

Then it came to him, simple and clear.

He said, "Well, just make sure to go over to Ops tomorrow and register this as an emergency-backup hop machine with Ops. Then you'll be allowed to have it, without one of those pesky "firing squad" situations getting in the way. What do you think?"

Ephraim gave a drunken scowl, peeved at the thought of officially registering his new, secret baby. His scowl faded as he gave it further thought. Over the next half-minute, his face went through a variety of contortions and mood changes. At least it showed he was giving the suggestion serious consideration, despite his initial reaction.

For a moment, Jeff thought Ephraim might just poo-poo the idea and invite him to screw off. Instead, wavering but standing relatively vertical and upright, he said, "Umm, 'kay, that'll work. Sounz good," and flipped the power switch off. The fields dropped and dissipated, and without further debate or comment, he made for the liquid refreshments once more.

Jeff mumbled, "Crisis averted. Now *I* need a drink."

# 14

General Ramey was not having a good day. As expected, the newspapers hadn't let go of the old story, and refused to accept the new version. Beyond that, they continued to push to find others who wished to be interviewed. Oh, sure, they were *printing* the new story, but the way they presented it said it all. They didn't believe it. Most of the people interviewed by reporters said, "One day they've got a flying saucer, and the next day they've got a balloon? *A BALLOON?* They expect us to believe that?"

*Newspaper people aren't known for being stupid. They can smell that this story stinks,* he thought, reading the headlines. *Who could begrudge honest, hardworking people for doing their jobs, and for showing integrity by doing them well?* Integrity was always at a premium, and he admired those who showed it. He looked for it in the people who worked under him. But now it seemed the fates had conspired to place him in an untenable position, forced to follow orders to subvert veracity, to make a mockery of honesty, to twist the truth into a lie. Worse than that, he had to suffer playing a part in ruining the lives of those so unfortunate as to have attracted the attention of Wren and his ilk. Bile rose in his throat at the thought of Wren having his way, wreaking havoc upon the lives of decent, honest folk.

Under his breath, he swore. *"Damn it."*

His aide popped his head into the doorway. "General, Mr. Wren is on the line for you."

"Put him through," he said, and picked up the receiver. "Mr. Wren, what can I do for you?"

"Good afternoon, General Ramey. I take it you've seen the newspapers today?"

"I have. It appears they're *not* buying what we're selling." He took some small amount of satisfaction in that knowledge.

"Nonsense. The plan is going very smoothly, General. It takes time for this sort of thing to happen. All the necessary components are in place, and working beautifully. With some diligence and mop-up work, it should all go as planned. In my estimation, it couldn't be going any better right now."

"I agree with your words, Mr. Wren, but the meaning I take from them is undoubtedly different from your own."

"Undoubtedly, General. I'm aware that you would rather the public didn't buy our story. But you let *me* worry about that. The reason I've called is to talk to you about what we're planning on doing with the wreckage. You're aware of the base at Groom Lake?"

"I'm aware of its existence, yes. Why?"

"We've decided to re-assign Groom Lake as a fully classified secret base. Highest levels of clearance, a place to store important items, like the wreckage, the research; the whole ball of wax. I need you to know about it so that you can start screening your people for possible transfer with the wreckage to support these activities. They'll need clearance."

"That shouldn't present a problem, Mr. Wren. Quite a number of people under my command have the necessary clearances for such a project. But I do have a question for you."

"I'll be happy to answer it, General."

"Why on earth did you call me on an unsecured phone line to

discuss such matters? I would have expected a visit from you and a briefing. The situation *must* have warranted a much higher level of security than this."

"For the wreckage of a weather balloon? Come now, General. You'll be properly briefed on our needs for the development of this secure area, and we'll have a chance to talk more then."

Ramey opened his mouth to respond, but thought better of it. Wren was up to something. He'd referred to the wreckage as a weather balloon. Warning bells and flashing red lights went off in Ramey's head. This call was not at all what it seemed to be. Until he knew more, he would go with the flow.

"Then I'll look forward to the briefing on the new project, Mr. Wren. Good day."

# 15

"Wake up, Jeff," Rose said, shaking him considerably harder than was necessary. "What happened? I didn't hear a peep from you last night. I thought you were coming by."

"Ooooh … Rose. I was coming over, but Eph got to me first." He shook his head, and regretted doing so immediately when his eyes lost focus from the pain. "He—uh, we—had some potato whiskey. Ooh, my head is *killing* me. Whoa. Bad. Ouch. This is bad. Bad bad bad. . ."

As it seemed he'd chosen drinking over spending time with her, Rose raised her voice, shook him harder yet, and made sure he felt it. "Serves you right! Well, it's a whole new day. Let's go. You ready to go to work?"

"Shhh … shhh," he begged, almost whimpering, and wincing pitifully. "Please, for the love of God, quiet down. I'll work. I'll work, okay? Just—just—shhh. . ."

She was plenty miffed with Ephraim before this happened, so Jeff knew that, in Ephraim's absence, he was in her crosshairs, and her full wrath would be focused upon him. As a woman in a mood to

91

exercise her prerogative, she wasn't inclined to offer much in the way of mercy. She intended that he would suffer through, with as much emphasis as possible on the 'suffer' part. Waving in surrender, he sat up, and moaned, "I'm up, I'm up. See? Give me five minutes."

The Ops center was busy when they arrived, so they went directly to Jeff's station, where he was scheduled to link up to the communications device. He wasn't feeling much better, but he could function adequately.

Rose asked, "Have we heard anything from Flash yet?"

"No, nothing yet. I hope to gain enough visibility, or notoriety, or anything else I can generate that might help him to notice me. Some of the folks I've chatted with are exchanging personal messages with me."

"Have you learned anything new? Anything that can help us find the wreckage before 2015?"

"No, not so far. I'm stashing whatever comes in. We're collating all data for reference in case it can help us to cross-reference other pertinent information. For instance, this guy who helped us find Warehouse 15, that was pure gold; it helped us to recover Hop 206 and its crew. The information from the warehouse might be valuable as well. I heard that Clayton authorized the fabrication of some weather tight containers to move larger volumes of the documentation by burying it out behind Hangar 5. No matter what happens from this point forward, this communications link to the year 2000 can be considered a resounding success."

Rose asked, "Are you going to tell your contact that we found the warehouse?"

Jeff shook his head. "No. That wouldn't be wise. If somebody knew we were actually going to be there, it might change what we find. That would be risky, don't you think?"

She couldn't deny the potential risk. She weighed the alternative, thinking out loud. "But if he knew we followed his advice, and that we were successful, he might supply us with more information— something more substantial. I suppose that's worth thinking about."

Jeff said, "We'll have to be more forthcoming about their future if

I'm to expect more in return. That much is certain."

"So, be more forthcoming. It doesn't have to be the truth, or at least, not *all* of it. Make some stuff up. You told me you like to contradict yourself and stir them up. So, start stirring. We need more information, and we need it yesterday."

He turned back to his console. "Information yesterday … okey-dokey, coming right up. Here. I found some articles written around 2009 talking about how Mad Cow Disease had progressed a measurable amount since the nineteen-nineties. Nothing big, but I thought I could make some reference to Mad Cow becoming an epidemic in—what? Say, 2012? I think I'll warn them not to eat or use products from any animals that are fed parts of animals that died from unknown causes. You know, chickens that eat recycled chicken parts, beef cattle that eat feed containing recycled cattle bones. That sounds good, eh?"

He scribbled notes on his pad as he talked. Then he gestured toward her notepad. "What ideas do you have? Whatever you have, we might be able to use it, even if it's not too important. We can give almost anything a twist if there was public interest in it."

She turned a page on her notepad. "Not much in the way of that, but I have other subjects I need to touch upon. Are you really going to make reference to the war? I saw your notes on the new capital after the war ended. How are you going to explain predictions that don't come true in the near future?"

He said, "I've worked up some double-talk and gobbledygook about time-travel actually being dimensional travel, and I'm going to use this term I like for it: *divergence*. Anytime something changes, the time line *diverges*, and if a butterfly flaps its wings in Australia, then this civil war I'm predicting in 2005 won't happen the way I said it would."

She raised an eyebrow. "So, when it doesn't happen the way you said, it's not your fault that somebody else tooted at another table on another world, and spoiled the whole party. Is that it? And the war?"

In spite of the dreadful headache plaguing him, he chuckled at her interpretations—which he had to admit were pretty good. "Right on the money. And I think it's important to talk with them about the war. Information like that just might give some of them incentive to funnel more information my way."

"But Omaha, Nebraska, the new capital of the United States? Land of wheat and Minuteman missile silos? Omaha, of the State of Nebraska, where nothing will live or grow again for the next five thousand years?"

"I know that, and you know that. It's obvious to us why that area is scorched. But, to catch Flash's eye, I have to maintain some level of irrational affirmation here."

"Waldron, you are without shame," she said, in her 'boss voice,' and pointed her finger at him, and the next time she spoke, the stern tone in her voice was unmistakable. "But I draw the line here. No. You're *not* to discuss the war. Not a word."

Jeff rolled his eyes in frustration at that, still suffering from his hangover. *There's going to be trouble.* "Oh, Rose—I already put it out there, all right? I can't just go back in there and say I got it wrong. Besides, I did it so Flash would see it, and understand that it had to be us to write something like that. That situation is becoming critical. Flash is *way* overdue on his contact."

"So, you just informed people in the year 2001 that in fourteen years a nuclear war will break out? Why didn't you just go ahead and tell them their world will end on September fifteenth? Or *did* you?"

"You're making it sound worse than it is. Most of them won't believe me anyway, and even if they do—"

Rose jumped up, yelling. "*TELL* me that you didn't give them the date. And tell me you didn't let them know what caused it."

"I didn't, Rose, I wouldn't do th—"

She interrupted, "Do you have any idea how dangerous that stunt was?" The elevating volume became a harbinger of her impending fury, and the pain from that fury further compounded his hangover. She slapped her notepad down. "The reason I questioned your notes was because I was going to *shoot down* your little scheme. And now I find out you've already *told* them. Perfect!" she yelled, throwing her notepad down and swinging her hands toward to the ceiling.

The stress, coupled with the headache, was too much for him. He yelled back, "But you just *told* me to take a chance, to give them some more info, and now you're mad because I went ahead and *did* it?"

"I didn't tell you to disclose that there would be a nuclear war in 2015, though, did I? *Shit!*" she yelled, slamming her hand down on a stack of papers. She wheeled and stomped out, leaving Jeff and a room of stunned Ops technicians behind in the protracted silence, a pregnant pause extended further yet because not a soul in that command center wanted to be the first to break it. Quiet fingers ticked away on keyboards as others wisely chose to turn back to their work.

Thirty long, tense seconds passed before Clayton spoke, his voice soft and measured. "Well, it seems she chewed your ass *clean* off and didn't leave anything for me, Mr. Waldron. What a pity, thinking of all the fun I would've had going up one side of you and down the other for a stupid stunt like that. Do you have anything you'd like to say?"

The silent techs waited along with the colonel, expecting a contrite apology for making such a monumental misstep. Jeff's head hung, and it felt as though it might split in two as he backed out of his station and turned his wheelchair, until he faced the colonel. It was then his face turned dour, taking on a surly look. He'd had all he could take.

He snapped, "I figure it's better to ask for forgiveness than permission, sir." Without another word, and without waiting for a response from the colonel, he wheeled his chair back around and tucked into his station.

Heads snapped back to their screens, as none of the techs wanted to be caught gaping at what had just transpired. They would have preferred to be invisible right then, in fact.

Clayton said nothing. Jeff's actions indicated a desire for neither forgiveness nor permission, and both were out of character for the young man. The wisest course of action was to allow the situation to defuse—for now. It would be addressed later, in private.

The rest of the day passed without further incident, but twenty minutes before his shift ended, Jeff decided to leave early and "walk" home. Shutting down his station without a word to anyone, he rolled his chair out into the cold night air. It was about a mile to his building. Along the way home, he passed Alabama Place, the street that led to Rose's apartment complex. The mid-January night air was crisp, frozen, and fresh—and relatively warm at about twenty degrees below zero. The worst of his hangover had passed, but the dehydration left a world-class headache entrenched and pounding away with enthusiasm. After a while, the exercise and the cold began to numb his headache and reduce his anger over the day's events, and he began to calm down.

When an Ops team vehicle came up the street from behind, and passed by, he couldn't see inside the dark vehicle, but was sure it was Rose checking up on him. He didn't know why, but just the idea that she was doing so instantly refreshed his anger. But it wasn't anger for Rose, it was an anger that dwelled deep inside him, an anger he normally kept buried.

He didn't think about it a lot, but on the occasions when he did, it stayed with him. There was a reason he'd commiserated with Ephraim last night, long into the night. They were both miserable, because, unlike Rose, Colonel Clayton, and pretty much every other person beside them on this base, it seemed they were the only two guys whose choices were made for them. Others decided what Jeff and Ephraim could and couldn't do. People around them controlled their actions. On the rare occasions he allowed himself to ponder the situation, it infuriated him.

Forgetting for that moment the contributions Rose made to the program, forgetting how hard she'd worked, and that she was, technically, his ranking superior officer, Jeff rationalized that he and Ephraim were the sole reasons this program existed.

His reasons for such rationalizations were based in truth, but only true because they were taken out of context, and viewed exclusive of other factors; the most prominent being the hard work so many others put into the program. At the moment, exploring others' perspectives mattered little to him, as it held the potential to interfere with his plans to remain pissed off for the foreseeable future.

The way he saw it, it was he and Ephraim; *their* hard work made all of this possible, and without them, the program most certainly would still have been in mothballs, still deemed "impossible." They had made the impossible possible, and yet every move they made was watched, judged, controlled. Manipulated.

Jeff understood that Ephraim did bear watching. *The man has a tendency upon occasion to climb out on a limb, quite a bit farther than most others would. But that's Ephraim. That's what he is; the man who pushes the envelope in so many ways. A few years back, he pushed a rickety old hop machine too far and lost a power coupling at the far end of the sprint. He ended up over the wall, and planted the machine way out in the potato field. But that was all in good fun. Killed a few potatoes, but nobody was hurt. Dinged his pride a little. Maybe.*

And then there was Rose, who went overboard protecting him at times. Sometimes she treated him like he was a little kid. Normally, he liked the extra attention.

Normally.

He thought, *Well, I'm not a little boy any more. I'm thirty-four years old, and I don't need protecting. If she didn't see it before, she should have—after the Portland trip. I kept my cool, and I saved her life. And what the hell was all that about today? They **expect** me to gather information. It's my job. How else am I going to get it? I have to use my imagination to make it happen, and they think they can tell me how I'm to do it every minute. They might just as well tie one hand behind my back. I've got news for them all. I've had it with this treatment. It's time they all learned, I won't put up with it any more. Starting with her.*

Rolling into his room, he picked up the phone. "Hello, Mr. Dennis? This is Jeff Waldron. Could you come up to my room? I need your help for a few minutes. Yes, I'll be here. Thanks."

\* \* \*

*January 5th, 2099*

"Ms. Rios. Where's Mr. Waldron?" Clayton asked.

"I've been trying his number, sir. I'm not getting an answer."

"I thought you picked him up and you two rode in together every day."

"Not *every* day, sir."

"You know what I mean. I'm sure you have a key. Maybe you should go and check on him."

Rose's face burned red, and she didn't respond.

"Rose, did you hear me?"

Her breath left her explosively. "Yes, sir, I heard you. I already *tried* to check on him, when I tried to pick him up this morning."

She hoped he would leave it at that that, but that wasn't going to happen.

"And?"

She surrendered the new breath she was holding, and said, "And, the locks were changed, sir. I couldn't get in, and he wouldn't answer the door."

Technically, she wasn't Jeff's girlfriend, so therefore she *should* have been exempt from what otherwise would be the standard gossip which would inevitably follow. Even so, her face burned a bright red as she imagined the furtively whispered comments.

"I see," Clayton said. "Very well."

She turned and hurried from the room, determined to find work elsewhere in the building for the day.

That night, when she hoped a call would come from Jeff, the phone remained silent.

The next day was the same. So was the next night.

After that, she didn't try Jeff's door any more.

Later in the week, Clayton called her to his office. He looked unhappy. Scowling, sitting on the edge of his desk, he handed a paper to her and said, "That's a transfer request. He's asking for a transfer, from here to any other fort. He says he'll leave anyway, if we don't grant it. Jesus. I don't need this kind of crap right now. What the hell happened between you two, Rose?"

She had no idea how everything could have gone so very bad, so quickly. None. Stunned speechless, she read the paper, over and over, trying to find something on it that might shed some light on the situation. But a transfer request was just a transfer request, standard issue 101-704-TR, and no matter how many times she looked, it told her nothing—except that Jeff wanted to be anywhere else but with her.

She didn't think she could stand the pain that seized her then. Not without dying.

"Rose, did you hear me?"

With a start, she came back to the present. Badly disoriented, she looked around the room; for a second or two unsure where she was. The colonel rose from the desk and stood in front of her. "Rose?"

She looked up, into his face, and the full impact of the situation hit her, overwhelmed her. "Sir?" she uttered, shaking, as an uncontrollable grimace of pain seized her, and when she took a step, at first it seemed she might fall. He stepped forward to steady the devastated young woman, who buried her face in his chest, and sobbed her heart out.

# 16

Jeff handed Ephraim another wrench, and they talked as Ephraim worked.

Ephraim asked, "So where was Hop 206 returning from?"

"It was a truck run. The hop crew had just purchased a new truck. They'd just bolted the hop machine into the bed, and were bringing it home."

"Oh, yeah, I heard about that one. They had me adjust the fields to fit that truck. They bought it from military surplus. A 1946 maroon Ford pickup, almost like new."

Jeff said, "It should have been. They bought it in 1949. It still had the 1946 plates on it. Expired when we bought it, but we were planning on running some missions in 1947, and I think the goal was to see if we could get to the wreckage before anybody knew it was there, before it was found."

"Well, *that* didn't exactly pan out, did it? One thing bugs me, though."

"What's that?"

"If it was military surplus, why was it maroon? I'd think it would be army green, like everything else they have."

Jeff pondered that. "Hmmm. Yeah, you'd think so."

After the third awkward moment of silence that morning, Ephraim finally cut to the chase, and addressed the real subject on their minds. "Okay, enough beating around the bush. You really did it, didn't you? You filed that transfer request."

After a short hesitation, Jeff said, "Yeah. Just this morning."

"You're *sure* you've thought this all the way through?"

"I have. I've had it with this crap."

"Oh, you have, have you?" Ephraim said, from under the platform. "Try designing and building the fastest vehicles in the galaxy, and then being told you can't take one out for a ride, even though it seems damn near every other person on the base *can*. No, son, it's, *me* who's had it with this crap, ten times over. But you don't see *me* filing for a transfer, do you? Think about it. Do you *ever* wonder why I get into so much trouble, why I piss so many people off? The answer's easy. It's because they piss *me* off. I do it to let off steam, to unwind, and if I'm honest about it, sometimes I like to get a little bit even with them for treating me like a—a *possession.*"

Jeff was surprised. Never for a moment had he considered the possibility that Ephraim's wild antics might be premeditated, much less carefully planned. "But I thought you—"

"You and everybody else, buddy-boy," his friend said, and pulled himself out from under the platform to look at Jeff. "I'm the smartest guy within three thousand miles in any direction, with the most education, too. I've got more degrees than anyone I've ever met. Do you think this level of education just comes to someone who hasn't learned how to discipline himself? Without learning how to function in the real world? I'm as domesticated as any person you know. If I wanted to cause some *real* trouble, I could do so, without much effort, and you can be sure my name wouldn't be associated with it. The things I do make a limited statement: *You don't own me.* Someday, they'll take me seriously; until then, I'll just keep sending my small-but-annoying messages."

He sat up, and leaned back against the hop machine. "The one thing I *won't* do is put this program at risk. I can't. The entire world is counting on what we do here, and as much as I whine and carry on, I don't suppose my wants and needs are more important than saving the whole world. Last I knew, saving the whole world is the reason we're all here. Right? Do you think I couldn't transfer out? Sure I could, just like you. I could do it *with* you. Then we'd be out of this damn program.

"Problem solved, right? *Wrong.* What we'd *really* be doing is risking everything and everyone we care about. Oh, I know, they can be real dicks sometimes, but we're all here doing a job. A job we *have* to work together on to try and save the world, even when it sucks sometimes."

A voice spoke from the dark corners of the shelving area. "Just for the record, Mr. Caine, you don't fool me with your antics. I knew everything about you before I restarted this program. And I know damn well why you act out. But, my first priority is this program and its security. I'd love to send you out on a lark to another time, I really would. You deserve it, more than any of us. But the risk is too great. So I must say no."

Ephraim listened to what the colonel said, and turned slightly toward the voice. "Colonel Clayton. I won't ask how long you've been here."

Clayton stepped out and walked toward them. "Long enough. I followed Jeff here. It figures he'd be hanging around *you.* Misery loves company."

Jeff, still sullen, asked, "Why did you follow me?"

Clayton handed him a paper. "To give you this," he said, and turned and walked away.

"What is it?" Jeff asked, suspicious of what it might be.

"Read it, and you'll see. Transfer approved, effective immediately. You think *you've* had enough? I have too. I've had it with you. Pack your bags. You leave tomorrow." Though tossed over his shoulder, the cold tone reaffirmed his parting words.

Jeff was stunned. He'd dropped the request on the colonel's aide's desk no more than an hour ago. It should have been weeks, even months, before the process even *started*. There should have been an interview process, to determine whether a transfer is necessary, or if the applicant had some complaint, etc. The list went on from there. They usually first tried to determine whether the applicant's concerns might be satisfied without a transfer.

That would be the case, of course, assuming the applicant offered any amount of significant value to the program. This turn of events left him dumbfounded, as did the unexpected depreciation of him as an asset, the only possible reason that could have so dramatically hastened the process.

Ephraim slowly shook his head. "Wow. You *really* stepped in it this time."

Stunned, Jeff mumbled, "What the hell just happened, Eph?"

"He called your bluff, son. Held a better hand, cleaned you out. This poker game is *over*. And it looks like I just lost my friend."

"Your *best* friend," Jeff said absently.

"What's the difference? Best or not, gone is gone."

"I don't believe this."

"Yeah, well. . . don't forget to write."

\* \* \*

There was a gentle tapping at the office door. "Good afternoon, Colonel Clayton. May, ahh, may I speak to you, sir?" Jeff asked, sheepishly.

Clayton didn't even bother to look up. "Why are *you* still here? We've said all there is to say, Mr. Waldron. I meant what I said. There's a transport leaving in the morning. I want you on it."

"But, sir—"

The steely gaze snapped up and met the younger man's eyes. Jeff *felt* the anger when Clayton snarled, "But, *nothing!* I won't have some *civilian* working under me who puts the program at risk because he's decided to cop an attitude. You were out of line. You failed to follow mission protocol; to have your plans approved by your superior. If you were in the military, I'd bust your ass *clean* to buck private, or airman. But you aren't *in* the military, are you? So I can't *do* that. What I *can* do is ship your ass *and* your attitude out of my fortress, where you can't do any further damage to my program."

*Or my people,* he thought.

Jeff released the breath he held. Clayton was right. He'd pushed it too far. Worse than that, he liked and respected Clayton more than anyone he knew. Hell, if not for Clayton coming to Portland to find him, bringing him inside, he'd be on the streets right now, wishing he had a life—assuming, of course, that he'd somehow managed to survive all this time, and that would be one big assumption.

"I came to apologize, Colonel. You're right—about all of it."

"*Am* I, now?"

"Yes, sir. I copped an attitude, and I failed to submit a plan before doing something that clearly posed a risk to the program."

As the colonel slowly rose to his feet, still scowling, his jaundiced gaze never left Jeff. He walked around his desk, then behind Jeff, then around again, until he stood behind Jeff yet again.

He spoke again, but this time, it was a growl, spoken low and mean, over Jeff's shoulder. "Now, you hear me, and you hear me *good*, Mister, because I don't intend to repeat myself ever again on this subject. This is your first—and your last—warning. If I *ever* have to deal with this again, there won't *be* a transfer. There won't be a review, there won't *be* an apology. You won't continue eating our food, and you will no longer have the privilege or protection of living behind these walls. You'll be escorted to the gates of this fortress, and given your former life back, with everything you brought with you when you came to us," and he grabbed the chair, spinning it around until his face was directly in front of Jeff's. "Which, as I recall, was *NOTHING!*" he barked the last words, and slammed his fist down on the desk, though emphasis was hardly required. He leaned closer to Jeff, until his face was barely three inches away. He reached for a paper on his desk and grabbed it up. It crumpled in his grasp. "*Do not* make me sorry I rescinded this transfer, Mr. Waldron."

He straightened, turned, and walked around his desk, tossing a quick "Dismissed" over his shoulder.

"Colonel, you won't be sorry. I—I promise," Jeff wheezed, breathless and trembling as he worked to wheel his chair around and out of the office. He had quite a bit of difficulty pushing the chair, as he was dizzy and shaking violently, and more than a little nauseous. The shakes slowly subsided as he made his way down the hall toward Ops.

About then, he remembered to breathe. At the door, he swiped his card, but the door wouldn't open. He tried it again. *The swipe card isn't working. Jesus. He was serious. I was out. He was transferring me.* The shakes, not quite gone, started again in earnest. That was when the door opened. Fred Arnold, who worked two stations down from him, stepped into the doorway between Jeff and the room. Jeff looked up at him, and said, "Thanks, Fred. My, uh, card isn't working. I guess I have to have it reactivated in the morning."

Fred didn't move. Jeff leaned to the side and looked around Fred's hip. Across the command center, he saw Rose and the others watching them. None of them moved or spoke. All eyes were on Jeff and Fred. "Sorry, Jeff," Fred said, "I'm sorry to be the one to tell you this. I don't like it any more than you do. Your security clearance is rescinded. You're out of Ops. The colonel has reassigned you to R&D. I'm to collect your card, your keys, and any security clearance items you have."

Jeff heard the words, but didn't believe them, even as he handed his card to the man. "Assigned to R&D? There's been a mistake. Here, let me in, and I'll call the colonel and straighten this out." He tried to go around Fred, but the man blocked him yet again.

"There's no mistake, Jeff. It came straight from the colonel's mouth. The regret at having to say it showed in Fred's face.

He stepped back inside.

All of the other members of the Ops team watched; watched Jeff's face redden with the burgeoning embarrassment. Watched as Fred pushed the button to close the door. Rose's eyes locked with Jeff's for a second. He tried to smile and look confident, waved, and said, "I'm sure it'll all be straightened out by tomorrow. Just a glitch. I—I'll see you all then, okay?" but the closing door cut him off, placing emphasis upon the decree of his exile, and refuting his resolve to return. Shaking almost uncontrollably, breathing faster and feeling more nauseous than when he'd left the colonel a few minutes ago, he rolled once again to the colonel's office, his stomach tied in knots. On the way, he pictured once again the prospect of trying to live on the outside as a wheelchair-bound man. The thought frightened him beyond all words.

Entering the office, he tried to sound confident, but was unable to keep the desperation from his voice. "Lieutenant, I—I need to see the colonel. There's been a terrible mix-up."

"I'm sorry, Mr. Waldron. The colonel is out."

"No, he's not. I—I can see him from here."

"No, you can't. Be-cause he's out."

"Wha—? What is this? I need to see him; there's been a mix-up. I've been barred from Ops. I need to see him, just for a second—"

"Barred from Ops?"

"Yes. Barred."

"Card not working?"

"That's right, it's—"

"Security clearance revoked?"

"Oh, I guess you've already heard—"

"Reassigned to R&D?"

"Uh, yes, that's right—"

The aide chirped brightly, "Nope. No mix-up. You're reduced to the lowest level of project clearance. You're to report to R&D immediately, to be outfitted for your mechanics coveralls, and to pick up your new lower-security clearance card. Is this clear?"

"Y-yes, it's—it's clear," Jeff answered, his voice no more than a whisper.

"Good. If you have no more questions, Civilian Contractor Waldron, here are your orders, with directions and bus routes to get there. I hear it *can* be difficult to find."

"I already know where ... where Ephraim's lab is," Jeff said, now beaten down completely, and immersed entirely in gloom. He took the papers. "Thank you, Lieutenant."

Still bright and chipper the aide responded, "You're welcome, Mr. Waldron. Good luck with your new assignment."

Clayton came out after Jeff departed. "How did he take it?"

"About as well as I did, sir," the aide said, his chipper demeanor reduced to sounding sad and miserable.

"That's why we pay you those medium-level bucks, Lieutenant."

"I earned them today, sir, that's for sure. If I had to do that to somebody every day, I'd just—I'd just *shoot* myself. And calling him Civilian Contractor Waldron? Brutal, sir."

"Painful—and necessary—but it should have the desired effect. I'd hate like hell to lose that young man. He personifies this program, you know. A lot of people on this base depend on him. One in particular."

"Sir? If he personifies this program, why are we barring him from it? Won't it harm the program?"

"The program needs him, but it needs him one hundred percent invested. Just this morning, he was playing at leaving, talking himself into believing he could do without the program, requesting a transfer. So I gave him what he thought he wanted. He wanted out the door, so I kicked him out the door—*hard.* That woke him up.

"Now here he is, crawling back and apologizing, and he thinks he can just slide back into his cushy job, no harm done. Instead, I've kicked him out the door again, and made it clear that this program doesn't need *him.* I'll call him back, but he needs to feel like an outcast for a while, to appreciate what he had here."

"That's the reason you get paid the bigger bucks, sir. Those are some ballsy moves."

"Pure strategy, Lieutenant."

"Remind me to never play chess with you, sir."

*     *     *

*R&D Lab*
*January 27ᵗʰ, 2099*

"Same wrench as last time."

"Here you go."

"Thanks. Ahh—damn. No, guess it's the other one."

It was a familiar scene, ever more so over the past three weeks, since Jeff's reassignment at the lab. One man sat in a wheelchair, handing wrenches to the other man working on one glitchy hop machine or another; a glitch, as often as not, located in the underbelly of the machine.

"So, have you heard anything from Ops? I thought you would have heard from them by now."

"No. Not a word. Besides, I figure *you'll* hear about it before I do. They'll notify you that you'll be losing your help."

Ephraim said, "Help? That's what you call this? I have to fix everything you work on. Some help."

Jeff grabbed the platform, rolled his mechanic's creeper out from under it, and said, "Well, if you don't like my work, get the hell out of my chair and I'll hand *you* wrenches for a while!"

Rolling Jeff's chair forward and back as though it were his own personal rocking chair, Ephraim said, "Sorry, sonny boy. No-can-do. Orders from the top. I'm to make your stay here as uncomfortable as possible, under threat of death, or even dismemberment. Or worse, the removal of my still."

"Your still? Crap. *That's* heartless. They aren't kidding around, are they? All right. That wrench. Right there. Yeah, thanks."

Ephraim sputtered as he handed off the wrench. "They ain't gettin' her. No way. I will put you straight through *hell* first. Besides, you have to admit; that lovely piece of technology has made your stay here tolerable, especially after hours."

Jeff agreed. "It takes the edge off, I'll give you that much."

"And after a few months of detoxification, your liver will probably start working again. Pretty well, anyway. Well ... all right, no promises."

Jeff grinned. "That doesn't matter. I'll probably keep dropping by after-hours once this is over. *If* they ever decide to put me back on the Ops team. If you don't mind, that is."

"No, I don't mind, always happy to have you. But why the hell do you want to spend your free time here? What about Rose?"

Jeff leaned against the hop machine, expelled a long, deep breath with a loud *whoosh,* and concentrated on a spot on the floor, or any place his eyes wouldn't have to meet Ephraim's. He shook his head, and said, "We're done, I'm afraid. Since that day, I haven't heard a word from her. I can't go see her. They locked me out, and she saw it happen. So, she already knows I can't go there. She knows I'm working here, but she hasn't come to see me, not even once since then. No, I think that's the end of that."

"Okay, so, you can't go to the Ops chamber. Forget about work. Didn't you spend most of your evenings at her place before all this? Did they lock you out of *there*, too? You forgot how to get there? What's the story?" he pressed.

"No, it's not that. It's just that ..."

"Oh, this should be *good.* Go ahead, I'm listening."

"Well, to tell the truth, I kinda locked her out of *mine.* So, I didn't think I should go to hers after that, unless she gives me a sign that it's cool again."

"Yeah, there was a rumor going around that you did that. Most decidedly *not* cool, Jeff. Weren't you the one who knew what to say around the ladies? I don't suppose it's occurred to you to go see her and give her keys to your new locks?"

"It's occurred to me, but I'm still ticked off at her for the way she chewed me out. I'm not too happy over the way I was treated, and not just by her."

"Oh, so the truth comes out. You're still sulking, and anyone can see how *well* that's been working for you. I don't know; maybe you could try something more constructive, like talking."

"Talking?"

"You know, move your lips, make them say some nice things,

maybe throw in a beer and some music. Talking. It's a new thing. They're trying it everywhere."

Jeff shook his head, ignoring the sharp prods and digs buried within Ephraim's humor. "No, I think the time for talking's in the past. If she wanted to be with me, she knew where I was."

Ephraim put on an announcer's voice, and said, "King Jeff has spoken. If the lass wants him, she shall attend his court, and curtsey properly. So it is written, so it shall be done." He dropped the voice, and his tone softened. "You know, you're being kind of a *dick,* Jeff."

"Drop it, Eph. Conversation over. Pick another subject."

"I pick *throwing it all away.*"

Jeff took a deep breath, and sighed in resignation. He pointed, held out his hand, and said, "That wrench right there. Yeah, that one. C'mon, hand it over."

It seemed Ephraim wasn't the only one who had learned how to run away whenever the subject matter wasn't to his liking.

# 17

Only Rose and Fred remained in the Ops chamber. The lights were dimmed, the system was in hibernation mode, and all the other techs had long since called it a day.

"You working late into the night again, Rose?"

She nodded in affirmation, leafing through a file. "Yeah. Go on home. We might get a late hop in, and I still have a ton of paperwork to sift through."

She often worked nights now. The others, who saw and knew why she was distracted, had tried to get her to go out to the usual haunts, and for a short while she went along with them, hoping to find Jeff sitting in their regular booth, waiting for her. After a week, that stopped. He wasn't frequenting their regular spots. She pictured him in some cozy, tucked-away little joint, relaxing in the back with some new female friend, with that old, familiar, happy look on his face, wrapping his new lady's heart around his little finger, just like he'd always done with her.

*I deserve it. I watched them lock him out of Ops, and I didn't lift a finger to stop them. That hurt look on his face when they told him he*

113

*didn't work there anymore. Even the memory of it tears at my heart. I didn't go after him. Who else did he have to turn to? He's out there somewhere, nursing his wounds with somebody who is there for him, somebody who deserves him.*

At home in her apartment, she cried over him, for her loss. She wished he would come by, if only to say what she knew he would say to her, to make it final, to put her out of her misery. Each time she thought of that, she cried again.

But she didn't always cry. There were nights she found herself angry at him for being so selfish, for requesting that transfer without so much as a word of discussion with her. But she had to face it: There *was* nothing official about them.

There never had been. He'd never brought up the subject of taking their relationship to the next level, and she'd never stepped up, had never dared. She cursed herself for being so strong and tough at work, but dropping the ball when her future happiness hinged upon it. Lowering the boom on Jeff at work was something she would have found difficult to do at home, like crossing an invisible line.

Lowering the boom on Jeff. She shook her head at the thought of it. Oh, how she hated that memory. Her last conversation with Jeff, and she had to be spitting-mad at him. Surely, he understood that, as his supervisor, she had no choice. Didn't he? But if he did, why did he leave early, and push his chair home in the cold? He must have recognized her car when she drove slowly by, but he didn't wave or give any sign. Since he didn't wave, she didn't stop. And perhaps the most confusing question of all; what could she possibly have done to offend him so deeply that he would change his locks?

She climbed into bed each night, exhausted, and remembered the times he had slept with her. Always the gentleman, always on top of the covers, keeping her warm and safe while she slept. *So* safe. Now she shivered through the nights, colder than she'd felt in years, and alone. *So* alone. And so empty.

"Oh, Jeff," she said to the still, quiet room, "Where are you? What *happened* to you?"

* * *

Jeff and Ephraim finished their shift, and hung outside for a few minutes, arguing. The hour was late, and the frigid night air showed the cold with every word they spoke.

Ephraim said, "Don't deny it. You miss her. You just want to stay mad at her. And I thought *I* was stupid-stubborn. You take the cake, my friend. Did you guys fight all the time? Is that what this is?"

Jeff countered, "No, we hardly ever argued. We always got along well. What *is* it with you? You act like you're some sort of expert on women."

Ephraim said, "More like the expert on what *not* to do with women, so you don't end up like me. The only woman in my life is Esperanza; she's the only one willing to put up with me."

"Really? I didn't know you had a girl. Maybe I was wrong about you."

"Yes, indeed. Esperanza. My potato whiskey still."

"You—you named your still Esperanza. Why does that make some kind of strange sense to me? Why does that not even surprise me?"

# 18

"Reporting for duty, Colonel."

"Is it that time already, Mr. Waldron? It was so nice and quiet here without you, too. Ah, well, take your station, please. It's just as you left it. I trust you have a clear understanding of my expectations?"

"Crystal clear, Colonel," he said, his face burning with embarrassment over this fresh public humiliation. He rolled into his station.

From the adjacent station, Rose watched him from the corner of her eye. He felt her furtive gazes when she thought he wasn't looking. After a few minutes, she tested the waters. "It's good to have you back, Jeff." She hoped he might at least speak to her as a co-worker.

Her comment served only to remind him that she'd witnessed this new public humiliation firsthand. It seemed every single time he was humiliated, she was right there, watching or playing a part in it.

"I'll bet it is," he snapped, without so much as a glance in her direction, and cracked open a notebook, burying his face in it, much as an ostrich might bury its head in the sand.

Of course, she had no way of knowing how the first conversation would go, but she hadn't foreseen a scenario where she would be the recipient of such a cutting rebuff. It stunned her, and stung much more than she had anticipated. Shaken, she turned back to her work, and for the next few minutes, she stared at her screen, unseeing, fighting back the tears.

From his vantage point in his director's chair, Clayton watched the scene unfold. Fully a month had passed since he exiled Jeff to R&D. He had hoped the disciplining would change things. It was a surprising development when the news reached him about Jeff developing such venom toward Rose. At the colonel's request, Ephraim had done his best to cajole Jeff into putting aside his bitter feelings for her. But if anything, he only held onto it tighter.

Ever since the day she saw the transfer request, Rose was a different person. *More fragile,* he thought. She showed up every day, and performed her duties as expected, but Clayton had some doubts as to whether she could perform adequately in a real emergency.

He'd hoped that Jeff would find his way over to her place and patch things up during the long absence, but according to Ephraim, any mention of Rose or suggestion that Jeff should visit or communicate with Rose met with smoldering anger, immediate shutdown, and a change of subject.

Any colonel wore many hats, and learned his people; learned how to work with them, how to manage them. He'd known Jeff now for many, many years. And Rose, aside from being the smartest, and probably the most beautiful woman in the northeast, might as well have been his own daughter, he cared for her so much.

He knew love when he saw it, and these two had it. Something was wrong. Seriously wrong. He'd done all he could to keep Jeff from leaving the compound, but something was broken here. Something was broken, and it appeared he might be unable to fix it; not as a colonel, nor as a father-figure. He'd seen it more than a few times. Sometimes it just happened. Something broke and came apart too hard, too fast, and too painfully to pull it back together again, or to pick up the pieces.

"Rose, do you have those mission reports for me?" he asked.

She turned toward him when he called her name, but she was deep in her thoughts and at first didn't comprehend what he asked her. "Wha—? Oh. Yes, Colonel, they're right here." She shuffled through her stack of paperwork, located the reports, and walked them over to the colonel. "Sorry, sir, I was, uh, distracted."

"I saw that. I'm not going to pry, Rose. Would it be better if we moved you to another station?"

"No!" she blurted out, and realized she'd reacted too quickly. Her eyes darted to the left and the right, but she saw nobody watching. Lowering her voice to a frantic whisper, she said, "Please, sir. Please. I—I know there are some problems right now, but that station, it's the only chance—" and she suddenly turned a dark red when she realized that the colonel wasn't about to give a damn about her proximity to her boyfriend. He had an Ops program to run. She felt trapped, with no way out. Her eyes brimmed over, and she looked at the floor, desperately aware she'd said too much, certain she'd just offered absolute proof that she was unfit to perform her duties under these conditions.

Clayton, in a whisper as quiet as hers, said, "I agree, Rose. We can't give up on him now. We've got him right where we want him." He reached out, and laid his hand over hers.

Stunned at the colonel's un-military actions, she realized he knew all about what was going on, and still cared. She looked up at him in dazed wonder, daring not to hope it meant what she thought it did. "Sir?"

He leaned forward and whispered, "This is going to take time, Rose. We may not be there yet, but we're not giving up, okay? We'll find a way. We'll think of something. Now, go and take care of that," he brushed two fingers down his cheek a few times to indicate her wet cheeks.

"Yes, sir," she said, and smiled through her tears, feeling a momentary thrill that somebody else cared about this—that someone else actually cared about *her*. The colonel had no choice when she first broke down and sobbed on him. She figured he'd endured it like a good soldier, caught in an awkward situation. And no doubt, he did. But now she knew; that wasn't the whole story.

A tremendous weight had been lifted from her. When she returned, her face was washed, her eyes were made up. And when she took her station, she was more like the old Rose. The colonel was right; whatever form this process took, it was also going to take some time to work through. But whatever happened, she was no longer alone in it. For over a decade, she'd had no one other than Jeff. Nobody to turn to, no one to confide in. Nobody who knew how alone and scared—no, not scared; how *terrified*—she felt at times, because she never told Jeff about how frightened she was of being alone, like she was when she was a little girl—Rosita—and how that little girl still resided within her. She didn't dare, for fear of scaring him off.

Over the past weeks, she'd realized that you can never truly prepare yourself for losing a loved one, however it happens. She'd depended entirely upon Jeff—as much as she had ever depended on anybody—with no backup support system, nobody else to turn to for moral support. Most of their friends were Jeff's friends as much as hers. But she was the superior at work, and senior to virtually all of the co-workers they socialized with, so as close as they would ever get would be to share a few drinks.

She'd long thought that the colonel must have known just how she felt about Jeff, but when he showed her the transfer request in private, she couldn't rule out that calling her in to confer on it might simply be standard protocol, should a transfer request come across his desk. After all, she *was* Jeff's immediate supervisor, as their last actual conversation so vividly demonstrated. Since the day of the transfer request, until ten minutes ago, she'd felt utterly alone in her life and in the world.

Jeff had wasted no time screwing up and stepping right back into it. He'd rolled back into Ops for the first time in a month and acted the complete jerk. Remorseful, he waited at his station for her return, so he could tell her so. He regretted snapping at her, and mentally kicked himself hard for it. It fell wholly upon him to find a way to make things right.

She returned from whatever task the colonel had given her, sat down at her station with an armload of papers, and began sorting through them.

He turned to her. "Umm, about before. I was out of li—"

She wheeled on him. "I know *exactly* what you were doing, Civilian Contractor Waldron, and it occurred to me that you probably don't have enough to do. I've taken the liberty of gathering the past two months' security reports for you. They'll need to be completed immediately."

She slammed the hefty pile onto his desk. "*And* this month's general activity reports you didn't file so far." She dropped an even heftier pile on top of the first.

"But—but I wasn't here to do them."

"Well, you're here *now*, aren't you? I want those completed and on my desk today. *All* of them. Let me know when you're done with them. There's more for you to do. *Much* more."

She stood, and turned briskly to walk out. When she was halfway to the door, the colonel caught her eye. He grinned and nodded, and gave her a wink. *Way to go, young lady. I couldn't have brought him up any shorter myself,* he thought.

She gave him a big smile, and strode purposefully out the door.

# 19

*Eighth Air Force Headquarters*
*Fort Worth AAF*
*July 9ᵗʰ, 1947*

With a full complement of officers and visiting officials present, the general's briefing room was standing room only. The plainclothes agents spaced casually throughout the crowd hinted to those in attendance that something outside of the ordinary might be going on.

Of course, times were such that something extraordinary wouldn't really stand out at this point in time. Since the crash at Roswell, normal was turned on its ear, and finding anything truly ordinary on base was less and less commonplace. As to the focus of today's meeting, rampant rumors circulated through the attendees. But that's all it was—rumors. Casual questioning yielded plenty of speculation, but no solid information. Whatever was going on had yet to reach the scuttlebutt superhighway.

Wren appeared in the doorway of the general's office, and strode briskly to the podium, prepared to address those assembled. No small talk, no chit chat.

"Good morning, all. I'm sorry to call you in on such a hot day. We hope to finish this briefing before it becomes stifling hot in here, so we can all move on to more comfortable locations."

Walking to the easel, he flipped the front page over the top. "I'd like to call your attention to this aerial photo of the facility at Groom Lake, in Nevada. We've officially reclassified this area as secure with a high-level clearance required. It has another name, which we are going to use unofficially from this point forward. Area 51. Please— pay close attention here, because some of the things I'll tell you will seem to contradict other things I say.

"Area 51 does not officially exist. That being said, when you do mention it, please make sure you refer to it *as* Area 51. When asked about it, you will deny any knowledge of its existence, and you will do so by stating *that you have no comment about Area 51.*

"I know these orders seem to contradict each other, but I ask you to follow them to the letter. In a normal high-security environment, this contradicts our typical response policy for such questions. But this is not a normal situation, and the design of these orders does not contradict our intentions in this specific instance. And it's important that you know this in advance; you *will* be asked about it many times in the future. Okay, moving along—"

And the morning wore on. Wren addressed mundane, nuts-and-bolts issues of upgrading the base's clearance and security levels, who the tasks would be delegated to, and timeframes. When he finally dismissed the briefing, he approached Ramey. "General, after the room clears, I'll need a private briefing with you and several of my men."

Ramey nodded, "Of course. I'll clear my schedule," and nodded at his aide, who opened the ever-present schedule book and made the changes, after which he left the room to make some calls.

Once the room emptied, Wren walked to the back and opened a door, gesturing three men inside. The men, who had not attended the briefing, entered and sat down opposite the general.

"General Ramey, I'd like to introduce you to three of my agents. They'll be stirring up some trouble around Area 51. On my orders, they'll be drawing the public eye toward the goings-on there. A couple of words you might not have heard used a great deal before this will eventually become commonplace, and the words are *conspiracy theorist*. Each of these men has undergone rigorous, specialized training. Their job is to infiltrate certain activist groups and stir them up."

Ramey said, "I assume they're part of your little crusade to make the public believe our new story."

"Quite the opposite, actually."

"Excuse me?"

"They'll be establishing conspiracy theorist groups. Their goal is to incite disbelief of the government, spread disinformation, and create conflict. They'll urge the groups to follow the original story, and to monitor the activity at Area 51. They'll claim they've gathered intelligence that indicates the wreckage will be kept there, and that the research on the wreckage and the bodies will take place there."

Ramey was struck nearly speechless. Ever since Wren came on the scene, the base—the general's entire *world*, for that matter—had been in upheaval, bringing an inordinate amount of stress with it.

But now, he was convinced the man was crazy as a bedbug.

Ramey said, "Well, I guess they should have pretty good luck with their accuracy, considering the source of their information. I don't know what you're up to, Wren. But, as of right now, I officially want nothing whatsoever to do with you. *You* changed the story in the first place. Since then I have reports coming across my desk that you've threatened both civilians and military personnel to keep it that way. Now, we're building a 'secret base' in Nevada to hold and research the wreckage and the aliens, to keep our secrets. Yet, you're sending men out there to spread that around, to tell those very secrets. You, Mr. Wren, are a loon of incredible magnitude. Stay away from me. Good day, gentlemen," he said, and made for the exit door, rather than his office.

He needed some fresh air, in the worst way.

When he heard Wren's men trying unsuccessfully to restrain their laughter, he thought, *Give me an enemy that's shooting at me any day, I can handle that. Anything but bureaucrats and politicians and plainclothes agents and their insane agendas,* and he hurried out, leaving the madness behind him.

He couldn't pretend to understand Wren. The phone call he received from the man was way out of bounds, as though Wren didn't care about the secretive nature of what they were doing. Then today, Wren gave all of the officers in the briefing orders to not discuss Area 51, because it didn't officially exist, but to refer to it *by name* as they denied its existence. And then there were those—what did he call them?—*conspiracy theorists*—he was planting out there. Maybe tomorrow, orders would come down to place billboards all along the highway from Fort Worth to D.C., detailing everything they needed to keep secret. It would make just about as much sense.

\* \* \*

*Fort Worth AAF*
*July 9th, 1947*
*11:00 AM*

Oliver "Pappy" Henderson arrived at the Fort Worth Army Air Field, and was bound for the flight office to sign in and report his arrival. As he rounded the corner, he heard a familiar voice off to his side.

"Pappy. Over here."

The pilot spotted general Ramey walking toward him. "General," he said, and snapped to attention, with a grin and a crisp salute.

"All right, Pappy, that'll do," Ramey said with a smile and a barely-there salute in return, and extended his hand to greet his old friend. "I've got something here for you, and you're going to love it. Just the kind of stuff you can't get enough of."

"You mean, you're about to put me through some kind of fresh new hell?"

"Something like that. Let's talk in my office. I have some scotch in there you might like."

"I assume you're talking about the scotch you won from me."

"Can't slip anything past you. Anyway, that's why I thought

you'd like some," Ramey said, and slapped the other man on the back.

Once Pappy checked in, the two men chatted amiably on their way to the general's office. The two had worked together during the war, and since then on various aspects of the Manhattan Project. Long enough to know there were some things to be discussed only behind closed doors. Pappy knew the look in Ramey's eyes. What he had to say would be revealed only when they were well away from prying eyes and ears.

A few minutes later, they relaxed in Ramey's office with a couple fingers of scotch for liquid refreshment.

The general's fingers unconsciously tapped out a distress message against the side of his glass, while he weighed his words before speaking; something he'd been doing a lot of lately.

As Pappy waited patiently, he watched the rattling, ineffective fan in the corner as it slowly turned from side to side, moving the warm, sticky air around the room, and did nothing at all to alleviate the pervasive heat and humidity. He knew the general would speak when he was ready.

Ramey said, "I'm in it—but good—this time, Pappy."

Pappy nodded over his as-yet-untouched glass, and said, "I figured as much, when I saw you were having something to calm your nerves in the middle of the day. I didn't want to say anything."

That drew Ramey's attention to the glass of Scotch whiskey in his hand, and he raised an eyebrow as he regarded it with a look of chagrin. Had it not been Pappy sitting in front of him, he would have found himself embarrassed. As it was, he simply placed it on his desk and pushed it to the side. Pappy placed his glass next to it, still untouched.

"Sorry, Pappy. I'm a little distracted."

"I'm listening, Roger. Anything I can do, just ask."

Ramey let out an audible sigh. "Right now, and for the foreseeable future, I need people around me that I can trust. That's why I called you in on this. You've heard about Roswell?"

"Who hasn't? The scuttlebutt's everywhere. Flying saucers, alien bodies, stuff you wouldn't believe."

Ramey tilted his head a little, cracked a tired, ironic smile, and said, "I wish I *didn't* believe it, Pappy. Hell, I wish I didn't know a damn thing about it. I'm the whipping boy they've placed in charge of the whole thing, and the word has come down from above. It never happened, and I'm to make sure of it. It's like putting the cat back in the bag. We're talking about civilians here. These people know what they saw. And not just a few."

He exhaled forcibly, in frustration. "You can't believe the measures the brass are willing to take to keep this a secret."

Pappy raised an eyebrow. "So, they're not just rumors. You *really* found one. And they're dropping a curtain on it."

"We have one, and some big headaches to go along with it. And now, *I'm* on the hook for the whole deal. They've got people from Washington running around here, with orders to put a lid on it and seal it up tight."

"Yeah, I saw one of them when I was walking in. William Wren. He's an Army Counterintelligence Corps agent. They'll let anybody on a military base these days. That guy gives bottom feeders a bad name. Nasty as they come. Mean as a snake. He answers only to General Trudeau at the Pentagon."

"Oh, you know Wren? Army Counterintelligence Corps, eh? That figures."

Pappy nodded. "He has one purpose; whatever needs doing, he gets it done, and I can promise you, he doesn't care who he has to use up to do it. He's one of those people who could walk through a crowd, and nobody would ever remember him being there. Not one person. But once you *know* who he is, you know he's been there—by the goose bumps on your arms, and the feeling that something's not right. If they're putting a lid on something and screwing it down tight, it's no surprise at all to learn that he's involved."

"Yep, that's him, you've got him pegged. *He's* the reason I called you in. I need my best people on this, people I can trust. There's no way I can do it alone."

"Just ask. Whatever I can do."

"We're preparing a C-54 with a load of highly classified cargo. There may be more loads, too. I need my best pilot on this one. It goes where it needs to, and no exceptions. Security protocols, the works. We're setting up a secure location in Nevada, but it won't be ready for a while. Everything's going to a secure warehouse at Wright Army Air Field in Dayton. After the South Pacific, for you, this should be a cake run."

"What am I moving? Can I see it?"

Ramey shrugged, "I don't see why not. You've delivered nuclear bombs, so your clearance is top-level. Let's go over there, and you can have a look-see."

Once Ramey had the guards clear nonessential personnel from the hangar, he took Pappy to the pile of crates and cases, next to which they found three metallic cylinders, next to a crate made ready for them. They worked the releases and popped one cylinder open.

Pappy said, "Whew. It stinks. What's this blue liquid-gel stuff?"

"It's a phenol and glycerin-based preservative. I'm told the blue color is a result of the reaction with the tissue."

"I see. Well, they don't look *all* that different from us, except they don't seem to have any real muscle structure. Little guys. Big heads, though. How many are there?"

"Three. These three here. Well, you'll be transporting three. One survived, and they're trying to keep it alive, but it's in bad shape. So far it doesn't show any signs of recovering. I'll be surprised if it doesn't follow the others pretty soon."

"What's this? I'm delivering a pickup truck? Or, what's left of one, it looks like."

"It was somehow involved in the crash. It's still something of a mystery. So, until they say otherwise, it goes with the rest."

Pappy looked around him. "I don't see anything radioactive. Just crates and stuff. Like you said, it should be a cake run, sir. *I* don't foresee any problems."

"I have a man who'll be tagging along with you. Warrant Officer Newton. He has clearance. He's to accompany the cargo where it goes. That's another story. One minute he's working for me, keeping an eye on *them,* and the next minute, *they've* acquired him. Sons of bitches," he growled. "I hope I can keep you on my team, Pappy. If I can't, remember it wasn't in my plan."

"No matter who I work for, General, I'll always be a part of your team."

\* \* \*

Pappy's C-54 rolled up to the secure warehouse at Wright Army Air Field, and, one by one, shut down her four radial engines. The doors opened, and a contingent of men surged forward with forklift trucks and all the equipment needed to make quick work of unloading and situating the classified cargo.

Pappy climbed down through the door under the cockpit, followed by Newton, and obtained the requisite signature from the loadmaster sergeant. Except for reporting the successful run back to Ramey, Pappy's part of the job was finished, and the way he saw it, not a moment too soon. He was glad to wash his hands of it.

A few minutes later, he shook hands with Newton and they parted ways. Newton would stay and babysit Washington's shipment to its final destination, while Pappy was to return to Fort Worth. He taxied his plane across the apron, and waited for the tower to clear him for takeoff. Off to the side, he spotted an official XC-35 military transport plane offloading its single passenger.

William Wren.

Pappy thought, *what a coincidence.*

\* \* \*

The secure warehouse at Wright Field generated a great deal of interest and speculation after the wreckage arrived. Everybody knew about it. It didn't matter how. In the military, people always seemed to know about whatever it was, precisely because nobody was supposed to know about it. You could count on that being the norm, rather than the exception.

Any soldier assigned to guard the warehouse and its top-secret contents considered it to be a great honor. But, around one or two o'clock in the morning, when the boredom overwhelmed them with yawns and the ever-increasing threat of sleep, even the finest soldiers found it difficult to stay alert. Anything that helped to stave off sleep was most welcome, especially a familiar face.

"Corporal Benson. How are things going here?"

"Major Corso. What brings you here?"

"You mentioned earlier that I might want to stop by if I was still on-base at this hour. And, as luck would have it, here I am. What's new?" the major asked, curious. Earlier that morning, the corporal had dropped a few hints that left him with the impression that there might be something of interest here.

"You should come with me, Major," Benson said. He unlocked the door and walked into the warehouse. "It's time for me to make my rounds, anyway. Now, you were never here, and you have to swear to me that you won't tell anybody I showed you, okay?"

"It'll stay between us, Corporal. You have my word on that. Are we alone in here?"

"There's one way in, and one way out, sir. All the other doors are locked and chained-up tight. I hope you don't mind my asking, sir, but I heard from some of the boys that you saved ten thousand Jews during the war?"

"I didn't do it alone, Benson. I helped to implement a plan to get them to safety, and we were lucky, I guess. A lot of people worked with me."

"Well, you and those people did real fine, sir. I'm proud to be able to say I know you. Ahh, here we are. It's this crate right here. I'll need you to open those clasps there at that end, and help me lift the lid off the crate."

Corso complied with the corporal's request, but as they laid the lid down, he asked, "Do your orders allow you access to these crates?"

Benson looked nervous as hell at the question, but he fessed up.

"No, Major. In fact, my orders are specific that I am not to touch *anything* within this warehouse. That should let you know how important this is, that, after I defied my direct orders, I told a major I did it. But, you've *got* to see this, sir."

For a brief second, Corso experienced a fleeting deer in the headlights feeling, but a moment's thought brought him to the conclusion that it was a little late for worrying now. He said, "This is already a court martial offense, so I might as well know why I'm risking my pension. Go ahead."

"This one right here, sir. It's some sort of casket, or sarcophagus. It smells pretty bad, so you might want to hold your breath. Hold onto this torch so you can see it. Here goes." He reached down into the large crate and released the locking clasps on the metal cylinder. He grabbed an edge and lifted the lid, and flipped it over to the other side, revealing the contents within.

Inside was a bipedal humanoid, most of which was immersed in a clear, blue liquid. The skin they could see above the liquid was a mottled tan and brown in color. Overall, it looked very much like an Egyptian mummy one might see in the museum. There was no appreciable exterior genitalia, other than some vestigial bits of flesh. It had recognizable hands and feet, but didn't appear to be too tall. The entire body was spare of flesh, and lacked muscle definition. The head was the most remarkable aspect. Huge in size compared to the thin, wasted body and limbs, the cranium was round at the top, and narrow at the bottom, *shaped almost like an incandescent light bulb,* he thought. There was a line, nothing more than a slit, which appeared to be the mouth. The nose barely protruded from the face, slightly below the eyes. He saw two nostril holes below that, also not much more than slits. The eyes were where Corso's senses told him they should have been, though somewhat slanted, and they protruded somewhat; large, and black, with no visible eyelids. *The same as us, but not the same at all,* he thought, leaning closer to see more.

It was then he smelled it, and without warning, his stomach rose into his throat. He backed away and took deep breaths, hoping to avoid leaving any splashes of evidence that might testify to his having visited. Leaning forward, hands on his knees, he hyperventilated for the better part of a minute, until his breathing slowed, and an involuntary trembling seized him. Still concentrating on the drab, unremarkable floor, he managed to ask, "Jesus, Benson. Is that a— an alien?"

"They don't tell me nothin', sir, but if you ask me, then yes, sir, I—I think it's an alien. There's three of them in these cylinders. Don't feel bad, sir, you did better than me the first time. I had to go get a mop. Don't you worry, I can close that cylinder up without help."

Until that moment, Corso didn't fully appreciate the amount of trouble they were in, nor the amount they *would* be in if they didn't button up that crate and get the hell out of there, before somebody caught them there.

Suitably inspired to abandon his patch of tranquil, nondescript floor, he returned to the cylinder, over which, thankfully, Benson already had the lid laid back in place. He reached in to secure the clasps on his end, and then helped lift the lid of the crate into place. Hurrying to snap down clamps nearest him, he said to Benson, "Let's get this closed up. Being in here is a *bad* idea. I'll keep your secret. Don't tell anyone else about this, and whatever you do, *do not* show this to another living soul. I have a feeling that a lot more than our pensions would be on the line. Are we clear?"

He didn't wait for an answer, walking quickly away in the direction from which they first came.

Benson snapped down the last of the clamps on his side, and hurried to join Corso in his hasty retreat. They both felt the warehouse closing in on them. He caught himself looking into the shadows around them, feeling the invisible eyes each shadow now harbored, and all were upon them. Suddenly feeling a chill, he shuddered.

"It don't get no clearer, Major."

\* \* \*

Lieutenant Colonel Arthur Exon was well known on base. He could
go where he wanted, with few exceptions. There was one notable
exception, and it galled him that he was denied entry. Wright Field
was buzzing from end to end with the rumors of the contents of the
restricted warehouse, each story more enticing than the last, and all of
the stories involved aliens.

Dire warnings were issued base-wide. No personnel were to
attempt entry without top-level security clearance, unless they were
hoping to get up-close and personal with the MPs and a stockade cell.

Exon viewed that as a challenge, and waited until it was late at
night, and the base was quiet. Approaching the warehouse, he was
challenged by the night guard, who appeared to be somewhat nervous
and jittery. "Who goes there—oh, it's you, Colonel. Can I help you?"

Exon got right to the point. "You can show me what's in there,
Corporal—" he leaned forward to read the name tag.

"Benson. Corporal Benson, sir. And I have to ask you for your
clearance authorization before I can allow that, sir." Benson blanched,
more than a little apprehensive about the situation, especially since
the night before. Still shaky over Corso's visit last night, he worried
that things could easily get out of hand. Corso was right; he risked a
court-martial by letting anybody without clearance see this. His
career—no, hell, more than just that; his *freedom* would be on the
line.

Once challenged, responsibility immediately fell upon Exon to
present the proper evidence of clearance, and when he didn't do so,
Benson snapped to, stepped back, and offered the business end of his
rifle, escalating the situation by presenting an armed pose not to be
ignored. Still, at this point, the weapon wasn't pointed straight at the
colonel. Not yet, anyway.

Benson knew two things at that moment. First, he'd heard the
scuttlebutt that Exon intended to find a way in to see what was in the
warehouse. Second, and significantly more ominous for him; he also
knew Exon possessed no clearance for the warehouse. If he allowed
the colonel to pass, he could kiss his career goodbye. At this point, he
was also honor-bound to report the incident, and the colonel. He

probably should have radioed for the MPs by now. This Exon character wasn't backing down.

Exon held up a hand, still feeling cocky and confident, and continued to slowly saunter toward the guard. "Easy, Benson, *easy*. I was just hoping you might see your way clear to allowing me a peek. It would just take a min—"

Benson snapped the bolt home on his rifle, shouldered it, aimed, and said, "Not one step closer Colonel, or you're going to have more trouble than you can handle. I know you're curious, but I have a job to do. Walk away while you can, sir. I like you, but I'll do what I have to. Walk away. NOW, sir, before I have to do something more than just put you on report. Right now, and that's the best way this is gonna end. Go on, now. Move it, sir."

The reality of the moment sunk in as Exon looked straight down the rifle barrel, pointed directly into his face. This guard was serious about guarding the warehouse, and more than a little edgy. Without another word, he turned, and quickly melted into the darkness.

He replayed and weighed the situation in his mind. This was no innocent transgression, and there was no way he could paint it that way, should he end up on report now. Accusing a guard of being paranoid and threatening to shoot you won't get you far, particularly when he's *supposed* to shoot you for trying to get past him. And he *had* tried to get past him, more than once. Maybe the guard would be disciplined for *not* shooting him, but that would in no way mitigate any charges against him for the attempted trespass. His arrogance and ardent curiosity, it seemed, were about to cost him dearly, and he saw no way out. To his credit, it never occurred to him to simply lie and claim he was never there.

The next morning, his desk phone rang. "Lieutenant Colonel Exon. Who? Oh, hey, Phil, what's up? Oh, uh, yeah. Oh, boy. That was a, uh, a big misunderstanding, Phil. I'd sure appreciate it if you could keep that off the ... Yeah? You can? That's *great*. Lunch? Sure, sounds good, and you can bet I'm buying. Yeah. I know that place. Eleven-thirty? I'll be there. See you then." He hung up, and almost fell face-first onto his desk in utter relief. He wasn't going on report.

Instead, he had to wait all morning to learn what the lunch meeting was about, or just as likely, what it was going to cost him to keep things this way. *Whatever it costs me, it's a pretty fair trade for keeping my career,* he thought.

Upon entering the diner, he took a minute to allow his eyes to adjust. At a booth near the far end of the place he saw Phil Corso, a major from the base, and the man responsible for making sure his name didn't end up on last night's security report. He literally owed this man his career. "Phil, good to see you," he said with a smile, and sat down opposite him.

Corso shook his hand, and said, "Sorry for the cloak and dagger stuff, Arthur."

Exon said, "Call me Art. I was curious as to what this was about."

"Benson told me what happened last night. I know you're curious, so I'm going to tell you what's in the warehouse. And what I'm about to tell you? I never told you. It never happened."

Exon nodded. "It never happened. You never even spoke to me, much less told me a thing."

Corso looked directly at him, and his piercing gaze remained fixed upon the man long enough that Exon felt like squirming, though, to his credit, he managed to maintain a cool facade.

Satisfied, Corso looked off into the distance, and went into his story, describing in detail what he saw in the warehouse. Exon paid rapt attention to every word. But one word captured his attention beyond all the others.

*Aliens.*

# 20

*Mack Brazel's place*
*July 11ᵗʰ, 1947*

"What's in the bag, Daddy?" Vernon asked.

Mack Brazel looked at his son and said, "I was out riding yesterday, and I found it scattered about the range. Not much, just some bits and pieces. This is all that's left. All the real interesting stuff from the southeast ridge is gone. They picked it clean."

Vernon touched the pieces, feeling the textures, bending the resilient solid sticks, running his hand over the material. As he handled the pieces, without looking up, he said, "I don't want anything from the place with the dead people, anyway. But the Army people didn't let us keep *any* of the other stuff." He looked up at his father. "Can I have some of these, Daddy?"

After a moment's thought, Mack said, "Sure, I guess so. I can't see the harm in it. Just keep them to yourself, and don't tell anyone. We're not really supposed to have *any* of this, y'know."

Vernon dumped the bag onto the kitchen floor, and started sorting through it, finding choice bits for his personal collection of neat kid's stuff.

He didn't appear to be listening, but then he said, "Like we're not supposed to know that the little people died in that crash?"

Mack turned around and faced the boy. "Now, I'm serious about this, Vernon. We have to treat it like it never happened. The government made me promise. I suppose we can do *that* much for them."

"But isn't that like lying, Daddy?" the boy asked with sincerity, his eyes clear and innocent. He was raised to always tell the truth. He knew how to lie, of course. Any kid knew that he stood a good chance of getting an extra cookie by lying, innocently claiming he hadn't yet eaten all three he was allotted. He also chanced being apprehended and getting a stern—and usually amused—look if he was caught. But saying he never saw that crash—that seemed like too big a lie to him, something altogether different, like something real bad might happen if one were caught telling it.

Mack looked with genuine pride and affection at his son, and glanced over at his wife, Maggie, who was less than amused by the turn the conversation was taking.

He said to the boy, "You're right. It's a lie son, and we all know it. But it's not *our* lie, and they're *not* giving us a choice. They aren't taking no for an answer. So, if anybody asks, all we saw was a little material and some sticks. They must have good reason for not wanting this to get out. Your mama and I think it's better if we all just go along with their story. You can do that, can't you?"

The boy looked down, trying to hide the disappointment showing on his face. *Grownups,* he thought, *they can always do what they want, even when it isn't what they say a kid should do.* He said, "But WE know there were people. WE saw them. You, me, and Dee, WE know the truth. Right, Daddy?"

Mack couldn't come down hard on his boy for believing his own eyes, or for wanting to reject this lie now forced upon them. He crouched, and took Vernon by the shoulders, and looked directly into his eyes. "Right, son. *We* know the truth. But we can't talk about it, not outside this house, and not to anybody else. We just *can't.* You understand that, don't you?"

The boy understood completely. He had from the start. So much like his father in so many ways, this was just one more similarity. They both had a natural aversion to dishonest behavior. He would comply, but he didn't have to like it. He looked back into his father's loving eyes and said, "Yes. I promise, Daddy."

Mack gave Maggie a tired, wan smile, and she smiled back briefly at him. That man; how he loved his children. Such a good father, and a hard worker. He'd do anything to keep them safe and happy. She knew he now regretted ever reporting that … that *thing*, whatever it was he found.

Now they wanted him to lie about it if asked. Mack Brazel wasn't much for lying, and she saw how it ate into him, having to do so. Frank Joyce, the manager in town at KFGL, the local radio station, had pursued him until he'd agreed to give a radio interview. She'd listened while he gave the phone interview, and could sense how it galled him to minimize the story.

The military men told him it was his patriotic duty to keep it a secret, to go along with their made-up story. And so, he did it. He hated doing it. He didn't *say* he hated it, but she knew her Mack.

They were about to sit down for dinner, when there came a pounding on the door. Mack answered it, and two soldiers entered. They were accompanied by a nondescript man in a suit, who immediately started asking questions. "Mr. Brazel, is it true that you gave an interview to the radio station this morning?"

For a moment, Mack said nothing, while he evaluated his possible answers. Once he decided that there was no other good answer to give, he responded. "Yes, I gave a phone interview. Why?"

The man in the suit nodded to the others, and said, "Mr. Brazel, we need you to come with us, to answer some questions. We have a serious situation, and your presence is required."

The men moved to either side of Mack, and the man in the suit asked, "We're not going to have any trouble, are we, Mr. Brazel?"

He gave a look of disdain to the man. "I'll go with you. You don't need your men to drag me out," and then, turning to kiss his wife, he said, "Maggie, I'll be home as soon as I can."

"Where are you taking him?" she asked the man, frightened and trembling. "Who are you? What are your names? What did he do that you have to do this?"

"My name is Wren, Mrs. Brazel. William Wren. We're taking your husband to the base, on a matter related to ... to what he found on his ranch."

The poured-out contents of the bag on the kitchen floor caught his eye, and he said, "Is— is that more of the material? How—where did you find it?"

Mack shrugged and said, "Blowing around. Lying around. Out on the same range. I didn't want my stock getting into it. No telling what it would do to them if they swallowed any of it."

Wren pointed and snapped, "You two! Gather all that up and bring it along."

Standing three feet from the distracted Wren, young Vernon casually reached behind him, and stuffed two handfuls of sticks and material into his pockets. Then, just as nonchalantly, he eased his shirttail out, and used it to cover the treasures his daddy told him he could keep.

*   *   *

William Wren walked in circles around Mack Brazel's chair, in the middle of a small, dark room. There was only one desk-lamp, and for some reason they were shining it straight into Mack's face. Because it blinded him, and prevented him from seeing anything else, he closed his eyes, and listened. He noticed that the man dragged one foot slightly. Not much, but enough that he heard it when the man walked.

*Thump. Swish. Thump. Swish.*

He wasn't tied to the chair. It was wooden, rickety, and perhaps the least comfortable chair he'd ever sat in. Tied to it or not, they'd made it clear that he wasn't leaving it until they decided he could. Wren continued to walk in circles as he asked questions— incessantly—and they seemed to be the same questions, asked over and over, each time in a different way.

*Thump. Swish. Thump. Swish.*

Mack was a kind and gentle man, but he was as tough as any rancher in the southwest, and he knew what he'd seen. He wasn't going to say otherwise. They *knew* he knew what he'd seen, and they *knew* he'd agreed not to discuss it elsewhere. That was the reason he talked about having found nothing more than some material and sticks that morning during the interview.

*Thump. Swish.*

Wren intended to set an example with this rancher, make the man a poster boy for his cause. He no longer had any real need to make the crash go away, but he was determined to prevent Mack from gaining any celebrity from the crash, or anything that might encourage him to open up about it. As Wren saw it, it was never too early or too late to plant the seeds of fear throughout the populace. To take the first step toward achieving that, he needed to break this man.

He thought, *I think I'm going to enjoy this.*

Over the next four days and nights, he and others alternated, browbeating Brazel, exhausting him and browbeating him more, and then doing it all over again, and again. On the third day, they took him down to town and walked him along the main street, while Wren whispered questions to him, asking him if he cared about all these people, his friends and neighbors. Mack understood instinctively that anyone perceived to be his friend could be in real danger, once these men learned of it.

Several times, he brushed past old friends as though he didn't recognize them, ignoring their attempts to greet him. When they encountered Dee's mother, Loretta, he sped up and rushed past her before she could speak to him, and quickly walked away. By the time they returned with him to the base and the small room, he was again physically and mentally exhausted. But there was no respite. The questioning started once more, and continued late into the night.

*Thump. Swish.*

But the rugged rancher wouldn't break, wouldn't beg them to

stop. He answered the questions with the same honest answers, again and again, and on the fourth day, Wren realized he'd picked the wrong man for this type of brainwashing. Mack's constitution was too strong. Refusing to admit defeat, Wren stepped up the level of interrogation. In doing so, he knew he went directly against General Ramey's orders. That didn't give him so much as a moment's hesitation, and he thought, *I don't **answer** to General Ramey.*

He no longer cared what Ramey wanted. All he cared about was results.

"Mack. May I call you Mack?"

"No, Wren. *You* can call me Mr. Brazel."

"Great, Mack. You've got a nice little family there. It would be a shame if something bad were to happen to you folks."

"Oh yeah? Are you threatening my family now?"

"Oh, no, I'd never do that. But bad things happen sometimes. For instance, the IRS might find you in arrears on your taxes and foreclose on your land."

"I don't own that land, I lease it from Mr. Foster, and manage the rest for him. Nice try, though."

"It could still be foreclosed on, *whoever* owns it. You'd have to find another place to live and work."

"What a shame, and miss out on all of this? I'd be heartbroken."

"I hear you have a son, Bill? In—where is it?—Albuquerque?— who owns his own home? It would be a shame if a series of unfortunate financial problems should arise for him, don't you think?"

"Whatever you do, he'll survive. We'll all get through it. Now I've already told you, you and I both know damn well what I found out there. I haven't told a soul. I'm sticking to my part of the agreement, so—why are you doing this to me?"

By now, Wren was nearly as tired as his prisoner. What the rancher saw, or didn't see, *none* of that was any longer the point. Somebody was going to walk away from this the winner, and somebody the loser. And the loser would *damn* sure be Mack Brazel, whatever it took.

He dismissed the guards from the room, and waited for them to leave.

*Thump. Swish.*

"Mr. Brazel, I think we need to have a meeting of the minds here, and to be honest, I'm losing my patience with the whole situation. Either this situation goes away, and you admit there was no crash, and nothing more than a weather balloon, or I'm going to have at least one member of your family killed. It'll appear to be an accident, but you can be sure, I *can* make it happen. In fact, I'll eliminate family members of anybody who appears to be helping you to perpetuate this ridiculous story about a crashed alien ship. How am I doing *now,* Mr. Brazel?"

Brazel looked straight forward, blinked, and said nothing. Up until now, he'd believed that as an American citizen, he was immune to this kind of thing, and would remain so unless he committed some sort of heinous crime.

This Wren was so like the Nazi SS officers he'd heard about, that, in that moment, he truly believed that this man *would* harm his family. His family was all he really had in the world. He was just a simple rancher, but his family made him a rich man.

He took a deep breath, and trembling almost uncontrollably, said, "I'm listening, Wren. What do you need from me?"

\* \* \*

The sheriff was outside when Brazel walked out into the sun, looking exhausted. He climbed into the car with Wilcox and asked, "Do you know where we're going?"

"Yes. I heard we're going to have an escort, too."

"Yeah. Just ... drive," Mack said, gesturing forward.

The Sheriff drove to Roswell, to the KFGL radio station, and accompanied Brazel inside, where soldiers had already taken up positions. The regular programming was already interrupted, and Brazel walked into Frank Joyce's office, the Owner/ Manager and friend, who had interviewed Mack several days ago.

"I have a prepared statement I'd like to make, if you'll introduce me, Mr. Joyce."

"Sure, Mack, let me take a look at it."

He read it, and his mouth dropped open. "Why, Mack, this ain't *nothing* like the story you told us the other day; are you sure you want to say this? And who the hell are these soldiers?"

Brazel took him aside, leaned close, and said, "Look son, you keep this to yourself. They told me to come in here and tell you this story or it would go hard on both me and you. *Awfully* hard. Let's just get through this. Will you introduce me?"

Joyce saw that Mack was under duress, so, loud enough for the soldiers to hear, he said, "Why sure, Mack, anything you need. Come on in and I'll work up an intro for you. Bring that paper. It'll just take a second, with your help."

They went into his office, and Mack wasted no time. "Frank. Look, just do what they say, and introduce me, and ask a few light-duty questions throughout. Then I need you to do me a favor. It might cost you, though, so don't say yes, unless you're sure."

"Name it."

After Mack whispered his request, he asked, "Will you do that for me?"

Joyce looked him in the eye. "Just try and stop me."

Three minutes later, at the top of the hour, they were on the air. Joyce welcomed Mack back. The rancher read the relatively brief statement that assured folks he hadn't seen as much as he first thought he'd seen, and that he'd made a mistake, and the military had assured him that all that they found was a weather balloon, and nothing more.

Once the rancher wrapped up his statement, Joyce speculated aloud as to why there were soldiers in the radio station while Mack read his statement.

"I couldn't say," Mack responded, "but, they insisted."

Joyce added a few comments about how disappointed he was that they weren't going to hear any stories about little green men.

"They weren't green," Mack stated.

"And that's Mack Brazel, folks. We'd like to thank him for coming in today and spending a little more time with us." He turned to Mack and said, "And … we're off the air."

"And in hot water, Frank. I hope they don't go too hard on you."

"I'll be okay, Mack. Give my best to Maggie."

Escorted by the soldiers, Mack walked out the door with the sheriff, where he saw Wren standing, with his car radio playing. The man's face was so red it was almost purple. Mack strode over to the detestable government man, and said, *"That* was the first time I've said anything about it, Wren, because up until now, I stuck to the deal I made. You threaten me or my family one more time, hurt somebody I love, or so much as *talk* to anybody I love, and all bets are off. The whole damned world will know, and I'll be the one who makes sure of it."

He turned on his heel, strode over to the sheriff's car, climbed in, and away they drove.

Wilcox said, "You should know, that Wren character was in my office, asking me questions about Vernon, Mack. Somehow he got wind of the fact that Vernon was with you."

Mack nodded. He understood now. He thought, *this isn't over; this will **never** be over,* and asked, "Please tell me he didn't ask about anyone else."

"He didn't. Hopefully he'll never hear about Dee. He won't hear it from me, Mack. You have my word on it."

"Thanks, George. That boy and his mama are good people. They don't need to be in the middle of this, though I can't be positive any more that we'll be able to keep them out of it."

Wilcox said, "You know, when you first came into my office, I didn't believe a word of what you told me. Figured you were full of it. I thought maybe you'd been drinking."

"I wish to hell I *had* been drinking."

Neither spoke another word for the rest of the drive home, not even when Mack climbed out of the cruiser, and walked slowly across the yard to his house. Wilcox had never seen Brazel walk any way but bolt upright and tall, the same way he sat in his saddle.

Not tonight. The rancher's shoulders were tired and bent, and he walked like a man burdened, carrying the whole world.

A single light burned in the kitchen. "Mrs. Brazel, I'm home," he said, and felt his strength leave him. His legs grew rubbery, and he grew faint.

"Mack? Oh Mack, what—what did they do to you?" she said, rising from her work at the table and rushing to him, and threw his arm over her shoulders. "I've got you. Come in here, sit on the sofa, that's right, I've got you."

She helped lower him onto the sofa, and sat next to him, worried. He sat for a minute or two, saying nothing, and staring straight ahead. When he finally moved, it was to turn to her, with desperate, hollow, sunken eyes. "Oh. Oh, my, Maggie," he said, and looked around, confused and disoriented. "I— I don't know what we're going to do. I just don't know what we're going to do," he said, trembling. The tears threatened, and then brimmed over.

"Oh, my Mack, my dear Mack. My poor husband, what did they do to you?" she cried, and held him tight against her while the sobs wracked his body, and his shoulders rose and fell. She held him for a long while, until he succumbed to it all, and collapsed there beside her. She straightened him out as best she could, pulled off his boots, covered him with a blanket, and pulled her chair over next to him.

Several times during the night, he sat upright and cried out in alarm, calling her name, and the children's, and it sounded to her like he was warning them of something. Each time, she soothed his brow and laid him back down. When he eventually fell into a deep sleep, she remained awake, watching and worrying about him until the morning sun crested the hills, warming the morning sky. He never stirred until the sun started to wane, late in the day. When he woke, he appeared haggard, and disoriented.

For forty-eight years, the truth had been the man's center, his pillar of strength. In Roswell, New Mexico, anyone who knew him, knew the truth walked with Mack Brazel. His handshake was his word, and his bond. Nobody could imagine any scenario so extreme as to ever cause him to tell a lie.

But they would *all* learn in the many dark days yet to come; in Roswell, New Mexico, the truth was no more.

# 21

*The Pentagon*
*Office of General Trudeau*
*July 15ᵗʰ, 1947*

"Let me get this straight, Wren. You're proposing that we create a whole new branch of the armed services to create enough chaos to provide a smokescreen for you, because you need it to move some classified materials around?"

Wren opened his folder, laid it in front of General Trudeau, and said, "That's a bit oversimplified, General, but yes. Others have proposed it; I'd be heading up the implementation. You have to admit that there is a growing need for this transition. The Army doesn't enjoy sharing its budget with the Army Air Corp, and feels its programs are suffering from the expansion of air development projects.

"The proponents of a separate Air Force—that's what they hope to call it—feel that with the increasing air activity by foreign countries, and others visitors to our airspace that are quite possibly not from this world, there exists a real need for an armed service dedicated to focusing on these unique, potential threats to our national security. The groundwork has already been laid.

149

"Add those ever-present needs to our more, ahh, surreptitious endeavors, and I feel it presents a perfect opportunity to conceal the movements of the wreckage from Roswell, and secure it elsewhere, undetected, and wholly unsuspected by anyone. Every minute we wait, the more likely it is that we will lose our window of opportunity, and the greater the potential risk. We must make all possible haste to study what providence has placed in our hands."

Trudeau thought about it, scratching his head. Wren was a continual pain in the ass, but he was right about this. This was an opportunity they couldn't pass up. Not only would it achieve everything Wren had listed off to him, but it would place the Air Force in sole control of any advanced alien technology, and instantly make the Air Force the elite branch of the service. The funds would flow uninterrupted for many years to come.

He began to populate a mental list of the people he hoped to bring into the situation. The man he believed would make a perfect first secretary of the Air Force came to mind; his old friend, and an avid Air Force proponent, Stuart Symington.

"Not bad, Wren. Not bad. It has potential. Let me start making calls. If we're going to make this happen, we'll need the right people behind us."

Wren laid another thick folder on Trudeau's desk. "You'll see here that a comprehensive evaluation has already been completed. It includes the projected use of personnel, many of whom I'm sure you'll find to your liking, along with a strong recommendation for the President to consider one Stuart Symington for the position of first secretary. The President has his mind set on Carl Spaatz for the first Chief of Staff. He's a strong general, though I'm not sure he's willing to be a team player for us. Time will tell."

Trudeau asked, "Who did you have in mind for the Chief of Staff?"

"Hoyt Vandenberg. He was on board with the idea of a transition to a dedicated Air Force right from the start. And I can say with some certainty that he'll work with us."

"This implies that the President has already been briefed and is already onboard with this, is that correct?"

"Yes, sir, he is; in theory, anyway. The politics are well underway. He can look forward to receiving high praise for his vision and foresight, so, for all intents and purposes, it's a done deal."

"I see," Trudeau said as he leafed through the folder. "Very good. Let's keep Vandenberg high on the list, then. We'll need good people." He looked up from the folder. "When did you find time to do all this? The work done to perform these evaluations must have taken months."

To his knowledge, something like this had only been in the theoretical stages. "If this is as complete as it appears to be, we'll be able to move ahead with this right away, Wren. I'm impressed."

"Wonderful, General. I'll look forward to working with you."

\* \* \*

*The Pentagon*
*July 26ᵗʰ, 1947*
*Three weeks after the Roswell Crash*

Wren presented a copy to General Trudeau, and announced, "Aboard the Sacred Cow, President Truman just signed Executive Order 9877, and I quote:

"Executive Order 9877 assigns the primary functions and responsibilities of the armed forces. The United States Air Force is charged to organize, train and equip air forces for air operations including joint operations; to gain and maintain general air superiority; to establish local air superiority where and as required; to develop a strategic air force and conduct strategic air reconnaissance operations; to provide airlift and support for airborne operations; to furnish air support to land and naval forces including support of occupation forces; and to provide air transport for the armed forces except as provided by the Navy for its own use."

He lowered his copy, and said, "In other words, the Air Force is now an autonomous, dedicated branch of the United States Military."

Trudeau looked pleased. "So, where does this place us now?"

Wren sat in the chair in front of the general's desk. "With your permission, sir, I'd like to implement the *other* side of our plan, and utilize the impending chaos to hide our movements. The packages in question are scheduled to be moved from Wright Field to an undisclosed secure location. I say "undisclosed" because I've already leaked that information through our operatives, and they'll be watching Groom Lake—Area 51—like a hawk."

He handed Trudeau a folder. "With the creation of the United States Air Force, and the need for dedicated Air Forces bases, the entire contents of many military bases are going to be transported from base to base. With the average number of shipments presently leaving bases by plane and truck every day, a determined person could sort out one shipment from another. This massive reconfiguration of our military bases will create chaos on a scale never before seen, and will also enable us to insert operatives and trusted personnel with relative ease."

He handed over one last folder, and said, "While the rest of the world is looking at Area 51 and hoping to glimpse the, ahh, packages we've moved there, we'll already have the items in question safe and secure in our underground facility in South Dakota, a secret base we call Warehouse 15. This will take a concerted effort to pull off, but I feel we can best protect our packages by spiriting them away in this fashion."

Trudeau looked up from the papers. "I'm going to give you carte blanche on this, Wren. You've pulled off the creation of an entire new branch of our military, so I'm guessing you can find a way to move a few crates around while nobody's looking. You have my authorization, and best of luck to you. I'll keep my fingers crossed."

"Thank you, General."

# 22

Jeff asked, "How come you still have me working under here? I work back at Ops now, so technically, *you* should be the one under here."

Ephraim said, "Because you're good at it." He found himself wondering whether Jeff had read The Adventures of Tom Sawyer.

Jeff said, "As I recall, you complained that you had to go back and fix everything I worked on. How does that make me *good* at it? Or were you just lying?"

"Okay. You were getting much better. I lied a little. But I have some whitewash here."

"Whitewash?"

"Nah, forget it. It's nothing."

"Okay. I have a question, Eph. Once T.I.T.O.R. takes a hop out and screws something up, why can't we just go right back again and do it again; fix it right away? That would seem to make more sense, but they never do that."

"You'd think it would, but we only have three operational hop machines—"

"Not counting your hot rod."

"Not counting my hot rod. The point is, they're always spoken for, and they're always out on missions. Even if they *weren't* out on missions, you can't take a hop machine back to the same time twice."

"Yeah, why is that?"

"Want to see the math? There are some pretty cool algorithms that go with that."

"What? Math? Algori— no. Besides, what I'm saying is that it makes no sense. With all the missions we run, they'd be useless in a matter of months. We'd have to build new machines all the time."

Ephraim said, "Pretty much. What do you think I'm always working on? When a hop machine reaches saturation—that's what we call it when it's used up most of its available time slots—we have two choices. The first is to build a new machine. Then there's the alternative. We can completely recalibrate an existing machine to a new frequency, so that its "signature" is completely different. That job alone takes nearly a month of work to achieve. But a month is a whole lot faster than building a new machine from scratch.

"Even then, it requires pulling all the generators off, rebuilding, resetting, and recalibrating them to a new signature. Every generator must match the others *perfectly*. It's tedious, and it's time-consuming job. But that's not all."

Jeff said, "There's *more?*"

Ephraim nodded. "There's red tape. The Board. They decide upon and approve every hop, and even when a hop comes back where they inadvertently caused a problem, they deliberate on it for weeks, sometimes months, before sending anyone back. Once they decide to send a hop back, one of the machines must be clear to be in that time. If not—"

Jeff was quick to catch on. "If not, the hop has to wait until 'fresh' machines are available."

"If not, the hop has to wait. You got it. Now, figure a month per machine to rebuild it, three machines, reset each one four times a year. Now you know why I'm always here."

"Now I know why you drink so much."

Ephraim laughed. "You should read about some of the missions the Board decides are important sometime. *Then* you'll know why I drink."

"I work in Ops. I've seen it. Heard the comments. Heard the colonel. I've even made the odd comment myself."

"Morons with power, incapable of rational thought. Most of what they do is reaction, not prevention. Kind of defeats the purpose of time travel and correcting historical errors."

"Rose says the same thing."

"Oh, good. Are you two lovebirds talking again?"

Jeff pushed and pulled himself into a sitting position up against the hop framework, and tossed his wrench down in disgust. "Lovebirds. Right. No. Not only are we *not* talking, she's got it out for me. She's out to make me pay."

"Really? What did you do now?" Ephraim asked, a bit too gleefully for Jeff's liking.

"*Nothing.* Not a *thing,* I swear, Eph. I even tried to apologize to her, but she wasn't having any of it. I'm screwed," he said with a deep sigh, underscoring his underlying nervousness by unconsciously running his fingers back through his hair a few times. He pulled the hair as he did so, and sucked air through his teeth.

He continued. "Clayton says if I screw up just one more time, he's going to escort me to the gate. And Rose—she seems determined to make sure I do just that."

Only then did Ephraim see how distraught he was. "I'm sorry, Jeff. I didn't mean to laugh. But I'm sure Clayton didn't mean that when he said it."

"You didn't see the look in his eyes when he said it. He meant it."

"But Rose, Jeff? I don't think Rose could *ever* be out to get you."

"Yeah. I would never have believed it myself. Until I saw it."

"That bad?"

"Yeah. That bad," he groaned.

"Sounds like you've got some serious apologizing to do."

"Nope. I tried that."

"Try again. I'm serious. You need to keep at it. Let her know you really mean it. You two had something special. It's worth fighting for."

Not unexpectedly, Jeff dug his heels in. "Whatever we had, it's gone. I don't know what her problem is, but I'm getting to the point where I no longer care."

"Yes, you do. You know you do. Hell, even *I* know you do. Go on, stop by her place. Tell her you're sorry. Tell her you know you have a lot to make up for. You guys were so close. I can't believe that it's suddenly all over."

Jeff wavered, and muttered, "Oh, I don't know—"

"See? *You* can't believe it, either. You'll hate yourself if you don't try. I'll bet she's waiting for you to go that extra mile, to prove that you know changing your locks was a major stupid thing to do. And we both know that *was* major stupid, don't we?"

Jeff didn't even try to disagree. "You think so? You think she's waiting for me to step up and admit it?"

"I think she is. She's not going to make it easy for you, but I'm right, or my gal's name isn't Esperanza."

"*Not* helping," Jeff said. After giving the matter some thought, he wiped his hands, pulled himself up into his chair, and said, "Well, I suppose I'd better get on home. I have to be in Ops extra-early tomorrow. The old man's bringing in some bigwig from Port Angeles, and it seems that I volunteered to be their tour guide, or babysitter, or *something* like that. They actually used the word *volunteer,*" he sighed. "Ever since I screwed up, I get *all* the crap jobs."

"I won't say that you don't deserve it. Sorry, but friends don't B.S. friends. Look, promise me you'll at least think about talking with Rose. I'm serious."

"Mmm-hmmm," he responded, absently, and wheeled toward the door. "Night, Eph."

"Night, Jeff. See you soon."

"Not if I see you first." Wheeling down the drive and onto the sidewalk, he maneuvered around the accumulated windblown drifts, and arrived at the bus stop. It was bitter cold out, and he looked for a bus. Soon, he saw one coming the other way. It wasn't his bus, and it was going the other way. His eyes came to rest on the bus stop across the street, kitty-corner, a couple of hundred feet from him. He checked his watch.

Before he was conscious of the decision he'd made, he wheeled his chair off the curb and into the street, determined to make it to the opposing bus stop and catch that bus, which he knew would go past Rose's place.

Minutes later, he relaxed in the comparative warmth of the bus, and with some satisfaction, noted, *I made it.*

The bus deposited him at Alabama Place, leaving him shivering in the bitter cold again. But this time, he wasn't chilled. He was more scared than cold. *This is crazy. It's been too long, I waited too long. I shouldn't be doing this.* But the bus that dropped him off was gone.

Already committed, he wheeled down the street, up the walk to her building, and using the key he still carried, entered the building. His shakes grew more pronounced when he reached her floor, and he approached her room by sheer willpower, forcing his trembling hands to push, as they didn't seem to want to roll the chair those final feet.

Five full minutes passed, while he silently debated the pros and cons of being there, his upper half fully as paralyzed by doubts as his lower half was by injury. Suddenly, without warning, his hand reached out and knocked on the door. There was no going back now.

Hearing the familiar rustling noises of Rose approaching the viewing window in the door, he looked up at it, the way he had a thousand times before, and tried to smile, like he did then. All at once, it hit him. He thought, *Why did I wait so long to do this? This is all I've wanted to do every single night. It's not living without her. It's just—existing. Ephraim was right, I need to make this right, and I need to do it tonight. Good old Eph—*

"Jeff? What are *you* doing here?" Rose spoke sharply as she peered through the narrow opening, with the door cracked open to the end of the chain. "What do you want?"

He had so much to say. "Rose, I came to talk to you. Can I come in?"

"I don't think that's a good idea. You shouldn't be here. Please leave."

"Please, Rose, I—"

The door closed, and he heard the bolt snap into place with a solid 'thunk.' He knocked again. "Rose, please. I'm sorry. I know I was wrong. Rose?"

He heard no sounds behind the door, and raised his hand to knock again. It was then he saw the time on his watch, and withdrew his hand. The last bus of the night would run by the stop outside in just a few minutes, and he had a snowy hill to contend with.

The choices left him torn. He could make that bus, or roll all the way home in the bitter cold. There certainly was no chance of him staying here tonight. Placing his hand against the door one last time, he said, "I'm *so* sorry, Rose." In silence, hand on the door, he waited for half a minute for her to return, for the door to crack open again. The thoughts of leaving her, of letting go, they tore at him. But she wasn't coming back. Heaving a sigh of resignation, he rolled down the hall to the elevator.

Inside her apartment, she sat with her back against the arm of the sofa, knees to her chest, with a pillow hugged tightly to her, covering her mouth. She had no idea why. Was she afraid she might answer him? Call back to him? Ask him to stay? All of the above, because she wanted him there beside her *so* badly, she could barely stand it.

But she wanted to be angry with him, too. *He's so sorry. I'll bet he is. He should be.* She wanted him to hurt the way she had, all those nights, waiting for him to come and be with her, the way he had *always* come to be with her before—before it all happened. She wanted him to know what it felt like to know that somebody he loved would not be there with him tonight, the way that she was going to be without *him* tonight—

*"BRRRINNGG!"*

The ringing of the phone next to her gave her a violent jolt, bringing her back to her surroundings, leaving her briefly disoriented.

It took several rings for her to recover from the initial fright. Still somewhat dazed, she answered, "Hello?"

"Hi Rose, this is Ephraim."

"Why are *you* calling me?" she snapped, as much from still-raw nerves as anger. Even so, their last conversation had ended abruptly, due mostly to Ephraim's stellar people skills. She hadn't yet forgotten it, and given the slightest chance, intended to exercise her woman's prerogative not to, for as long as possible.

Ephraim knew he deserved that, and accepted his lumps so he could move on to the reason why he called. "I'm calling about Jeff, Rose."

"Jeff?" she asked, caught off-balance by the combination of his arrival, departure, and now Ephraim calling to talk about him.

"Yes, about Jeff. He's been upset for a long time now. He misses you, but you know how guys are; we're too stubborn for our own good. Tonight he was really in bad shape over it, and I think I talked him into going to see you, and trying to make up for the way he behaved. Anyway, it's possible that he might be dropping by to see you. I thought you'd like to know."

She muttered, "He was already here. I sent him away."

"Oh, uh … I'm … sorry to hear that. He, uh, *told* me you didn't want anything to do with him anymore. I guess—I guess I just couldn't believe that, with all the history you two have. Well, you can blame me for sending him over, Rose. I talked him into it. He knew what was going on between you two, better than I did. Ahh, I'm sorry for bothering you. Good night."

"That's okay. G'night," she said, no longer angry, sensing that Ephraim was truly concerned for both her and Jeff. *That was nice.* She hung up the phone in a daze, confused over some of the things Ephraim had said.

*He really missed me? He was in really bad shape over this? And he thinks I don't want to have anything to do with him? After all our history together?*

She sat straight up. "Oh, God. I sent him away. He's going *away!*" she cried, as she leapt from the sofa and ran to the door, throwing the lock bolts and pulling the chains off, her voice frantic, praying as she unfastened them. "Please, God, let him still be here!" The hall was empty. "Jeff! Jeff, wait!" She sprang down the hall, and hit the elevator button.

Rocking nervously from foot to foot, and wringing her hands, she waited fifteen seconds, then thirty, then she could stand still no longer, and sprinted for the stairwell at the end of the hallway, down the stairs, and slammed the bar, running straight out the door into the street.

Up the hill, at the end of the street, the bus slowed to pull up to the bus stop. She sprinted as fast as she could, yelling his name, begging for it to wait.

As she neared, the bus pulled away. She knew she couldn't catch it. Running alone in the middle of the snowy street, she slowed, stopped, and watched in despair as the red taillights faded in the distance, taking Jeff away from her—again.

A searing pain in her feet drew her attention, and she looked down to see her bare feet in the snow, and that she was wearing nothing more than pajamas. At thirty degrees below zero, the wind cut through her like a knife. The freeze-burning continued as she ran back to the building, and she realized her keys were upstairs, on the table by her door.

She hopped in place, trying to stay warm, frantically pushing buttons, until some kind soul buzzed her in. Embarrassed, she woke the building superintendent, who stumbled out of bed, and let her back into her room. Thankfully, he was too groggy to be upset, and departed without saying anything to make her feel any worse than she already did.

In her room, she curled up on the couch again, shivering from cold, and inches from breaking down and crying. Instead, she found herself at a much more serious place in her mind. For the first time, through the tears, the anger, and the reprisals (yes, she'd told herself over and over that saddling Jeff with the crap jobs and the endless piles of forms at work weren't a form of revenge, but that was B.S.), it became clear that though she loved him with all her heart and soul, that they were in danger of being lost to each other.

*This has gone too far. It has to stop. First thing in the morning, I'll talk with him.* Nothing was more important than finding their way back to each other. *Nothing,* she thought, as a single tear trickled down her cheek.

The following morning, she arrived early at Jeff's place, only to discover he'd already left. Hurrying into Ops, she remained resolute in her decision. She would follow through on her plan from last night. But Jeff wasn't anywhere to be seen in the command center when she dropped her things at her station. No matter. It was important to tell Clayton what she had decided anyway, before Jeff returned.

Before she covered half the distance to the command chair, the door slid open. In rolled Jeff, and alongside him strode a tall, attractive blonde woman. Rose tried not to stare, but it was hard not to notice the woman's stunning figure, and *impossibly* long legs.

The blonde held her attention long enough for Jeff to spot Rose. Still feeling the sting from last night, he quickly veered off to his station, choosing discretion as the better part of the day's valor.

The blonde continued to walk toward Rose, when Clayton spoke. "Rose! I'd like you to meet my niece, Samantha Clayton. Sam's come to spend a few months, or maybe a year with us. I promised my brother I'd give her a try in Ops, since she has a Doctorate in quantum physics. I believe she'll be an excellent fit for our program. Sam, this is Rose Rios."

He said to Rose, "I've paired Sam up with Jeff. He's volunteered to show her around and help familiarize her with the place, give her the lay of the land, so to speak. If there's anything I've forgotten, Rose, let me know. Let's make Sam comfortable here on her first day."

Samantha smiled, and to Rose's further dismay, displayed a bright white, perfect set of teeth as she extended her hand. "Rose, I've read and heard *so* much about you. I'm honored to be working here with you. This is all pretty exciting for me. Imagine, I'm going to be working on the famous T.I.T.O.R. project."

Rose managed a distracted smile, and mumbled something that resembled a welcome. After the introductions, Samantha walked over and took her place at the next station on the *other* side of Jeff, of all places, and she struck up a conversation with him. Rose, unaware she was still standing alone in the middle of the floor, watched the scene unfold.

Their conversation animated, they laughed and joked, and then Samantha lowered her head and tossed her long, blonde hair back over her shoulder.

In that moment, last night played out again in Rose's head. She saw Jeff knocking, and the hopeful look on his face. His falling face when she sent him away etched itself in her mind. And there would be no chance of forgetting how she found herself alone, half-dressed and half-frozen in the street, just a stone's throw from the bus stop.

Unsure of what to do, she chose to flee, and hurried from the command center, to find work elsewhere for the day.

As the doors of the command center closed behind her, she heard a rushing noise in her ears, louder and louder. Perhaps it was the blood pounding through her veins.

Or, maybe it was the sound of everything she'd ever loved or cared about being destroyed; swept away from her by a blonde force of nature.

* * *

Samantha stacked the last file, and asked, "So, what's next?"

"How does lunch sound?" Jeff answered.

She answered with a beaming smile, "Perfect. I can't wait. Let me drop these files off with Uncle—ah, I mean, the colonel, and I'm finished here."

He closed his notebook, and backed out of his station. "Me too. I'm starving." On the way out the door, he said, "The food here's nothing to write home about, but they do a pretty fair job. Sure beats cooking for myself."

As they ate, Samantha decided to learn a little more about him. "You said the food here beats cooking for yourself. I take it you're single?"

"Yeah. Single." He looked out the window, and under his breath, muttered, "That's me." After a moment's thought, he turned to her and said, "I guess you'll hear about this anyway. You remember Rose, who you met this morning. She—I—we—used to be close, for a very long time. That's all over now."

As he spoke, she watched his face. "You don't sound happy about that. I'm sorry to bring up something painful to you."

He looked at her and shook his head. "There's no way you could have known. I made a mistake, screwed up, and that's that. We're through. No talks, no more phone calls." He looked off into the distance, mentally revisiting the recent past. "I thought maybe—maybe if I went to her and threw myself on the mercy of the court; maybe we could patch things up."

Though she waited, he stopped there without continuing, so she said, "Well, don't leave me hanging here. What happened?"

His face took on a pained look. "I went to her place, and knocked on the door, and I asked her to talk. She told me to go away, and closed the door. You know, Samantha, I hear it over and over again in my head; the bolt, slamming home on that lock. It was like ..." he shook his head, as though he couldn't stand having the memory occupying his thoughts.

"I understand. I've been there myself."

"Yeah?"

"Oh, yeah. Change a few details of the story and the names, and you have the reason why I'm here."

A kindred spirit. He looked her quickly up and down, and said, "Now, who the hell would get rid of somebody like you? You look like a keeper to me. What was he, crazy?"

"Not crazy," she said, smiling in appreciation at the freely offered compliment, "but not smart enough to throw himself on the mercy of the court. Hell, he never even bothered to show up for court," she admitted. Her face fell. It was her turn to take on a distant and distraught look.

He asked, "I'm guessing that you would have forgiven him?"

"Yeah, probably. I think so."

The irony caused him to chuckle. "Well, here we sit; we're quite the pair, aren't we? Tell you what. I'll make a deal with you. When it gets to the point where you need someone to talk to, you call me to come cheer you up. And I'll call you when I need somebody, too. How does that sound, Samantha?"

She looked into his kind eyes for a few seconds, and said, "My friends call me Sam. Remember that, friend. Because you've got a deal." Without any warning, she leaned over and kissed him on the cheek. "And now, it's sealed," she said, flashing another one of her dazzling smiles.

He couldn't help but smile back. And when he did, he couldn't help but feel better. A little bit, for the moment, at least.

Across the cafeteria, Rose felt her world rock when she saw Samantha kiss Jeff, and the smiles that followed.

Everybody else saw it, too.

# 23

The Northwestern Fortress was located in Port Angeles, Washington. It was there that Samantha was brought up by her close family, which, in her younger years, consisted of her mom, her uncle Marcus, and her dad, General Conrad Clayton. Prior to traveling to her uncle's fortress in northern Maine, she'd lived her entire life within the walls of the Northwestern fortress.

A good-sized city in its own right, Port Angeles was more of a "normal" city than any of the other fortresses dotting the U.S. countryside, due primarily to its access to the shipping lanes. That enabled the region to support many more types of businesses than it otherwise could have supported. Once the nuclear attack took place in 2015, the same geographic elements and prevailing winds that previously held the pacific rains at bay acted similarly to keep the densest radioactive fallout clear of Port Angeles. Accordingly, it remained one of the most unaffected spots in the country. In spite of the blackened skies and deadly sunshine unfiltered by ozone, the surrounding countryside remained relatively pristine. In fact, of the entire nation, eighty-five years later, Port Angeles remained the location displaying the least severe damage from the ravages of nuclear war.

Port Angeles boasted PAP, Port Angeles Polytechnic; a small but highly-accredited college, from which Samantha had earned her

Doctorate in Quantum Physics.

Life in Port Angeles was pleasant enough for her, though others would have considered it exceptional. To look at her, tall, extraordinarily beautiful, always smiling, one might never believe it, but she had her own burdens to bear. As the daughter of the general who ran the largest fortress in the country, effectually the military leader running the complex that housed the government of the surviving United States, the everyday expectations placed upon her were formidable. Though her father loved her, everyone and everything else imaginable competed and clamored for his attention. He made every effort, but more often than not, she came out second best. Too many birthdays were spent alone, and graduation ceremonies were spent scanning the faces in the audience, in hopes that, just that once, his ever-changing schedule didn't prevent him from attending the important event.

College, though demanding—or, perhaps because it *was* demanding—was a welcome distraction for her. During the last three years of school, her spare hours were spent with a young man who, after many hints and no small amount of prodding, asked her to marry him. Steve Tarken, one of her classmates, was a well-liked, promising young scientist who, by all appearances, had everything in common with her. Until the day they graduated, the day all that changed. The day Tarken vanished from her life.

He didn't die. There were plenty of signs of life. His mother, who often spoke to him, simply wouldn't reveal his whereabouts. Perhaps it spoke more to the real feelings Samantha had for him that she never searched for him, never visited their old haunts, never took advantage of her father's influence and connections, which would have enabled her to track him down in a matter of hours. To be sure, she was hurt by Tarken's sudden departure. But nothing more than that drove her or gripped her. He was gone, and even she was surprised to find that she was more than satisfied with that.

But it did bring other questions to light. Why *was* she so easily satisfied with that? What did that say about her? The introspection began, and soon the inescapable truth surfaced. Tarken wasn't enough for her, and never had been. Perhaps he'd seen it for himself, and knew what might lie in the future if they remained together. By everyday standards, he was considered highly intelligent, but Samantha was so brilliant that even Tarken saw it. By comparison, he was ordinary, and even he considered himself to be boring compared to Sam. Though he could have found a better way to leave her, she had to admit that he had found a way to effectively address the most important issue they faced.

They didn't belong together.

After his disappearance, some months passed before she announced that she had outgrown Port Angeles. Whether that was true or not didn't matter. It wasn't exactly a revelation. She no longer wanted to be there. The unambiguous feeling that she had outgrown the fortress was sufficient to fit her needs. She'd grown larger than the fortress walls, and it was time to leave.

General Clayton was not much of a family patriarch in some ways. Clearly, he didn't excel at being an at-home Dad, but he could more than make up for it in other ways. For instance, he could make things happen. Now that Sam had stated her intentions to leave, his formerly vexing high-raking military position and power offered tools, custom made to serve her purposes.

So, when she asked to go and live at the Great Northeastern Fortress with her uncle for a time, it happened with the speed only a five-star general could bring to bear upon the situation. One week later found her sitting in the lunchroom at Loring, commiserating with her new coworker and good friend Jeff, who seemed to be a wonderful listener. She felt so comfortable with him. Just feeling *something* again was an improvement, and she felt better than she had in months. She had found a friend, and felt comfortable. The rest would come.

After lunch, as they ran errands around the base, she asked, "So, what are you going to show me this afternoon?"

"I thought we'd drop by R&D. That's the research and development lab. I'll introduce you to my best friend, Ephraim."

"Any friend of yours is a friend of mine," she said.

"You say that now, but you might want to reserve your opinion for later. Ephraim, he's a—" he leaned his head back and gazed skyward, hesitating in his search for the right words, "an acquired taste, I guess you'd say. He has a habit of rubbing people the wrong way. It's the rebel in him, I guess."

"But you said he's your best friend."

"He is at that."

"Unconditional?"

"Unconditional."

"He's lucky to have you for a friend."

"I like to think that I'm the lucky one. That's the parking lot. Pull in here."

Wrenches could be heard clanging to the floor as they entered the building, and Jeff attempted to stifle an uncontrollable giggle. Samantha wondered why he was giggling, when the air turned blue with cusswords. After that, she had to place her hand over her own mouth as well.

"Eph, put a cork in it. I brought a lady into your realm. Time to show some couth."

"You calling me uncouth?"

"I calls 'em like I sees 'em." They entered the work bay. "Samantha Clayton, I'd like you to meet our resident mad scientist and social misfit, and someone who I'm not *terribly* ashamed to admit is my best friend, Ephraim Caine. Eph, this is the colonel's niece, Samantha, who has come to our humble fortress to work with us on the T.I.T.O.R. program. Since you're a friend of mine, you can call her Sam."

"So, I finally get to meet the infamous Ephraim Caine," she said with a grin, and extended her hand. "You're all they talk about in Port Angeles. Jeff seems to think quite highly of you, too."

"That alone should warn you off. But I guess he's harmless. Pleased to meet you, Sam." He stopped short when he looked into her eyes, and said, "Wow. You're pretty." He meant no harm; when he thought she was pretty, it came out.

"You'll have to forgive Eph. When he thinks something, the

words just sorta fall out of his mouth unchecked," Jeff said, in way of an apology.

She flashed one of her smiles at Ephraim, and said, "I'll never fault a man for saying what he thinks."

Ephraim pointed a thumb off of his shoulder at Samantha, and said, "See? Now, I like the way *this* one thinks. You were bound to stumble across a good one sooner or later."

He beckoned them inside, anxious to show them some of his newer projects. Samantha followed, eager to see what Ephraim was up to. She asked a lot of questions throughout the afternoon, and her curiosity never wavered. Ephraim delighted in sharing and detailing the specifics of his work with somebody who understood all of it; a fellow physicist. It didn't hurt at all that she was drop-dead gorgeous.

Later that night, Jeff stopped by for his usual visit. Ephraim looked a little surprised when he rolled in. "I thought you'd be with Sam. You two looked like you were getting along great."

"We were, but we only just met. Besides, I'm *assigned* to be with her for the time being, to help her get used to the place. I don't think she needs me in her lap every minute."

Ephraim said, "Say what you like; somebody's going to set their sights on *that* lady when you're not looking, and you'll be on the outside looking in, my friend."

"Did you just call her a lady?"

"I said it, and I meant it. So, sue me."

Jeff said, "Whatever happens, if she's happy, I'll be happy."

"Then, be advised, I may have to move in on you. That's one beautiful woman. Brilliant, too."

Jeff snorted. "I'll believe *that* when I see it, Eph. *You*, taking the time to chase a woman? Maybe if she were shaped like a hop machine … *maybe*. Otherwise, not a chance."

"You think so, eh? We'll see about that."

"Ooooo. This is me being worried. Threatened, even."

* * *

Samantha carried the reports from her station back to the colonel. "Colonel, these are the reports you requested."

"Fine. Thank you. So, Sam, how are you getting along?"

"Oh, just fine. Busy. I'm sorry we haven't gotten to see much of each other since I arrived, Uncle Mark. Jeff's kept me on the move, but I'm learning my way around."

Clayton waved it off. "There'll be plenty of time for that, young lady. We'll make sure of it. How are you finding our fortress to the north?"

"Cold. It's cold enough, I'll give you that. And different. I'm used to everything being spread out, like Port Angeles. You have lots of the same things here, but fewer of them, and everything is tucked away inside of a building, or underground. I guess it has a more military feel to it. But it's homey, and the people all seem close-knit. I didn't think I'd like it here, but you picked the right man for the job. Jeff has shown me everything I'm going to need to live here."

Clayton raised an eyebrow. "Are you saying that you've made up your mind that you want to stay here? It's barely been a month since you arrived."

She smiled, and said, "I'm saying that I'd like to stay here, and be a part of your program, if you'll have me."

"If I'll—well, of *course* I'll have you, Sam. You've impressed a lot of people around here, and they all feel you'd be a valuable addition to our team. I didn't encourage them to hold their breaths on this, though. You arrived here in the winter. Our summers are pleasant enough here, but our winters are stark, and bitter cold. Most newcomers don't stay long, once they taste our winters. I think I'll make the announcement before you change your mind."

He stood up, and announced, "May I have your attention, people? I'm pleased to announce that we have a new team member. Sam Clayton has asked for her temporary assignment to us to become permanent. Let's welcome Sam to her new home!" and he led a round of applause.

Jeff rolled toward Sam with the rest of the crowd to congratulate her, and expressed his delight over her decision to stay. Sam would enhance T.I.T.O.R. in a number of ways, and he thought the world of her. They'd grown close during her time there, and now his new friend would be staying. She was responsible for taking the edge off his loneliness, and he liked to think that he had reciprocated in that department.

One person didn't join the crowd rushing over to welcome Samantha. Instead, a flushed Rose snatched up some files from her desk and walked quickly out the door. She couldn't share their delight over Sam's decision to stay. Once outside the room, she hurried around the corner, leaned against the wall, tried to breathe again, and fought the tears. Until today, she'd clung to a single, desperate hope; that Sam might find their climate too extreme, and take her leave for Port Angeles. Or any other place in the world. Any place besides Loring. Anywhere that took her far away from Jeff.

It was too much to hope for, and now her hopes were dashed. To Rose, the task of trying to get her life back on track without Jeff seemed, at first glance at least, to be tough, but achievable. That didn't last long. To her utter dismay, she found that their old haunts now belonged to Samantha, who spent most nights having drinks with Jeff, and apparently got along with Ephraim quite well, as she was almost always with one or both of them.

When they spotted Rose in one of the old haunts, and made sure she saw them, she could barely stand it. The last time she walked in and found them already there, she thought, *how do I compete with the three musketeers here? Ephraim and I mix like cats and dogs. He's Jeff's best friend, and not only does Ms. Legs show up with all the goods, she gets along famously with him besides.*

She sighed, and thought, *I'm so screwed.*

Movement caught her eye. *Oh, look. Great. Jeff sees me. Is he—? No way. Crap. He's waving at me, waving me over there. Is he kidding? Yeah, hi, okay, here, I'm waving back. Bye.*

Jeff usually spotted Rose when she entered the pubs they were in. She always looked alone. No. That wasn't it. Lonely, she looked *lonely.* He felt so sad for her, and even though she couldn't stand him, he couldn't stand the thought of her looking—or feeling—lonely.

Most of the times, she looked away, or turned and left, or both. After a few weeks of that, he continued to try. One night, Ephraim and Sam were animated, joking and laughing as usual, when Jeff saw Rose walk in. He found himself monitoring the door far too often. He just couldn't forget her, and he didn't know how to ignore her. Rose entered, found a spot at the bar, and sat alone, nursing a drink. Jeff watched her for a few minutes, and could sense that she was aware of them.

Sam and Ephraim were occupied, so he raised his hand and waved at Rose. When he caught her eye, he waved her over, hoping she'd come and sit down. Instead, she waved back, stood up, and walked out the door without a backward glance.

Jeff excused himself, and rolled his way through the dense crowd and toward the door, hoping to catch her, to talk with her. The place was packed, and he pushed through all the way to the sidewalk, only to find the street empty.

Ephraim and Sam watched from their table. "That man has got it bad for her," Ephraim said.

Sam nodded. "And it's killing him an inch at a time. I'm trying to get through to him, but I'm not having much luck."

Ephraim said, "Me too. He's lost. Doesn't know what to do. She won't talk to him, she won't see him, and it just tears him up. Anybody can see he's flat-out in love with her."

A tear formed in the corner of Sam's eye. She tried to blink it away.

"Anyone but her," she choked out.

"You really care about him, don't you?" Ephraim asked.

Unable to speak, she just nodded, and the persistent teardrop finally freed itself and made its way down her cheek. "Yeah. I do."

Ephraim nudged her. "Softy."

She pushed back. "Jerk."

# 24

*Groom Lake – unofficially designated Area 51*
*Autumn - 1947*

The group gathered at the gate of the Groom Lake facility had grown in number each week, and now exceeded twenty agitated individuals.

"We know you're hiding something in there!"

"Yeah! We have the right to know. This is America!"

One of the men in front yelled, "What are you hiding? We heard you're keeping UFOs and aliens in there! Do you really think you can keep that quiet? People talk, you know!"

He yelled and stomped and waved his arms about. The others followed suit, absorbing and then repeating his accusations.

The others knew him as Ronald Locke, and he had a knack for stirring things up, for making people think about what was going on behind the scenes, for drawing them into the fray. Locke was a real party guy, always encouraging the group to bring their friends to make it a better party. Their numbers continued to grow, and so did his popularity.

Nobody knew his real name. Nobody around *there* did, in any case. Nothing about him so much as raised an eyebrow. When anyone checked his background, it turned up nothing but an average guy who was so obsessed with saving the planet that he stepped on the occasional military toes while demonstrating outside military bases. A nut case activist. A nobody. The typical person you'd expect to find demonstrating outside of a military base.

On the good days, he marched around in circles, chanting and waving signs. On his bad days, he liked to get himself arrested while attempting to scale the boundary fences with his camera. Those bad days often extended to three days—or sometimes a week—in a military cell, charged with trespass.

A car drove up to the gate, and after the credentials were checked, the vehicle was waved on through.

Seeing the guards were occupied with the car, Locke called for a huddle, and the others gathered around, like an oversized football team.

"I need two volunteers to go with me. We're going to reconnoiter. We'll need the others to stay here and keep the guards distracted."

Once his team was chosen, they broke the huddle, and the others returned to the forefront, chanting and shouting at the guards. Locke and his team slipped over the nearest hill, and hiked along the fence for a mile or so. In the distance, Locke's eye caught a gleam, and looked carefully to see whether they were being observed. Roaming guard teams were everywhere, and it took a sharp eye to see them first.

Satisfied, he hiked for another few minutes, then chose a spot along the fence. "Here. We'll go over here."

The others gave him a boost, and he was soon on the other side. "Okay, throw me my camera, and then it's your turn."

He caught the camera, and had just dropped the strap around his neck, when an amplified voice shouted, "You there! Stop! Military Police! Do not attempt to run!"

The others turned and looked at him, panic in their eyes. In a calm, urgent voice, he said, "Stay low. Run into the brush, stay in the brush. Go. Now!"

"What about you?"

"Nothing to do but the same thing on this side. Remember, stay in the brush and keep low. Now, go!" he said, and wheeled about, running for the nearest brush.

Forgetting everything he said, the others turned and ran, out in the open, straight back along the fence line, as fast as they could. Several minutes later, they remembered his advice, and cut off into the scrub. Some time had passed when they emerged from the scrub, hot, tired, scratched-up and dirty. They dreaded the coming walk of shame as they walked down the hill to rejoin their group near the gate, embarrassed to report that they'd left their fearless leader trapped inside the base fencing, under hot pursuit by the patrols.

Today was *not* going to be one of Locke's good days.

*   *   *

The cell was more of a room with a locked door. They'd provided him with a bowl of oranges and a pitcher of ice water, both presumably to be used to rehydrate himself after the hot chase through the thickets.

Locke sipped his water and relaxed, idly passing the time by counting the myriad holes in one of the ceiling tiles and tossing an orange into the air and catching it, until somebody showed up to deal with him.

When at last the lock was opened and somebody stepped inside, he had almost confirmed his first count with a second.

"Mr. Locke. So good to see you again."

"Good to see you too, Mr. Wren."

"I listened at the gate. You're doing a good job out there with the dissemination of misinformation. The crowd seems to be getting larger as well."

"Thank you, sir. We're holding regular meetings, and people are bringing their friends. A small group of our more literary members have banded together, and we're about to release a publication, warning the public about the government and the cover-ups."

"Excellent. Does this publication have a name?"

"It does. Truth Magazine."

Wren gave that a moment's thought, smirked, and raised one eyebrow. "Oh, my. How *entirely* inappropriate."

Locke grinned. "Ain't it, though?"

Wren almost smiled in return. Almost. Instead, he said, "Our next stage is about to begin. Your inside man at Wright field has just leaked the following critical information to you:

"Sometime in the next few months, the wreckage from the Roswell crash is to be shipped to the labs at Groom Lake, the top-secret restricted section they now call Area 51. That should do the trick. I want all eyes on Area 51, and none looking elsewhere. Can you make sure that receives prominent placement in your publication?"

"Absolutely, sir. Within four weeks, the grapevine will be buzzing with the news. I assume you'll provide the necessary leaks from Wright field to keep the focus on exactly which shipments will be coming here, and how we can identify them?"

"Your counterparts are making preparations as we speak." He stood, and picked up his hat. "You're an efficient man, Mr. Locke. I like that. You have a future with us."

"Thank you, sir. If I might ask, how long can I expect this assignment to last?"

"There's no time limit. Keeping eyes focused upon Area 51 will be a full-time job, with no end in sight. You'll continue to receive the extra pay as long as your assignment lasts. We'll have to adapt as the situation plays out. Your publication is the perfect example of that. Soon, you'll be working from an editor's desk. Demonstrating outside the gate will have been a stepping stone for you. You can delegate from there. Your cover will become your life, and you will have become this persona. In every way, and in every aspect of your life, you will be Ronald Locke."

Locke absorbed the information, and though he may not have liked it, he sucked it up, and said, "Yes, sir. I understand."

# 25

The convoy of two hundred trucks began to organize and line up, preparing for departure from Wright Field. Phil Corso was there, helping to orchestrate the exodus.

The re-designation of military bases to separate the Air Force from the Army, Navy, and Marines was an unending logistical nightmare. But that paled in comparison to the boondoggle forced upon them here at Wright field. Every single truck leaving the base had been driven through a building, where they sanded off every identifying number from the exterior, and painted with flat primer.

Only drivers with clearance were allowed. None of the drivers were told where they would be driving, nor were they permitted to tell anybody once their orders arrived. One armed agent rode shotgun in every truck to ensure those orders were followed to the letter.

All of the trucks were moved during the night prior to shipping out, and drivers were simply pointed to a truck. Once the engines were started, the agents in each truck would open the sealed orders on the seats. Even then, the drivers were not told their destinations, only the roads they would take to get to the rally point. Some had no instructions beyond that, other than to rally with and follow a particular convoy. No drivers would know their destinations until the day of arrival.

Out on the road, Locke's people scrutinized the exteriors of the trucks, looking for a specific identifying feature that would mark them as the trucks that held the wreckage and the aliens. The trucks carrying the "packages" bound for Area 51.

One asked, "Are you sure we'll be able to tell them from the others?"

"It rained last night, didn't it?" Locke said.

"Well, yeah. Why?"

"All of the trucks were parked outside last night, in the rain, right? The trucks we're looking for will be dry. They wouldn't leave them outside, their cargo is too valuable. Look for trucks that are dry."

"Well, how the hell did you know it was going to rain?"

"I have my ways."

Inside Wright field, thirty covered trucks pulled out of the classified hangar. Fifteen moved to the right, and fifteen moved to the left.

Corso said, "That's taken care of, Mr. Wren. What now?"

Wren pointed to the fifteen on his right. "Take hoses and wet those fifteen down. I want it to look like it rained on them last night."

"You heard him, Sergeant. Those fifteen on the right; take them over by those hoses and wet them down. We want them to look like … never mind. Look, just wet them down."

"Yes, sir. Wet them down. Okay, men, come with me," the sergeant called out, and hustled away.

Wren watched until the trucks were all wet down. The sun was creeping into the clear morning sky when he ordered engines started. The agents had 5 minutes to open orders and prepare for departure. Wren climbed into the lead truck on the right, and never even bothered to open his orders. He'd written them, and knew every word, every road, every inch of the route, frontwards and backwards.

He reached up, and pulled three times long and hard on the air-horn cord. Two hundred trucks answered the horn blasts with their own, and the convoy departed Wright Field.

At the gate, Locke's people instantly identified the fifteen dry trucks, and latched onto them, following them at a discreet distance. They needn't have bothered, but they couldn't have known that the drivers were hand-picked for the job, and that, to the last man, the drivers all worked for Wren. If the vehicles following them somehow lost them, they'd do whatever it took to make sure they were found again. It was imperative that Locke's people tracked those trucks all the way to Area 51, whatever it took.

Once they picked up their target vehicles, a poorly-played game of cat and mouse ensued across the countryside, while Locke's inept but determined rookie cohorts believed they were managing to stay within visual range of the elusive trucks. When they finally pulled over outside the Groom Lake gates in Nevada, they regaled their fellow conspiracy theorists with stories of repeated failed attempts by the truckers to lose them as they traveled cross-country to Area 51.

Locke led the first round of storytelling, and the others took their cue from him. The way he told it, the truckers were seasoned tricksters, but no match for his tenacious team of trackers. No doubt about it, the Roswell wreckage now resided, safe and sound, within the boundaries of Area 51. And they had proof. They'd followed it every inch of the way, with dogged determination, foiling even the cleverest attempts to lose them along the way.

And they told that to everybody who would listen.

\* \* \*

Northern Nebraska seemed to go on forever. Roads that stretched out forever into the distance, and fields that did the same. The frost made the morning grass sparkle like millions of diamonds in the bright sunrise.

Wren hated every moment of the trip. The drivers seemed to think that mornings were custom-made for them, and moved about slowly, drinking coffee, taking their time, shaving, cooking a hearty breakfast, and the whole morning routine.

Ironically, these fifteen drivers were ordinary, run-of-the-mill classified military truck drivers, who knew nothing of Wren, his agenda, or what they carried. As much as Wren may have wanted to crack the whip on them, he couldn't; not without drawing attention from the drivers by making what seemed like any ordinary day's standard shipment of classified equipment seem extraordinary.

So, he suffered in silence for days, until the convoy finally pulled into the overflow parking lot for Mount Rushmore, where the drivers were all thanked for another successful run, and the group was rewarded "for a stellar run" with five cases of Old Milwaukee beer.

The delighted drivers and their bonus beer were loaded into an empty truck, which departed for the closest military base, several hours away. Once there, they would probably have to be sobered up to be ferried on to wherever they would be needed most tomorrow in the ongoing nationwide military base shuffle. By then, they'd remember little about this run.

And that was the end of it. Fifteen drivers, who transported possibly the most classified cargo in the history of their country, never knew it. It was just another run in a blur of hundreds of runs that took place for thousands of drivers all over the country, during the establishing of a separate Air Force, and the subsequent re-designation of military bases all over America.

These ordinary men had helped to sweep the secret cargo away, undetected, to a location so clandestine that it existed on nobody's radar. And they did so unknowingly, with the help of the biggest smokescreen in history.

# 26

"Are you two packed and ready?" Clayton asked.

"You worry too much, Uncle Mark. We've got it under control."

"Your father trusts me to get you back home safely, young lady. He's excited that you'll be visiting."

"Dad? Excited? That'll be the day. I'll be lucky to get any visiting time at all during this trip."

"Make time for it."

"I'm not the one who needs to make time for it, Uncle Mark."

"Yes, well … give him a break. He's got a lot on his plate. How about you, Jeff? All ready?"

"Yes, sir. Thanks for picking me for this, sir."

"You're helping her move her things back here, Jeff. It's not a critical mission. Just busy-work. It's not a holiday, either, but try to have some fun while you're there. We'll see you two back here in a week."

"Yes, sir. We'll do that."

They exited the command center, wrapped up in organizing the trip, laughing and animated as they discussed the myriad details still to be addressed. Thus occupied, they were far too caught up to notice the eyes that followed them intently down the hall, until the doors closed and blocked their view.

Rose couldn't believe it. She'd finally come to terms with

Samantha's decision to stay. If that wasn't already bad enough, now the word was circulating that Samantha and Jeff were about to embark on an all-expense-paid vacation.

Rose wasn't superstitious, but she couldn't help but feel as though the fates were heavily stacked against her. Jeff and Ms. Legs, as she had taken to calling Sam in her mind, were off on a week-long trip to Port Angeles, purportedly one of the prettiest spots—if not *the* prettiest—in the country. Sent by Colonel Clayton, of all the people who could have sent them.

*This* was a part of his plan? *This* was how he was helping her? *This* would help her to get Jeff back?

*Not likely*, she thought. *Too much is at play right now. That plan no longer exists. How could it? Before, it behooved Clayton to help me get Jeff back. But that was before Ms. Legs showed up, and decided that she wanted Jeff for herself. She's Clayton's niece. We all know how the old saying goes; blood is thicker than water.*

She let out a deep sigh. It wasn't really Clayton's fault. Even if he did still want to help her, his brother was a *general*, for christ's sake. Not just *any* general, but the nation's ranking military officer, **the** five-star who ran the country's capital city, and protected the government leaders. The man took orders only from the commander-in-chief. What the general wanted, the general would get. Safe to assume that his brother would comply.

Rose stalked the halls for the next two hours, furious, frustrated, and completely at a loss as to what she should do about it. *This is bull. I can't stay here and watch this go on. In a week, they'll be back, and it'll start all over again.*

Just before noon, she walked into the colonel's office and spoke to his aide. "I have an appointment with the colonel. Rose Rios."

"He's expecting you, Ms. Rios."

The colonel stood and gave her a warm smile as she walked into his office.

She didn't trust it for a second.

"What can I do for you today, Rose? Is everything okay?"

She wanted to scream what she was thinking, *Is everything okay?*

*Are you kidding? You just sent my boyfriend on a week-long getaway to paradise with Ms. Legs, and you're asking me if everything's okay? What the hell do you* **think?**

She said, "Everything's just fine, colonel. I came to make a request. If I could, I'd like to be put on the active list to crew hop missions. I'm fully certified as a hops pilot, and I believe I have the right to exercise that option, if there's room."

"Well, of course you do, Rose. You're more than certified, you're a highly skilled pilot; one of our best. We'd hoped you would head up a team long before this. Why the sudden change?"

She thought for a moment, and said, "You said it, sir. Change. I think I need a change. If it won't create any problems, I'd like to start as soon as possible."

Clayton ran his finger across his desk calendar, and said, "Very well. Let's—yes, let's get you into the simulator for, say, two hours a day, staring this afternoon, can you do that? Good. If all goes well, we'll activate you on Monday, a week and a half from today. Jeff and Sam will be back by then, and I'll have them pick up where you leave off in Hop Ops. Is there anything else you want to talk about while you're here?"

"No, sir. Thank you, sir."

After she left, his aide came in with some papers to sign. "How are things going with her, sir?"

"Not too badly. Tough girl, as tough as I've ever seen. She's coming along, but she has a ways to go. She needs to see that if she's not willing to fight for it, then she's willing to let it go. It'll never work out, otherwise."

"Uh, are we talking about piloting a hop, or about Jeff?"

"Both. Think about it."

"And your niece?"

"She's grown fond of Jeff. That's why I sent him with her."

"I'm sure you know what you're doing, sir. I don't understand what's going on, so I'll leave it to you." He hesitated, and ventured, "It's just—"

"Yes?"

"It— it's just that this doesn't look good *at all* to me. It looks like it's all falling apart."

A trace of a grin crept across the colonel's face. "I can see where it would. Dismissed."

*   *   *

Clayton took the call. "Hello, Conrad. How are you?"

A lot of questions were forthcoming, and he answered them.

"They left this morning."

"Yes, Jeff is with her."

"No, he's done her a world of good. I thought you'd like to meet him."

"He won't be what you expect, let me say that much. But don't underestimate him, either. He's an exceptional young man, Conrad."

"His interest in her? I'd say that's rather between the two of them, wouldn't you? Oh, I see. Yes, sure. I understand your position."

"Well, perhaps, but don't go too hard on him. In his own way, he's as close to me as Sam is. He might just as well be family. And don't you forget that he's already done what you couldn't. Like I said, he's an exceptional young man."

"Good. Good. Well, they should be there within a few hours. I sent some men along on the transport. If you could give the men some accommodations … excellent. They'll be there on leave, until you need them to load up."

"Sounds good. Oh, and Conrad? Try to set aside some time for Sam. It would mean the world to her if you were there just for a few hours, or a nice dinner out. If you can take time off from saving the world. Yeah, well, who better than your brother to bring up your weak points? All right then. Take care."

He hung up, and chuckled.

*   *   *

Conrad Clayton called out, "Helloo, honey, I'm home!"

Samantha ran down the hallway. "Daddy, I didn't expect you until later. We're making an awful mess back there, and I'd hoped we'd have it cleaned up before you came home." She hugged him, and he held her at arm's length.

"Look at my girl. You're more beautiful than ever. Maine seems to agree with you. And what's *that?*" he said, pointing at the smile beaming from her face. "It's been some time since I've seen one of *those* on your face. I hope they keep coming."

She said, "Dad, I'd like to introduce you to my good friend, Jeff Waldron. He came with me to help me pack things up."

Jeff rolled forward, and extended his hand. "General, I'm pleased to meet you. Sam has told me all about you."

"I'm sure that was a short story," he said, with a smile. "My job has kept me away from my daughter all too often, and she's had to do almost everything without me. It's made her an amazingly strong young woman, and I'm so proud of her. But I've missed so much of her life. One thing I know is that she doesn't have an abundance of stories to tell about me."

"Oh, Dad, there's plenty to tell."

He looked at her, and the old soldier's eyes softened. "No. No, there isn't, baby girl. But we're going to spend time together this week, maybe add a few stories to your short list, if that's all right with you. It's the best I can do."

She beamed at him. "It's perfect, Daddy. I can hardly wait."

"Well, I'll let you get back to your packing. I had to sneak away from work to come see you, and no doubt, they're looking for me by now. I'd better get back to it. How about dinner tonight, my treat?"

Sam said, "Sounds great."

"Yes. It does," Jeff added.

"Wonderful. I'll pick you two up at four, and we'll go anywhere you like. Jeff, it was good to meet you."

As the general's car pulled away, Jeff said, "He seems nice."

Sam said, "My Dad's the best. He works so much, I never get to see much of him. But he's a good father."

"He's crazy about you. That's easy to see."

"For a lot of years now, he's been my only parent. My mom died when I was pretty young. Uncle Mark, he was here for a number of years, but then they gave him the Great Northeastern Fortress. Ever since then, all dad and I have had is each other."

"How did you lose your mom?"

"There was a pirate attack, almost thirty years ago. They fired on the city. My mom and I were caught in one of the blasts. She protected me, and took the brunt of it. I was just a little girl. I don't remember much about it, except for this," she said, and raised her shirt to show a mean-looking, lightning-bolt shaped scar that spread across her side, onto her ribs, and below them.

"Oh, Sam," Jeff said, "You were hurt bad."

"I almost died."

"I can't imagine what your dad must have felt."

"Later on, I'll show you what he felt. You can see for yourself."

A car arrived at four, sans the general. He sent word that he'd meet them at the restaurant just as quickly as he could.

At the restaurant, Sam explained that they should go ahead and order their meals, and make the best of it, because her dad very likely would not show. They had dinner, and Sam talked about what it was like growing up there in Port Angeles.

Afterward, Sam had the driver take them to the waterfront, where they walked along the water, enjoying the change of scenery from their fortress in Maine.

"Looks a little like Cape Elizabeth, in Maine. What are those?" Jeff asked, pointing at the hillside that ran along the shoreline, the top ridge of which was dotted with square cubes, partially buried in the hillside, spaced at regular intervals, and extending as far as the eye could see.

"Those are our defense pillboxes, our version of your great wall, ocean-style. They don't look like much, but they're our first line of defense. They use collective triangulation sighting technology," she said, and then turned, pointing up the hill. "Up that hill, out of view, are the big guns. You don't want them to get you in their sights.

There are some pretty large ships at the bottom of that channel out there, pirate ships that tried to attack Port Angeles in the past. Destroyers, tankers, pirates, you name it; they've all tried. No ship ever took more than two salvos to sink."

"You're pretty proud of these guns," Jeff said.

She smiled. "Sure I am. My dad set up these defenses, and I've watched with him from up on the hill during several incursions. Once the big guns speak, the whole thing's over in just a few minutes. I even know how to run the whole system."

Then, it hit Jeff. "Wait. Did your father build this system because of your mother's death?"

Sam nodded. "I knew you'd figure it out. Yes, he did. And I was with him the day he sent the raider that killed my mother to the bottom of the channel, and that day, the raider never got to fire a single shot. I pushed the button that day." She said, "It worked so well, that was how he got his stars."

"Funny how life works sometimes, isn't it?"

"Yeah. Funny."

Jeff looked out over the channel, and tried to picture such a scenario. The unobtrusive pillboxes, though deadly mechanisms of defense, didn't detract from the beauty of the spot. The smell of the ocean filled the air. Waves lapped persistently against the shore, as the gulls announced the arrival of the two trespassers, screeching at them from the air, while busy sandpipers skittered about the narrow stretch of sand, taking care of their business.

The natural beauty and vibrant wildlife in this pristine area gave stark contrast to the death-dealing guns hidden just out of sight.

Samantha took a deep breath of the sea air, leaned wistfully on the rail, and drank in the vista before her. "I used to come here with him. It's the one thing I do miss," she said, pulling her collar up to fend off the biting wind coming in off the channel.

"With your dad?"

"No. With Steve."

"I'm sorry. I should've taken the time to think. You're missing him."

"No, that's just it. I'm sitting here with you, and I don't miss him at all. What I've missed is taking in this view."

"Oh, I see. The view. So, we're good?"

"Oh, yes. We're good," she said, and kissed him on the cheek.

*     *     *

Late at night, Samantha had a craving for a spoonful of peanut butter, and wandered into the kitchen, where she found her father polishing off a sandwich. They migrated from there into the living room, where she sat beside him on the sofa.

Sitting on that sofa, they often talked late into the night, discussing their days. Many of their best memories were made right there. To anybody else, it might not have seemed like much, but Sam wouldn't have traded those memories for gold.

He asked, "So, tell me about this young man, Sam."

"Jeff is a good friend, Daddy. He's been good to me."

"Is he *more* than just a friend?"

"Yes, he is, but not in the way you're thinking. He helped me get through a rough time. Now, he's there for me when I need to talk. I'm there for him, too. We've grown close."

"You understand, I have concerns—"

"Why? Because he's in a wheelchair?"

"Maybe that too, but mostly because he's with my daughter. I know you're grown. I know I can't protect you the way I'd like—"

She interrupted, "You can't protect me, *period,* Daddy. There's always something out there that can find a way around you. Look at Steve Tarken. You *liked* him, because he had 'potential,' and look what *he* did to me. Here one day, gone the next, without a word."

"We *can* find him, you know. Anytime you want. I told you that before. In fact, we know where he is."

"I know where he is too, Daddy. He's gone. That's that. My point is; I know Jeff would never do something like that. Never. But Steve, I suppose I always knew he was capable of it."

He ran his hand down her hair, then hugged her. "Look at you; all grown up. Your mother would have been so proud of you. You're so much like your mother when I met her. She was *so* beautiful, and she knew her own mind too, just like you. I always wondered what a magnificent creature like her saw in a war horse like me."

"I know exactly what she saw in you, Daddy."

"Thank you, baby girl, you're sweet," he said, and, as general's tend to do, skillfully moved the conversation back on track. "So, you're serious about this new fellow, Jeff?"

She thought about that for a long time before answering, which suited him. He was a firm believer that one should find the truth before they spoke.

She leaned over and placed her head on his shoulder, and said, "If I *did* get serious about him, Daddy, I can tell you right now that he'd never hurt me, and you'd never have to worry about me. That's what a fine man he is."

He gave a small grunt of satisfaction. "That's a good answer, baby girl. If anything changes, you'll let me know?"

"I'll let you know, Daddy," she said, and wrapped herself around his arm, just the way she used to, and, safe and secure in the love of her father, faded off to sleep on his shoulder. Ever since she was a little girl, it let her know she was loved and protected.

But it went two ways. It also let *him* know he was the luckiest man in the world.

Early the next morning, Jeff rolled into the kitchen for breakfast, and met the general, who was ignoring his breakfast in favor of scanning through a stack of reports.

"You're up early, young man."

"I might say the same for you, sir."

"No rest for the weary. My car will be here at 6:30, as always."

"We've got a busy day planned too. But we figure we'll finish the packing by mid-afternoon. With everything packed up, we'll have the rest of the week to see more of Port Angeles. Sam has graciously offered to be my tour guide."

The general's demeanor turned serious. "Jeff. I want to talk to you about Samantha."

"Yes, sir?" he said, doing his best to appear casual, rather than scared and nervous.

"Whatever it is you're doing, it's made a world of difference to her. You just keep on doing it. My brother said you were an exceptional young man, and he was right. Thank you for being there for Sam when she's so far from home. Everybody else knows me as a fierce warrior, but when it comes to my little girl Sam, I'm just an old worrier. The last words I ever said to her mother were my promise that I'd take care of her. But it's a big world, and a father can't be everywhere. I suppose every father worries about that."

Jeff nodded in agreement. "Any father would. But, I promise you, sir, I'll look after her. Sam's safe with us at the northeastern fortress. She's already family, so we all look after her. Colonel Clayton would make sure of that, anyway. He's as doting an uncle as you are a father, though I doubt I have to tell you that."

"No, you don't. Marcus just adores Sam. He helped raise her after her mother passed away."

Just then, a horn tooted outside.

The general rose from the table. "That's my car. You two have a good time today, and if I might try again, let's make the same plan for tonight. Four o'clock, again?"

"Four o'clock it is. Sounds great, sir. I'll let Sam know."

As he watched the general's car drive off, he replayed their conversation through his head over and over, first pensive, then confused. Finally, he said out loud, "The colonel? Colonel Clayton said? Me? An exceptional young man? Huh. Well, if that doesn't beat all."

# 27

*Great Northeastern Fortress*

Led by Colonel Clayton, the hop crew entered the command center to the applause of all the technicians. He raised his arms and announced, "Gather round, people. Gather round."

He stood behind the hop crew, turned them to face the others, and placed his hand on the pilot's shoulder. "I'm pleased to announce our newest pilot has completed the requisite ten hops. Therefore, it's my honor to award full pilot status to Captain Rose Rios."

More applause followed, and Clayton continued. "As you all know, there is one requisite task yet to be completed. Therefore, I expect to see every single one of you at the celebration at Finnigan's Joint tonight. Are there any questions?"

The room full of people answered as one, "No, sir!"

"Are my instructions clear?"

"Yes, sir!"

Clayton gave them a broad smile. "Then that's a day. You're all dismissed, and I'll see you there. Congratulations, Captain Rios."

Rose beamed. "Thank you, sir," and shook the hand he offered.

"Don't thank me, Rose. You earned it. Now, go enjoy the celebration they're throwing in your honor. I'll see you there."

When Jeff arrived at the party, Finnigan's was bustling, and Rose was surrounded by a crowd of happy well-wishers, most of whom came more for the free drinks than to actually celebrate Rose's advancement. Even so, every single one of them understood that the price of the free drinks was to put on a good show of toasting Rose. Hell, it was free, and it was fun. Win-win.

That was just as well. Jeff hadn't a clue what he'd say to her, even if he *could* reach her. Someone called his name, and off to the side he saw Ephraim and Samantha waiting for him in a booth.

With free drinks on the menu, Ephraim was one of the first to show up, and the first to start celebrating Rose's new rank. Samantha arrived later than Ephraim, but was doing a fair job of closing the gap between them, and the jokes and anecdotes flowed as freely as the drinks. For the next hour or two, Jeff joined in, nursing a few beers and laughing at their jokes when he was supposed to.

Though he put on his own good show, the other two could tell he was more pensive than usual. Perhaps it was because Rose was the center of attention tonight. Wherever Rose went, whatever Rose did, Jeff's mind followed. Sam and Ephraim were the two souls he most enjoyed socializing with, so no matter what, he would always be made to feel at home at their table, even if as a fellow party-goer, his preoccupation left something to be desired.

As the night wore on, the air in the crowded room began to feel close to Jeff, so he made his way outside for some fresh air. The crisp air, the solitude, and the black, diamond-crusted sky helped to ease his troubled mind.

"Oh, I'm sorry. I didn't know anybody was out here. I didn't mean to disturb you," a voice behind him said, and Jeff turned to find Rose on the veranda with him. She said, "I'll leave you alone."

"No!" he said, "I— I mean, please join me. It was a bit crowded in there for me. I'm not used to it. I mean, it's been a while since, uh—"

"No need to explain. It's been a while since I've been out, too."

"That's understandable. You've been so busy, what with earning your full pilot's rating and all," Jeff said.

"The colonel's kept you busy as well, helping Ms. Le— ahh, Samantha to settle in here at the fort. She seems to have become very attached to you."

He said, "We've become friends, if that's what you mean—"

"It's none of my business, but it looks a like a lot more than friends, if you ask me."

Suddenly angry, Jeff spun his chair away, and rolled away, toward the front of the building. Over his shoulder he said, "You're right. It *is* none of your business. You've made sure of that. And nobody *asked* you." He pushed forward hard enough that he spun the wheels of the chair in the gravel parking lot. Turning the corner, he left Rose to stew in her own juices.

Her eyes followed him until he disappeared. Turning to return to the party inside, she was startled to find Samantha standing outside on the patio, not far from her. She thought, *how long has Ms. Legs been standing there? Long enough to witness our little exchange, I'll guess.*

Samantha said, "Hello, Rose. I'm sorry I wasn't able to congratulate you earlier on making full captain, but you were surrounded by quite a crowd in there."

Glad of the low light that hid her burning cheeks, Rose said, "It was a big night for me. Don't give it a second thought." She pointed toward the front of Finnigan's, and said, "If you're looking for your date, he went that way."

Sam said, "Did he, now?"

Ephraim emerged from the door, laughing and making his goodbyes. He made eye contact with Sam, and held up one finger, signaling to her that he'd just be a moment.

Rose gaped, struck dumb by the brief signal. There was no mistaking its meaning.

Sam caught the look of surprise on her face, and in a lowered voice said, "You know, I like you, Rose, but you're not very bright, are you?"

Startled, Rose recoiled further. Overwhelmed first by the comprehension of what she'd seen, and then Sam's less than subtle insult, her eyes blinked rapidly, and she remained mute when

Ephraim walked by and offered his arm to Sam. She accepted it with affection, and wrapped her own around it.

"Congratulations, Rose," he said amiably, unaware that anything had transpired between his date and the celebrated new captain. They walked away, chatting and laughing, while Rose witnessed, much to her own mounting discomfort, how relaxed and cozy they were together. For a couple to be that at ease with each other, they would need to be together for a while. If *they* were that cozy, then …

Her legs grew rubbery, and she dropped into a patio chair, trying to sort out her jumbled thoughts, in an attempt to reconcile them with what she'd just seen.

*How could I have been so stupid? Sam wasn't with Jeff and getting along with Ephraim, she's with Ephraim, and friends with Jeff. I only saw what I was afraid of.*

Her first impulse was to go after Jeff, and she did; but a quick check of the bus stop showed he was gone. She wasn't going to give up so easily this time, and next, she went to his place. But he hadn't yet returned, or still wasn't answering his door. With no key, she felt uncomfortable hanging around there, and made her way home.

The next day wasn't much better for her, but she had no time to dwell upon it, which was probably for the best. In her new position, she was responsible for all mission paperwork, and couldn't avoid the task of chasing down errant team members and taking them to task over incomplete reports and improperly filled-out forms.

The paperwork was only the tip of the iceberg. Every single, endless detail of both the last mission and the next mission were her responsibility. Since her team was still in transition, she hadn't yet selected one of them to delegate any measure of the work to. She'd wanted to keep busy, so she wouldn't have time to think about Jeff.

It worked. She would not be visiting Ops anytime soon.

The next day, she happened upon Jeff in the lunchroom. The second he spotted her, she saw his eyes turn dark. He wheeled his chair around angrily, and pushed off in the opposite direction. If that didn't sting enough, she saw Sam looking at her, shaking her head.

What little appetite she had left her entirely. She fled the crowded lunchroom, and sought the safety and isolation of her car.

She wiped her eyes, certain that others saw it when they looked at her; how stupid she was, how she'd messed everything up. Self-doubts tore at her. How could she come so far, become a hop pilot and a full crew captain, and still continue to screw up every damn thing in her own life?

After a while, the tears ceased, and she reluctantly left the quiet of her car to return to her office.

As the mission leader, her job didn't allow time for self-pity, and her crew depended upon her to get them home safely. She thought, *At least I haven't screwed **this** up yet,* as she immersed herself in the work.

Immersed in her work, and absorbed in her misery, the obvious eluded her; that those around her carried burdens, dealt with their own demons, put on their own strong faces to come to work. They went home to their families at night, struggled to balance the demands of both their jobs and lives, and dealt with problems within their marriages and relationships as best they could.

With no example to follow, she'd never learned the art of finding common ground, or the importance of fighting the determined fight to hold onto someone she loved. Or even the importance of simply saying, "I love you."

Jeff was busy in his own right, now that he and Samantha shared the extra burden of Rose's duties in Ops, and their own besides. Sitting next to each other, they talked all the time, about everything.

Everything but Rose.

Samantha tried to talk to him about it, but, almost as though he'd regressed to his time working at R&D with Ephraim, he went silent and dark at any mention of Rose. He continued to do a good job in Ops, but the happy, sociable Jeff Waldron they once knew was gone. Now, he was all command center business, with no interest in anything else.

Clayton couldn't complain about what could only be considered consistently flawless performance, and nothing Jeff did gave him any cause for concern for Ops. Officially, all of his criteria had been met, and as the colonel, he had no choice but to accept it at face value.

The tensions between Jeff and Rose were evident, but when Rose transitioned into hop crews, their workplaces separated, minimizing their encounters, and, from Clayton's perspective as their commander, any potential problems. It was far from the first time he'd seen a couple break up. But it was the first time he considered a couple's break up to be tragic in every respect.

"Mr. Waldron. I'm waiting for a report on that intel from your link. Is there any word from Flash?"

"No sir, nothing yet. He should have been in contact months ago, and we're still coming up empty."

"Very well. Keep me apprised."

"You'll be the first to know, sir."

The doors slid open, and Rose walked in. "Colonel Clayton, you sent for me?" she asked. As she approached the colonel, her eyes wandered off to the right, and for a split-second, her eyes locked with Jeff's. Her step faltered for only a second before she recovered and shifted her focus back to the colonel.

It was only a second, but a second was long enough for Clayton to see it, and he sensed the spark between the two. *Ahh,* he thought, *all is not lost after all.* He suppressed his grin by smiling pleasantly. "Yes, Rose. How's that new team of yours shaping up?"

Still flustered, she tried to use it to her advantage. She ran her hands back through her hair, feigning frustration, and shook her head. "Uh, well, sir, it's a mess, if I'm to be perfectly honest. The team members aren't as well trained as I'd hoped. They developed some sloppy habits under Captain Martin, enough to be dangerous under the right circumstances. Right now, they're doing labs and running drills, and that'll continue until I'm happy with the results."

"That sounds about right. I expected you'd need to whip them into shape, but I knew you were up to the task. To me, the challenge is half the fun. Besides, you wouldn't appreciate it if you didn't have to work for it, would you?" he said, raising an eyebrow.

It couldn't hurt to plant the seed.

"No, sir. I think you're right about that."

"I'm more than satisfied with your progress so far. Carry on, Captain Rios."

"Thank you, sir," she said, and crossed the chamber to leave. She allowed her eyes to wander over to look at Jeff for the briefest of moments, just long enough to confirm her suspicions. As expected, Jeff was looking back, and their eyes met.

*The first time meant nothing,* she told herself, *and he wasn't expecting me, so it caught* **him** *by surprise. But it felt like he was watching me the whole time I was here, and the second time, well, he would have avoided making eye contact if he didn't still ...*

Breathless, she didn't dare finish the thought, but with even more pieces of the puzzle in hand, and her heart in her throat, she couldn't help but wonder if they could ever find a way back to the cozy, comfortable Jeff and Rose who were once attached at the hip.

Before leaving the Ops chamber, she looked back, only to find another pair of eyes following her. Samantha watched the scene unfold, with an irritating Mona-Lisa smile on her face. Rose turned and dashed out the door, remembering their last conversation, and feeling the sting of Sam's words as they echoed once again in her ears, *You're not very bright, are you?*

Still scurrying, even as she made her way down the hall, she had to admit that, when it came to Jeff, Sam was right. More so than even Sam knew, because as much as Rose wanted to find a way through this, she hadn't the foggiest idea of what she could do, or how the Jeff and Rose she remembered and longed to bring back could ever be salvaged.

# 28

The man didn't visually belong in the dark, dank chamber, with walls of poured concrete, and no windows. Dressed in a crisp, spotless, well-pressed suit, his prim neatness gave stark contrast to both the chamber and the men working for him.

He asked, "So, how is our good friend, Mr. Gordon, today?"

Groaning in the middle of the chamber was an unconscious man, with forearms strapped to the wooden arms of a chair, his head hung limp, and his legs strapped to the chair legs.

In the dark corners, the steady *droip, droip, droip* of water droplets hitting the puddles on the floor ticked away the seconds and minutes like an old clock.

The source of the slow leak was anybody's guess; perhaps it was from the water pipes passing through the chamber, pipes whose seams and joints were overstressed by the untold number of men who, over time, were hung from them, and tortured.

Or, perhaps groundwater, traveling deep underground, found its way through the cracked, disintegrating concrete ceiling. Either was just as likely.

A putrid, malodorous mixture of urine, blood, and death permeated the air, so biting and thick that it seemed one could almost reach out and somehow touch it.

One of the men handed a clipboard to the agent, and said, "Still not cooperating. He's one tough son-of-a-bitch."

The agent scanned the paper, and said, "Keep at him, Baxter. It's time to take the gloves off. Take off a toe or two if you have to. Whatever it takes. He gave us information before that led us to the internet chat rooms. We can get more from him. I want to see some results, and soon."

Baxter said, "Yes, sir, Mr. Wren. We'll get you more. We're on it."

After Wren disappeared from view, Baxter grabbed a handful of Gordon's hair and lifted the subject's head. "Nah, he's still unconscious. It'll be a few minutes more before we can start again."

Letting the man's head drop back onto his chest, he leaned back against the bench, and tapped a cigarette from its pack. Snapping the filter off, he tossed it aside. Turning it around, he lit the end that formerly held the filter, and inhaled deeply. Smoking was his only real vice, but probably more relevant to his reasons for smoking was the fact that the unfiltered, strong menthol smoke temporarily displaced the thick, reeking air that saturated the chamber.

Exhaling, he asked, "So, Suarez, what do you think of our boss?"

Suarez shook his head, and said, "Wren? The guy gives me the creeps. He scares me. It's like he's got no soul. And that's just for starters."

"I thought *you* were the guy who gave *other* people the creeps, or at least the heebie-jeebies."

"Yeah, right? I pride myself in that. But something's—" he stopped and shuddered, "something's just not right about that guy."

"Rumor has it that *his* father was the agent in charge of the Roswell cover up. There wasn't anything he wouldn't do to you. They say that, compared to him, junior there is a regular boy scout."

"Well, that's one boy scout I could do without," Suarez said, whereupon he noticed Gordon stirring. "Good. He's coming around. Turn on the recorder. Let's get back to it. Wren's not in a waiting mood."

Speaking in a professional tone, Baxter said, "Resuming interrogation on subject Gordon. Thomas F. "Flash" Gordon."

The broken, bloody form in the chair stirred, and when the bucketful of cold water hit his face, shooting up his nostrils and down his throat, he coughed and retched, shaking the water and blood from his swollen, almost unrecognizable face.

Baxter said, "Welcome back, Thomas. Let's get started again, shall we?"

Through swollen lips, Flash said, "Screw you, Baxter," and spat blood, spraying his torturer's face. "I saved that up just for you, asswipe," he said, displaying a near-toothless grin of defiance. "You think *this* is tough? I grew up living in a room twice as bad as this, filled with rats and roaches. I've taken worse beatings from the kids in my neighborhood. You're a pussy."

Baxter ignored the insults, and looked at Suarez, who asked, "Hammer?"

Baxter nodded, and Suarez pulled Flash's head forward and used a rope to keep him tied there, bent over so that the prisoner could see only his feet, the floor in front of him, and Suarez.

He grabbed a hammer from the bench, and kneeled directly in front of Flash, inspecting the hammer. It was an Estwing framing hammer, and a big one at that. At twenty-eight ounces, with its striking surface crosscut for extra accuracy, it was the preferred framing hammer of carpenters everywhere.

The same crosscut surface and extra weight also made the tool a fearsome meat tenderizer. Running his thumb over the business end, Suarez gave Flash a savage grin, and laid the hammer down while he slowly removed Flash's socks, exposing his feet. He picked up the hammer, raised it high above his head, and remained poised there, waiting for the signal to strike. Flash had no choice but to watch, up close and personal.

Baxter said, "You know, Thomas, there's no need for this. Tell you what; tell us why you're radioactive. Tell us why you set off our Geiger counters, yet you're still healthy. Answer just that one question. We're going to get the information from you. Why not make it easy on yourself? End the pain. Tell us what we need to know, and we'll take you to the doctor and get you patched up."

Flash said, "Like the last time? And the time before that? I told you a few things then, and you patched me up, and here I am again. Nah, I'm done talking to you. You're gonna have to kill me. You're gonna kill me anyway."

Baxter thought about that for a second. A twisted smile slowly spread across his face.

This was the part he liked.

He crouched, allowing Flash to see his face, and said, "My friend, we're not going to kill you, and we're not going to stop. Not today, and not tomorrow, and not even when you scream like a little girl, begging me to kill you. Not until you tell us everything you know. Every last little scrap."

He grinned at Flash, leaned back, and then glanced at Suarez. A barely perceptible nod, and the hammer came down hard on Flash's smallest toe, smashing it to a flat, bloody pulp.

He screamed in agony, straining against his restraints as the screams and curses flooded from him, the cords standing out on his neck as he alternately cursed Baxter and his ilk, and shrieked from the endless pain. After several minutes of that, the chamber began to spin and go woozy, and he slid toward the merciful blackness.

Another bucket of ice water robbed him of that reprieve, and left him awake and terrified, stripped of the bravado he had displayed just two minutes before. Gritting his teeth against the pain, he tried to remain brave, and attempted to prepare himself for more questioning. He steeled himself, and looked up at his torturer.

But Baxter asked him no questions, and gave him no chance to defy him. Offered him no opportunity to answer him, or to fail to answer him. He waited until Flash looked up at him, and nodded again.

Suarez lined up on Flash's other foot, and brought the hammer down in a vicious swing on the big toe, which splattered like a ripe cherry tomato, leaving only a pulpy mess.

Suarez laughed, wiping bloody splatter from his own face.

It was then that Flash heard the distant screaming. Mad, insane screaming that came from somewhere else, some*one* else. And it didn't stop. On and on it went, while he felt the pain course up through his leg, and then his body. Only then did he realize that it was *he* who was shrieking, and crying, and swearing, begging and pleading with them to stop.

Suarez raised the hammer once more, and Flash screamed in terror, begging them to stop, pleading frantically, and swearing that he'd answer their questions.

The hammer hovered, wavering slightly in midair, waiting for Baxter to give the signal.

Flash fell silent, trying to stifle the whimper of pain that escaped him anyway, waiting to answer the questions, *wanting* to answer the questions, *any* questions at all, waiting for Baxter to start asking them. To just start asking them. For the torture to stop.

When their eyes met, Baxter smiled slightly, for he knew he'd won. Flash would tell him anything he asked, and gladly.

He nodded.

Bloodcurdling screams filled the air as the hammer fell.

\* \* \*

Alarms sounded, followed by shouts and gunfire, and within minutes, the facility was locked down. It was just one man, and they'd stopped him in his tracks. The facility was once again secure.

It was then Wren came running down the hallway, shouting, demanding a report. When he saw what had transpired, he was livid. "How could this happen? How could you let this happen?" he bellowed.

Baxter stood at attention, perspiring in fear. "I'm sorry, Mr. Wren. Nobody thought Gordon had the strength to walk, much less fight. He overpowered a guard and took his weapon, and he came out shooting and fired on four guards. They returned fire, and he was killed. None of the guards were injured in the escape attempt."

"Of course they weren't injured, you *idiot!*" Wren yelled. "You helped him commit suicide by firing squad. Your men couldn't shoot him in the legs? Do you have any idea what you've done? That man had priceless, irreplaceable information we desperately needed, and now he's useless to us. Useless!"

He paced around, staring at the bloody body on the ground before him, and paced back and forth, trying to think. He walked over to his aide and said, "Call a meeting for this afternoon. We'll have to take what we have, and see what we can do with it."

"Yes, sir. Right away."

"And do—something—with—this—stinking—piece—of—meat!" Wren bellowed, furious, half-crazed, and savagely kicking at Flash's bullet-riddled corpse with each word.

# 29

*Great Northern Fortress*

Rose looked at the names on the list of building residents, She was sure she had the right place.

Then she saw the tag; **E222 - Clayton, S**.

She reached for the bell, and pulled her hand back, thinking, *This is a bad idea, yeah, it's just a bad idea.*

Turning to walk away, she stopped, staring down at the packed snow at her feet. *It's Sunday,* she thought, *and you're **not** going to get another chance like this.* After another moment passed, she turned and rang the bell. Unsure as to what she'd say when the intercom came on, she only knew she'd do her best. Thankfully, she never had to work that out.

The door buzzed, she walked in, and found the second floor.

*Okay, second floor, East wing, number—222, this is it.*

She knocked gently on the door, and waited. Nobody answered, and she raised her hand to knock again, when the door swung open, surprising her.

Sam said, "Well, *Rose!* Hello! What brings you here?"

Rose wanted to run away without a word, wanted to not be there. But she'd made up her mind, and she would stay this course. A thought flashed through her head, *I hope my voice works.* She cleared her throat, and said, "Hello, Samantha. Would it be all right if I came in? I— I need to talk to you about something, and I don't know who else to turn to about it."

Samantha, sporting the usual (disturbing) Mona-Lisa smile that drove men (and Rose) crazy, suddenly broke into one of her dazzling smiles, and said, "Well, it's about time. Get in here, girl. Take off your coat. Just throw it over there. Pick a chair or the couch; they're all pretty comfy. How about a beer?"

Rose was overwhelmed by the friendly welcome, which disarmed her, and left her somewhat confused. But she remembered thinking right outside the door that she could use a beer right now. *Magic beer time. Presto digito; your wish is my command.*

"A beer sounds great. Thanks."

Sam brought two beers back from the kitchen, handed one over, and grabbed a cushion of the couch not far from Rose, tucking one leg underneath the other, and relaxing against the back. She said, "I'm really glad you came over. There aren't too many girls to hang out with here, and I've been waiting for months, hoping we'd become friends."

After a brief pause, Rose asked, "Even though I'm not too bright?" and issued something of a challenge to Sam over her statement during their last exchange of words.

Sam beamed, and said, "Even if you aren't, girl. Do you want to talk about it, or not?"

Her directness lacked any hostility, and once again, Rose found herself disarmed. *When in doubt, start at the beginning.* "I would. I've been wondering why you think I'm not too smart."

Sam thought about that, and said, "You're plenty smart. Book smart. But you refuse to see what's in front of you. I've only heard rumors about what happened to split you and Jeff up—"

"There was nothing to split up," Rose quickly interjected, a bit *too* quickly, in fact. "We were never a couple."

Sam said nothing, and looked her in the eye without comment. She wasn't accustomed to being interrupted, and being the general's daughter, she'd learned many ways of commanding attention with a look.

Rose flushed. "Sorry, go on." Sam was certainly formidable when she decided to be.

Sam continued. "I don't know what happened, but I know that both of you have made just about every mistake there is that can keep a couple apart. You're smart people, both of you. But when it comes to each other, neither of you are too bright. I don't know you very well, Rose, and that's your fault, but I won't pass judgment on you. On the other hand, I know Jeff very well. The boy is crazy about you. Always has been. Always will be. There'll never be anyone else for him.

"But, whatever's gotten between the two of you has caused him to park his ass squarely on his shoulders, and we can't get him to go to you and try to work it out. He's angry all the time, and that's not the Jeff we all know and love."

The tears flowed down Rose's cheeks, and she said, "I know. I miss him so much. But I don't know what to do about it. I've made such a mess of everything."

Sam leaned forward. "Talk about it, girl. Get it out. Between you and me, we'll find a way to make things right again."

Rose took the handkerchief that Sam handed her, and dabbed her eyes. "It's my fault. It's all my fault. Jeff came back. Ephraim talked him into trying one more time. He knocked on my door, and I sent him away," she said, sobbing in anguish. "But I ran after him. I did. I ran as fast as I could, but I couldn't catch the bus."

Some of what she said wasn't entirely comprehensible through her sobs of anguish, but Sam went with it. She knew the basic components of the story, but that was the first she'd heard of Rose running after Jeff. Of course, she'd only heard the story from Jeff's perspective before. That was the thing about perspectives; there was always another one to be found.

She reached toward Rose, and ran her hand down her hair. "Oh, sweetie, that kind of stuff happens to us all. It's bad, but you can't let it stop you. And let's get something straight right now. It's *never* all your fault, especially when a man's involved. That goes double if Ephraim or Jeff have anything at all to do with it."

For some reason, Rose found that hilarious, and it caught her off guard enough that, just when she was about to blow her snotty nose, she cracked up laughing instead. Sam joined in, and they fell together in screaming spasms of uncontrollable laughter.

A few minutes later, when the laughter, and giggles, and blowing of noses was finished, they fell quiet.

Rose said, "Thanks for being nice. I didn't know what to expect. I think we're going to get along fine. And, if we're going to be friends, I guess you should know. I gave you a nickname."

"Oh? What was it?" Sam asked, taking a swig.

"Ms. Legs."

Sam lurched forward in her seat, nearly snorted the beer out of her nose, managed to swallow it instead, and said, "I hope you don't mind if I *love* it!"

They fell together again, giggling.

Several minutes later, when things were more serious again, Rose asked, "What do you think I should do?"

Sam looked her in the eye. "Girl, you've *always* known what to do. He's a man. They're pretty simple organisms." She helup her hand and started counting fingers off. "Until you get another chance to feed him, drink with him, or sleep with him, tell him you love him. **Keep** telling him. Don't take no for an answer. And don't worry, we'll be giving him a push in the right direction."

*"We'll* be giving him a push?"

Sam nodded. "Ephraim and I. Don't worry, girl. We've got your back. We're behind you. There's nothing **our** team can't do."

Rose looked off in the distance, and said, "Then I'm going to talk to him, as soon as I get back from tomorrow's mission. And I won't give up until I get him back."

Her coach drilled her. "And what are you going to tell him?"

Rose blushed slightly at the thought. "I'm going to tell him— that I love him."

Sam grinned, and stood up. "This calls for another beer."

"Make that two, please."
"Coming right up."

\* \* \*

*August 2001*
*The Pentagon*

"But, why tell them about Warehouse 15? That'll lead them right to us."

William Wren, Jr. nodded in agreement. "Yes, it will, with any luck at all. And if it does, we'll have a platoon of men waiting for them. The variables involved are diverse, and we need to focus the situation to direct the possible outcomes. We'll give them information to follow, and no matter how they choose to follow it, we have to be prepared for every contingency."

The large, circular table was ringed with uniformed men, and the circular room held an outer ring of chairs for aides, the men and women who came and went as their personal scheduling devices required. None of those from the outer ring sported stars or birds on their shoulders. They didn't rate a table or a desk. None of the men seated around the inner ring of the table sported anything *less* than stars or birds on their uniform shoulders, except for one. Every eye in the room remained focused on William Wren Jr.

General Madsen, the most senior man in the room, was well known for his surly demeanor. But he'd earned a reputation for making prudent choices. He said, "I've been sitting at this table for thirty years, and I'm not ashamed to admit that I saw my first gleam of hope when I heard your father was stepping down. Now, we have a brand new William Wren here, and once again, we must question the wisdom of yet more of these convoluted plans. I fear no good can come of this."

Wren's familiar, slightly twisted smile was a trait passed down to him by his father, and it never failed to send chills down their spines.

"Your reservations are duly noted, General Madsen."

Other questions were broached to him, now that Madsen had broken the ice.

"What possibilities are you talking about?"

"You talk about setting a trap. That usually means there has to be bait. Who or what is going to be the bait?"

"How do you propose to catch one, when our military has never so much as gotten close?"

Wren stood and crossed to the podium, and pressed a button on the laptop there. On the screen, a presentation started.

"If these beings can find a way to create an information portal that gives them access to our world wide web from their world, they can find a way into anything we have, given time. The only way to protect ourselves is to acquire their technology, and find a way to use it to defend ourselves. I have a plan, and it's bold, and risky. They're not stupid. Information used as bait has to check out. We haven't got much information as to why, but what we have indicates that one of their major goals is to retrieve the Roswell wreckage, and it stands to reason that they're hoping to do so covertly."

"Maybe they just want their people back. That's not outside the realm of possibility. In the same situation, *we'd* want to repatriate ours. It seems to me that this would be an excellent opportunity for us to use their return as a first step toward mutual cooperation."

There were murmurs of agreement.

"Maybe so, but that's not going to happen. The frequency of related questions suggests that it's pretty important to them. Our information source dried up before we were able to get everything we needed, but from all indications, the Roswell wreckage continues to be the best bait."

He continued, "We have a verifiable link, a Warrant Officer Newton, who transferred into the program right at the outset. He ended up at Warehouse 15, with the materials from Roswell. His father was an engineer involved in the creation of Warehouse 15. Our man who is working the chat room is claiming to be a very old, retired Newton, and he's leaking quite a bit of relevant information to them, all designed to bring them to us."

A bird colonel spoke up. "What's the timeframe on this?"

Wren said, "That's an excellent, and highly relevant question. This is a long-term project. I don't know where—or when—these beings are operating from, but from their viewpoint, this is all taking place over a matter of months at most. Our estimate for full implementation is ten to fifteen years, conservatively."

"What if they decide to come sooner?"

"Judging from bits of information we gathered from our source, I'm confident that they won't come before we're ready."

"Why will it take so long to ready ourselves?"

Wren picked up his laser pointer, and drew a large circle on a map of a western state, and said, "Because we have to remove the population from this entire area, without causing a stir. This isn't like we're putting in a dam and claiming all the land upriver. We need this to remain a complete secret until the very end."

Madsen asked, "How do you propose to make that many people leave?"

Wren smiled one of his chilling smiles. "Bad luck. Bankruptcy. Stolen cars. Poisoned wells. Stolen equipment. Identity theft. Fires. The land will be repossessed by banks, after which we'll quietly buy it up under meticulously created shell corporations. It'll all take place gradually, over the next twelve to fifteen years."

Madsen's face flushed with anger. "I've had a belly full of you Wrens. Decade after decade, I've watched your father ruin the lives of American citizens and soldiers to further his ambitions. Hundreds of them. I guess that wasn't good enough for you. Now you want to ruin—what?—*thousands* of lives? And there's no other way you can achieve this goal?" he asked, and stood, leaning forward on the table. "You may get authorization to move forward with this travesty, but you'll need to go through me and these stars to get it done."

Though Wren smiled agreeably, his eyes turned cold and disturbing.

He said, "Certainly. Any way you feel is appropriate, General."

# 30

*September 15th, 2015*
*Northwest Nebraska*

Rose shivered and held her coffee cup with both hands, warming them in the chilly morning air. "I could get used to this place," she said, lifting her cup to gesture toward the mountains in the distance. "Who knew anything could be that beautiful? What do you think, McBride?"

Following Rose's lead, McBride warmed his hands on his cup, walked over, and sat on the same log, taking in the view. "I think if we do this right, we can *all* get used to it. Is that Montana?"

She said, "I'm pretty sure this is Nebraska, and that's Wyoming. So I guess Montana's that way, but even further north."

"What areas do you plan to search today?" McBride asked. "This is the third hop machine, and the third time we've searched. We're out of machines, and we run out of time today."

Rose picked up the map she was perusing. "Our coordinates show we're on a ridge in the Nebraska National Forest now. Right about … here. We've run every direct road between Area 51 and Mount Rushmore several times, with no luck. I think we should try alternate, indirect routes running through northeast Wyoming today. This road here—Route 450—that looks promising. Add that one to our list, Brian."

McBride leaned over to check out the map. "That's … Little Thunder Road. Route 450. Okay, I've got it."

Rose pored over the maps, and said, "From our position here, we'll be running north and west first, which will put the sun at our backs, so we can see everything. Good thing too. We're up against it, so everybody should be ready to leave as soon as possible. I need you all at your best today, so stay sharp. This may be our last chance for a long time. Months, maybe years."

"I'm ready," Schmidt said.

"Me too," Williams added.

McBride gave the thumbs-up and said, "Piece of cake."

She wished she shared their optimism, but eight days had passed, and searches of the target routes yielded nothing. Each successive day they managed to attract more attention than the day before, which in turn brought increasing numbers of military aircraft, all attempting to intercept them. And each time an aircraft attempted to intercept them, the hop machine went to full-fields, and auto-evaded.

The first evasive action deposited them over the Arctic Circle, then two times over Europe, and the other three times Australia, South America, and Africa, respectively, after which they would return to the search grid. It was inconvenient, time-consuming, and more than a little dangerous.

She said, "We need to change our tactics. Let's fly as close to treetop level as possible. We can't afford any more interruptions like those we had yesterday, not if we're going to have any success. Brian, you're our hotshot co-pilot; you're in the hot-seat. Keep us on the deck unless I say otherwise. I know it'll be demanding, but we only have a few hours left. Can you do that?"

"Consider it done."

"Same deal as the last two days. We're looking for any sort of convoy. Let's get in the air. Goggles on, everybody. If you see anything, holler out."

*  *  *

The soldier trotted down the line of parked trucks until he reached the tent nearest the fire pit. Entering the tent, he snapped to attention, and said, "Sir, the men are in position and ready, same as yesterday. Do you have any other orders for them?"

Colonel Larrabee looked around, and shook his head. "No. Carry on."

"Yes, sir," the soldier said, and ran off.

Larrabee perused his maps, and reviewed the reports from yesterday. He thought, *the flyboys chased the UFO's a number of times in the past two days, and they've returned repeatedly. They're around, and searching for something. Perfect.*

He didn't need confirmation that his plan was coming together. There would be no air patrols today, in order to encourage the mice to come out and play while the cat was away. The bait was set, and he was sure they would take it. And, not to put too fine a point on it, he and his men were the cheese.

"I think we can expect some visitors today," he said, to no one in particular. His whole body tingled with anticipation. This was the culmination of years of planning and hard work. And they'd chosen him to lead this mission.

*  *  *

"Where to next?" McBride asked.

"Route 450. Little Thunder Road. Head north from here."

"Got it."

Schmidt said, "I can't believe we haven't had to evade a single military aircraft all day. It's almost *too* quiet. Do you think we're going in the wrong direction? We should have spotted one or two by now."

Rose said, "No. We're on the right track. I can feel it. Besides, we've exhausted every other possibility. We're all a little bleary-eyed, but let's see this through. It's nearly time to leave now, but we can give it a few more minutes."

Schmidt called out, "Contact. Over there. Just off the road, I see a military convoy. See it, Brian?"

"I see it. We'll be on the ground in two minutes."

"Careful, Brian," Rose said. "Circle once, and look things over. See if *anything* looks out of place. Let's try to stay out of trouble."

"They have a fire over there. Some men are moving about. Things look pretty relaxed, from what I can see."

"Anybody see any weapons?"

Williams said, "Just one so far. There. By that big truck. Slung over his shoulder. But we'd expect at least one sentry."

Rose said, "I think this is as good as we could hope for, *if* this is even the right convoy. Here's hoping."

McBride asked, "Should we go a mile or two up the road and land, and drive the truck into their camp?"

While Rose thought about that, she took a deep breath, held it, and let it out. "No. We're out of time. Land in that open area to the right of the fire. Smiling faces, everybody. This is going to make a big first impression, but remember; we're friendly, and we're here to help. They may get a bit excited, but once they learn why we've come, they should relax. Reday? Okay, Brian, nice and easy."

McBride circled the camp one more time, this time directly overhead, low and slow. He maneuvered to the spot Rose picked, and settled toward the grass.

They were just a few feet above the ground, when a blinding flash lit the air around them, coming from both sides at once. No sooner had the initial intensity started to fade than another flash blinded everyone, and then another. The hop machine stuttered, stalled, and dropped the last foot to the ground, landing with a jolt on the four truck tires.

"Shut down the hop, Brian; kill the power *now,*" she shouted, fervently hoping that the hop wasn't damaged beyond repair by the pulses. "Everyone, cover your eyes! Don't look at the flashes!" Rose yelled to the others. They complied, and threw their arms over their eyes. Fortunately, thanks to Rose being a stickler for safety protocols, the whole team had their auto-darkening goggles on.

McBride felt the controls with his free hand, and going by touch, threw the main power breaker. "Done, Rose. She's shut down."

They heard soldiers running around them.

"No more flashes," she said. "Let's see what's going on."

They opened their eyes, and looked about them.

Fifty soldiers, wearing protective gear and armed with automatic weapons, had surrounded them. Her hop and crew, on the ground, unarmed, with the fields down, were completely exposed there on the bed of the truck, and they raised their hands.

Rose didn't raise hers.

"We need to speak to your commanding officer," she said.

"That would be me," Larrabee said, and stepped forward, removing his gas mask.

She removed her goggles, and moved to climb over the tailgate. When she did, a number of the soldiers tensed and several cocked their weapons, to let her know they were serious. She froze.

The officer held his hand up, and the men backed away, though they didn't lower their weapons.

"Hello, sir. My name is Rose Rios," she said, and extended her hand.

Larrabee didn't immediately respond with a handshake, and appeared cautious, considering whether he should or not. Overcoming his reservations, he shook her hand. "Colonel Larrabee."

She didn't waste any further time. "I'm pleased to meet you, Colonel Larrabee. Sorry to land without any warning, but we're here on urgent business. We're not sure why, or how it's going to happen, but we came to warn you that the Russians are after your cargo. I can't tell you exactly who we are, but I assure you, we're friends. We need to—"

The colonel held up his hand. "Ms. Rios," he said, "I'm afraid that we're not the least bit interested in your reasons for being here. I'm under orders to seize your time machine."

"Well, you should be—uh, wait a minute. What did you just call it?"

"Your time machine. We know all about it. We detonated those warheads to immobilize it. And now I'm taking possession of it."

"*You* detonated those?" she asked, raising her voice, pointing to the columns rising into the sky all around them. "Are you *crazy?*"

The colonel nodded to the men. They came forward and seized the stunned Rose and her crew, urging and pushing them toward the trucks.

"Wait. No. Are you kidding? Do you have any idea what you may have started?" Rose yelled over her shoulder. "You need to know what's going—unngh," she grunted, and fell to her knees as a gun butt in the solar plexus took the breath out of her, silencing her, and reinforcing the colonel's previous assertion. *Nobody* was interested in what she had to say.

Gasping for breath, she was lifted from the ground, and dragged along while the other members of her crew were hustled along. The soldiers stopped, and waved their weapons upward, indicating that the hop crew was to climb into the back of a tarp-covered truck.

The crew first helped her onto the bed of the truck, then climbed up with her. She remained there in agony for several minutes, writhing in pain, holding her gut, and gasping for breath.

When her breath returned, McBride and Schmidt helped her onto the bench seat, and held her until she could sit upright on her own. She sat up straight, moaning at the pain in her stomach muscles. "Bastards," she groaned, still dazed and traumatized by the treatment she'd received, but improved enough to move around, albeit slowly.

McBride leaned toward the back, and looked at the distressed sky through a gap in the tarp. "Jesus. I can't believe they'd do all this just to trap us."

Schmidt said, "Which makes this all the more confusing. How did the war start? I don't mind saying, I'm confused as hell right now. The war starts today, but it doesn't look like the Russians had anything to do with it. Maybe it has something to do with those nukes they just set off."

"I'm inclined to think the same thing," Rose said, and stood slowly. They held her arms until they knew she could stand alone without help. Making her way over to the tailgate, she pulled the tarp back two inches, and viewed the thin, angry, roiling columns rising high into the atmosphere.

She moved along the outside of the bed, peering through gaps in the tarp, and counting as she went. "I can't believe that they felt it was worth the risk of detonating, it looks like—what, six?—nuclear weapons on American soil just to get their hands on our hop machine. They didn't want to know who we were, where we were from, *nothing.* It was like they knew we'd be here. How the *hell* could they kno— **oh, my God in heaven,**" she cried, fearfully backing away from the gap.

"What? What's happening?" the others asked.

She was white as a sheet, and shaking in terror. Finding her voice, she said, "Look. Look at the sky. Beyond the columns from the detonations. All over the sky. The whole sky. They're everywhere."

They scrambled to the back, and pulled the tarp aside, looking up.

The sky was filling, from the ground up, with vertical white tracings, and every one grew taller by the second. At the top of every white trail, something was moving straight up— *fast.* Then they understood.

"Is that? Did they?"

"Oh, God."

"They did it. Oh, my God, they did it. We're too late."

"We're all dead."

They knew they were watching the contrails of hundreds and hundreds of Minuteman Intercontinental Ballistic Missiles, on the way to their targets.

On their way to Russia.

The nuclear war had begun.

And they were trapped, right in the middle of it.

# 31

"Today's the big day, eh?" Ephraim said, as he walked into the R&D lab. I thought you'd be in Ops, monitoring the screens and making sure you saved the world."

Jeff half-rolled his eyes. "After all the work I did, tracking down the wreckage, identifying likely places they'd find that convoy, what did they do? They sent *Rose* on the hop. Just wait. We'll *see* who gets all the glory if the world gets saved. No, I've got better things to do than babysit her hop crew. Besides, today's the last day of the last batch of hop machines. They've all reached saturation."

"Don't be so mean. Rose deserved the honor of piloting this mission. What else is on your agenda?"

"I need to go through these cases of paperwork from the warehouse. We haven't even scratched the surface yet."

"Well, you go ahead. I have to finish up the calibrations on my custom-deluxe, suped-up hop machine. I only have a few tweaks left, so I'll have it wrapped up this morning. After that, it can go anywhere."

"How did I know you'd find something else to do, so you could get out of the drudge-work?" Jeff said, shaking his head. "What a bum."

"What a sucker."

Jeff chuckled and cracked open another box. At the top of the pile, a photograph caught his eye. It was a crisp photo, probably eight by ten inches. Printed on the back were the words: *Bench Tests – 1980.*

A fully assembled hop field generator was displayed on a bench, complete with power couplings. It clearly showed a large section of the workbench missing. The edges were cleanly cut in a perfect half-circle, extending all the way to the floor below, as evidenced by the clean, semicircular cutout in the concrete of the floor.

There was no doubt about it; the researchers had managed to fire up the generator and establish a field. Whether they had any clue at the time just what they had there, Jeff held in his hands clear evidence that they'd experienced a breakthrough with the 'alien' technology. He gave a low whistle.

*1980,* he thought, *in order to have done what this photo showed, they would have to have learned enough to understand and integrate the microprocessor; that alone would've been an extremely advanced scientific breakthrough for the technology of that time.*

It was more than enough to be considered significant. He cleared a place on a nearby table, and started an 'important' pile.

As the morning wore on, he came across a number of similar photos. None of them were as remarkable as the first, but each time he laid one aside, it left him with a nagging feeling, as though he'd missed something.

Ephraim came in, and said, "It's about time for lunch. Don't forget, we promised Sam that we'd meet her at the Caribou. You ready?"

"Just about. Take a look at this, Eph. I found it in this bunch."

"Let's see. What is tha— oh. They fired up a generator. I guess one of the generators survived the crash."

"Looks that way. Something's bugging me, though. It's like I'm missing something. I can't put my finger on it. Take a look, maybe you'll see something." He handed them to Ephraim.

Ephraim looked them over, and said, "I don't see anything that catches my eye. In all of these photos, I only see one field generator that's functional. They were all taken there in that lab. Looks like standard experimental stuff. Sorry," he said, handing them back.

Jeff took them and laid them back in the box, and as he turned back to Ephraim, he stopped. "The same lab. They're all taken in the same lab. That's it. Do you still have the photos the search teams took under Rushmore?"

"Yeah, I have a set of them, right here. Why? What's up?"

Jeff looked at the photos, then grabbed up a few from his box. "That's it. Yep, that's what caught my eye. I'd seen the lab before. These photos were taken in the same place. The same lab."

"Is that important?"

He stared at them another few moments before he answered. "I doubt it. Not nearly as important as learning that they fired up a field generator, anyway. But it was bugging me for a while there," he said, slipping the photos into his coat pocket.

Ephraim urged, "Time for lunch. We'd better get a move on if we're going to meet Sam on time."

At the Caribou, they talked shop while they ate lunch.

Sam asked, "Do you have the photos? I'd like to see that."

Jeff checked his pockets. "Uh, yeah, I have a few here, uh, somewhere. The one where they fired the generator up was folded. I stuck it in one of my pockets. Here it is. Here's a few more," he said, producing various photos from various pockets.

"Nice filing system you've got there," Ephraim observed.

She inspected them. "You say these were taken in the same place as the others we took, in the lab under Rushmore?"

Jeff nodded. "Yes. There's one from our search, um, *there*. See? You can tell it's the same lab."

She looked disturbed. "But, this one has a date of 1980 on the back."

"Yeah, we saw that."

"So, isn't Rose out there trying to find the convoy that's moving the wreckage *to* Rushmore? If the wreckage was already under Rushmore in 1980, then why are they moving it there in 2015? That can't be right. We need to find out what's going on here."

She'd put her finger directly on the elusive issue eating at Jeff.

He said, "We need to get back to R&D and start digging for anything with dates, something that can tell us what they were up to in 2015. If Rose is about to walk into something dangerous, we need to know, and fast."

"Is there any way I can help?" Sam asked.

"The more eyes and hands we can get on this, the better," Jeff said.

"I'll call Unc— um, Colonel Clayton. He'll okay it."

Inside of an hour, they had every case open. The room looked like a paper avalanche had struck.

Ephraim held up a file. "These photos were taken in 1948. Same lab. I don't know how we missed this until now. That wreckage was under Rushmore, right from the start. Within a year of the crash, anyway." Staring at the photos, his brow knit in consternation. "This is wrong. This is all wrong."

Jeff said, "You think *that's* wrong. Take a look at this file."

Samantha read the cover, and picked a few pages out of the file to peruse. "Papillion. What does this have to do with Rose's crew—oh, my *God,*" she said, "Ephraim, you need to see this.

Ephraim took the folder from her, and perused it, flipping pages and quickly browsing through the contents. He looked up at Sam and Jeff. "We need to get these to Clayton, right away."

\*   \*   \*

The colonel's aide showed them in.

Clayton looked up. "Ephraim. Jeff. What can I do for you?"

Jeff said, "Sir, we think Rose and her crew are in danger. While we were sorting through the boxes of items from Rushmore, some alarming information surfaced."

"Let's hear it."

The files we've got here are all related to a project they were putting together. It started with a photo of a field generator they'd managed to fire up, and then we determined that the wreckage had been under Rushmore since 1948. Maybe since '47. The point is, sir, as near as we can tell, the wreckage was never *at* Area 51. We tried to figure out why the Russians were trying to intercept it, but we just kept coming back to the materials already being under Rushmore. What were they trying to intercept?"

The colonel stopped him. "Wait. You're saying the wreckage was never moved to Rushmore in 2015?"

"No, sir, it wasn't."

"But, we *found* it there."

"That's correct, sir, but that's the point; it was there all along. Think about what the Board was telling us. Logically, we should never have found it there, if it was intercepted en route. We looked into the possibility that the military might have made plans to move it from under Rushmore to some other location in 2015, but we found no evidence of that. Then we found these," he said, as he tossed a pile of files onto the desk.

The colonel looked at the thick pile, and said, "I assume you're going to sum up what you found rather than make me read all these?"

"Yes, sir. This program is called Papillion. That's French for butterfly—"

"I know what it means, Jeff. What was their objective?"

"*We* were their objective, sir. It seems they were onto us from 2001, when I was online and asking questions. They'd already determined that what they had was a time machine, and they'd connected the dots. They didn't know *who* we were, or exactly where we were from, but they'd pieced together enough that they believed that the UFOs they saw flying about were the same technology as the crash wreckage."

"Christ," the colonel growled, "so they *knew* what they had there."

"Yes, sir. Once they realized what the field generator was, it was just a matter of time until they figured out that an electromagnetic pulse of sufficient magnitude could disrupt the field and shut down a hop machine."

"Jesus!"

"They wanted our technology, and they formulated a plan to ambush us and steal it. We found plans to deploy a decoy convoy in mid-September of 2015. A hop machine started the war, sir, but it wasn't Hop 206. They're planning to hijack Rose's hop machine."

"Are you positive?"

Ephraim said, "It would be too big a coincidence, sir. Think about it. An ambush that requires a massive EM pulse, *and* a nuclear war starts on the same day? We need to send a crew back to stop Rose from intercepting that convoy. If we can't—"

Clayton snapped, "I get it, I get it. But we've got bigger problems than that. *Both* of the other hop machines have reached saturation for that time already, searching for that convoy. We have nothing available. So, we need to talk, Mr. Caine."

"Yes, sir?"

"You've built a second-generation hop machine that you keep in your shop?"

Ephraim's eyes darted furtively toward Jeff.

Jeff blurted out, "I didn't say anything. Last I knew, you were going to register it."

A sheepish Ephraim said, "Colonel—"

"Forget the bullshit, Ephraim. Is it true, or isn't it? Do you have a functional hop machine, or don't you?"

"Yes, sir, but it's actually *third* generation, and it's calibrated."

Clayton leaned forward and put his hands on the arms of his chair, as though he was about to jump up. He barked, "Then why the hell are you still standing here? You know where Rose is going, and you know what date and time, and from this," he picked up a file and tossed it forward, "you must have the approximate location."

"We do. But colonel, it wouldn't be a sanctioned hop—"

"What?" Clayton jumped up. "All of a sudden, you're by the *book?* The *Board* can't save that crew. *T.I.T.O.R.* can't save them. Your rogue hop machine is the only chance they've got. Move your ass, Mr. Caine. *NOW.*"

"We're on our way, sir," Ephraim said, and sprinted out the door with Jeff right behind him, pumping furiously to propel his wheelchair down the hall and keep up with Ephraim.

Clayton ambled out and watched as they dashed away down the hallway, and remained still after they disappeared from sight.

His aide heard him mumble; perhaps to himself (perhaps not), "I suppose I always knew it would come down to this. Those eggheads are the biggest pair of misfits in the country, and now the whole world depends on what they're about to do."

He took a deep breath, and a few seconds later he said, "Godspeed, boys. Bring 'em home."

Minutes later, Ephraim's truck screeched to a halt, and he grabbed Jeff's chair from the bed, snapped it open, and dropped it on the passenger side. He yanked open Jeff's door and said, "Get yourself in your chair. I'll get the hop out of that corner in the back."

"Okay. Lock those wheels first. Yeah, just like that. Both of them. That's it. Thanks. See you in a minute." Grabbing the truck door, he swung out, lowered himself into the chair, and followed Ephraim inside, where he heard the familiar, low, whirring noise emanating from the rogue hop as the lower fields fired up. The hop rose up and over the other machines and parts, and set down by the big door, resting on the four spring-loaded peds.

Ephraim shut the hop down, and as soon as the field dissipated, he leaped off, rolled the ramp against the side, and then ran about the shop, yelling to Jeff, and gathering things he thought he'd need. "We'll be gone a while. We'll need this—and this. Oh, this too."

Jeff rolled up the ramp onto the platform, and secured his chair with the special lockdowns Ephraim had built for him a while back, when they were making wild, crazy plans to actually take the hop out, on some unspecified, legendary day. Locked down, he began to stow the gear Ephraim tossed up, taking care that the rifle was clamped securely in its holder. He picked up a small canvas bag, and asked, "What's this?"

"It's a money bag. I have money from different eras in here."

"You think we'll need money?"

"You know for a fact that we won't?"

"Good point. I'll stow it."

Ephraim climbed aboard, and tossed Jeff a key-fob. "That's it. You're in charge of the overhead door, Mr. Waldron."

"Roger that, chief," Jeff said, and pushed the button. Ephraim took the controls, fired her up again, and seconds later they were moving through the doorway. Once outside, the machine hovered just above the ground while Ephraim actuated the upper fields. An intricately linked mechanical cage rose around them and locked together overhead, followed closely by a shimmering silver field which rolled up and around the outside of it.

The field's exterior offered a unique appearance. From any distance, it looked like a solid stainless steel shell; opaque under full power, but viewed from the inside, it was transparent. Excited ions within the fields created the reflective exterior visual effect. From the perspective of somebody viewing it from the ground below, it looked like an inverted saucer placed on an upright saucer. Like a UFO.

The precisely calibrated fields were positioned together, overlapping such that they offered the occupants protection far beyond that of any metal casing. Since Ephraim hadn't mounted the machine onto a truck bed, choosing instead to use only the original spring-loaded peds, the overall field size on this machine was much smaller, as it needed only to encompass the smaller hop framework, and not an entire pickup truck.

"Contact!" Ephraim said.

"What?" Jeff asked.

Ephraim sighed, and said, "Just say *Contact*, okay?"

"Oh, okay. Contact!"

Ephraim grinned, and guided the machine upward. As the machine moved upward, he set the destination date, time, and location, and engaged the auto-controls. They were under way. He relaxed, rechecked his seat belt, and monitored the screens. Looking back, they saw the earth rapidly growing smaller.

By design, the hop machine was built to cheat the laws of nature, and was capable of going straight up at full escape velocity almost from the second it was engaged. It also came equipped with acceleration governors and inertial dampeners to minimize the crushing forces upon the human body, which otherwise could never survive such instant acceleration.

Perhaps ten minutes passed before they emerged from the travel corridor and initiated re-entry. Five minutes more, and their descent slowed as they passed fifteen thousand feet.

"Slowing to a hover at twelve thousand feet," he reported. "Telemetry was sent, and showed all our systems are in order. Let's get our bearings and make sure we're on track. Everything looks pretty good so far."

"Where are we?"

"We're over northeast Nebraska—"

A flash consumed the sky in front of them, so brilliant that their auto-darkening goggles were not enough. Ephraim turned his back to the flash and simultaneously blocked for Jeff, and yelled, "Look away! Close your eyes. Don't look at the flashes from the blasts!"

Jeff threw his hands over his goggles, and said, "Tell me when I can look." Another flash came, followed seconds later by one more. He was alarmed when, with his goggles on, he could see bright light through his hands, and still saw the brightness with his eyes closed.

The hop machine started to shudder, and within seconds, the hover began to wobble and lose stability. For Jeff, it was a decidedly uncomfortable and scary feeling.

"You can look now, Jeff. Here we go," said Ephraim, and threw the main power breaker switch to the "OFF" position. A second later, they were exposed to the cold air at twelve thousand feet, and their hop machine dropped like a rock, straight down.

Jeff screamed in terror, "What are you doing? Eph?"

Ephraim couldn't hear him, with the wind tearing up through the vehicle at a hundred and twenty miles per hour. All Jeff could do was grab onto something, and hold on. After falling for a minute or two—which seemed to Jeff like hours—Ephraim reached for the control panel, and flipped up the red cover, exposing a red punch button. Jeff recognized the red button. It was the one he'd been told never to touch. Ephraim looked at Jeff, smiled a wicked, crazed smile, and slammed the button with his fist.

Four loud, simultaneous, percussive bangs signaled the deployment of the emergency chutes. After a violent yank that snapped them into their seats, the craft settled into a slow, easy sway, and Ephraim said, "EM pulse."

"EM pulse?" Jeff asked, still shaking.

"I knew that if we ended up in the vicinity of a nuclear blast, like on, oh, say, this particular day in history, that a strong enough electro-magnetic pulse could disable the hop machine. That's why it started sputtering up there; the field generators were being disrupted, so I shut the power down before the pulses damaged them. As you saw, without the fields, these hop machines have the approximate glide characteristics of a manhole cover. I had a bunch of these ballistic-deployment chutes around, and I decided to hedge our bets."

Jeff gave an astonished look. "And you were going to tell me this might happen, exactly *when?*"

Ephraim just smiled. "Gotcha."

"*Ass*hole," Jeff muttered, still shaking with adrenaline from the fright.

Ephraim grinned. "Now, we just have to hope that it doesn't land on a steep hill, or in a tree, or in a ravine. Steering isn't an option with this." He said, as he leaned over one, then the other side, trying to get a good look at the earth moving steadily toward them. "Oh, *yeah,*" he said, "Looks like a big wheat field below us. Still, we're going to land pretty hard, so you'll want to brace yourself."

He continued to give a play-by-play, and when they landed, it was with the expected bone-jarring jolt, dampened only slightly by the spring-loaded peds. But they were on the ground, intact and unharmed.

While Jeff unclamped the rifle and took the watch, Ephraim jumped down, and ran around the craft, unhooking the chutes and tossing them aside.

Jeff watched him releasing the chutes and asked," Um, what if we need them again, Eph?"

Ephraim shook his head, indicating, "No," and said, "These are one-shot deals, Jeff. One use only. It would take hours to replace the ballistic charges and repack them. At best, we have minutes."

Jeff understood. "Just try to avoid any more of those EM pulses."

"Believe me, I'll do my best," he said, checking his watch, then switching the mains back on to fire up the machine. Nothing happened. "It won't respond. Too much EM clutter still going on to establish a field. This is what *really* worried me; being knocked out of commission by an EM pulse, and then unable to get it back online in time."

"In time for what?"

"In time to avoid being vaporized. Within the next hour, hundreds of big-yield warheads will arrive from Russia. If historic estimates are correct, then we have maybe forty-five, fifty minutes from the moment those first detonations occurred, until the Russian ICBMs hit us. One hour at the outside, but that's probably *way* too optimistic."

He pointed upward. "Look all around us; do you see all those vapor trails going straight up, heading north? Those are outbound ICBMs, taking the direct route over the polar ice cap to Russia. You can bet that, once the Soviets are sure we've deployed ours, they'll send theirs."

"What, wait, *we* fired first? I thought the Board said the *Russians* started the war?" Jeff asked, confused and agitated.

"Another genius assumption made by our illustrious Board. And wrong, as usual. After reading through those files you found, I'm pretty sure I know how it happened. But, if we can't get this hop machine back up soon, it won't matter a damn which country started it."

"Oh. Right. Can I help with anything? How long has it been since those first blasts?"

Ephraim checked his watch. "Just about thirty minutes. We have, ahh, maybe twenty minutes left, and that's being optimistic."

Distraught, Jeff asked, "We're not going to be able to save Rose, are we?"

"I know you want to be all pie-in-the-sky about this, Jeff, but right now it's likely that we won't be able to save *ourselves*. We're in a bad spot here. If we can save Rose, you know I'll try. Right now, we're out of the game entirely," he said, emphasizing his statement by giving the uncooperative control box column an angry kick.

When he did, the machine grumbled, some lights flickered, and it went dark again. It wasn't much; no more than a flicker, a fleeting glimpse of the slimmest of chances. Would it fire up in time? Excited, he looked at Jeff. "Did you see that?" He ran the start sequence again, and the machine flashed and fluttered, then dropped out again.

He tried it once more, and after bucking once or twice, the fields fired up, smoothed out, and the machine lifted from the ground. He couldn't be sure all the generators had fired up, so he tentatively ran it northwest over the fields, and found the machine ran smoothly.

But they had no time to waste on tests. Ephraim said, "We won't make it in time unless we run at least four thousand feet altitude at full speed. If we lose our field generators again from four thousand feet … we won't have parachutes—"

Jeff said, "If Rose dies, I don't want to live, Eph. Step on it. Go. As fast as you can."

Ephraim already had the exact bearings. The blasts had left him with visuals that provided him with exactly what he needed, or at least, what he *thought* he needed. Switching to manual control, he went to full throttle.

At four thousand feet, traveling at a blistering thirty-eight thousand miles per hour, the passing landscape looked surreal, blending into a blur of colors. At such a speed, traveling so near the ground, anything could happen. Ephraim prayed nothing would get in their way. Sure, the machine would auto-evade and punch out, but that would be disastrous. They simply didn't have the time to recover from a punch-out, and still get to Rose.

Watching his controls carefully, he held the speed in the red. His jaw set showed the tremendous exertion such extreme concentration demanded. Yet, less than two minutes had passed when he throttled back, and took a long, deep breath. The blur slowed, and relaxed into something recognizable. But once they could identify the scene before them, they both found themselves wishing they could be somewhere else.

Just ahead, stretched from the ground below them to the sky far above them, six thin, ominous mushroom clouds wound their way up through the atmosphere, looking more like thin, wavering stems than mushrooms. Together, the columns created a circular cage with a diameter of thirty miles, contained at their tops only by the light cirrus clouds at sixty thousand feet.

The sight of it tied their stomachs in knots. Ephraim felt like he was somehow asleep, and flying in some dark, dreadful nightmare, and how he wished it were truly so. If only he *could* wake up, and watch it fade into the ether, dissipated by his warm, cozy bed.

But there would be no waking up.

Holding himself together, he maintained his course, steering directly between the two closest columns. The eerie, broiling vertical clouds, thin from a distance, were now several miles away from them on either side. The post-nuclear specters towered over them, filling their field of vision. This close to them, the columns were beyond massive, climbing from the earth all the way up into the sky, and they fought the feeling that they were squeezing through a rapidly closing gap. They had to. Somewhere in that circle of hell, Rose needed them.

"Do you have her yet?" Jeff asked.

"I'm betting my whole paycheck that right in the dead center of this nightmare is an Army convoy. We need to find that, and once we do, we should find Rose's hop machine there. One minute, tops. Get your eagle eyes ready."

"Your whole paycheck? They *pay* you?"

"Just—get ready, okay?"

Seconds later they spotted the convoy, at the exact center of the circle, where he expected it would be. Parked next to the convoy was a silver GMC truck, and they knew it had to be the truck in which Rose's hop machine was mounted.

When they landed next to it, soldiers swarmed out of the trucks and surrounded them.

Unlike Rose's hop crew, Jeff and Ephraim were not wholly

unprepared. When the fields lowered, Jeff had his assault rifle shouldered and at the ready, pointed back at them. He said," I need to speak to your commanding officer. *NOW!*"

An officer pushed through the armed soldiers and identified himself. "I'm Colonel Larrabee. I've already taken possession of that time machine and I've confined its crew. I'm now taking possession of your machine as well."

Jeff leveled his rifle on Larrabee, and trained it, unwavering, between the man's eyes. "Try it, Colonel. I dare you."

Larrabee ignored him, as though he wasn't there.

Ephraim spoke up. "You need to know, these hop machines belong to the United States of America."

"That's right," the Colonel responded.

Ephraim, irritated, stepped down off the hop machine. "Fields up, Jeff," he said.

With his free hand, Jeff threw the switch that turned the machine on. As the fields rose, the soldiers backed away from the expanding field. Inside the fields, he could see the soldiers, but they couldn't see him. All they saw was what appeared to be a solid, opaque stainless steel shell, shaped much like a saucer. For all intents and purposes, he was now bulletproof.

A soldier stepped forward and prodded the strange exterior with his gun barrel. Withdrawing the weapon, he gasped to find his gun barrel gone, consumed by the field. A second man stepped forward, and reached his hand out to touch it.

"If you like that hand, you won't do that," Jeff said from inside, and the first soldier, who had lost his gun barrel, moved quickly to intercept his comrade. The second soldier backed away, as did others who were close enough that they might risk touching it.

Ephraim, still outside, ignored the soldiers, knocking the gun barrels aside with his arm as he approached Larrabee. "No. You *don't* understand. My name is Ephraim Caine, and these machines don't belong to *these* United States, not here in the year 2015. They belong to *OUR* United States in the year *2099*. You're trying to steal technology from your own country. You have no idea what you've just done.

"Our program exists for one reason only; to try and stop you from destroying the Earth, today, now, here. Get it? All this time, we believed that the Russians caused the holocaust when trying to steal the Roswell wreckage from you. But the whole time, it was *you*, our own military, trying to hijack an American hop machine. For eighty-five years, our sole purpose has been to undo what you idiots have done today."

He looked around, and noticed that the soldiers looked far too relaxed for men who knew they were about to be vaporized in a nuclear attack. Did they have any idea at all of the death and destruction headed straight at them? He had to know. "Colonel, do you even *know* what's happening right now?"

Larrabee looked a bit confused. "What do you mean?"

"I mean, why the hell aren't you running for cover?"

"From what? *You?*"

"No, not us. Don't you have radios? Haven't you talked to your superiors?"

Larrabee looked at his lead radio man, who looked sheepish, and finally spoke, "I was going to tell you, sir. We can't. Our radios have been down since the detonations. They were all turned on, monitoring and reporting the first machine's approach, and coordinating the detonations. We're pretty sure the EMPs fried them."

Ephraim said, "Jesus, man. *Look.* Look all around us. Those are all outbound Minuteman-III ICBM con trails. Your forces were placed at DEFCON-II, due to all the UFO activity over the past two days, right? But *you* knew what those UFOs were, colonel. They were us, looking for you, and that's what you wanted. So, *you* weren't concerned about a DEFCON-II. But you forgot to take your satellites into account, didn't you?

"Let's walk through this, shall we? You've detonated multiple warheads to shut down that hop machine. What did you *think* would happen when our military satellites detected the detonations? Or did you think at all? Enlighten me, Colonel Larrabee; what *are* our defense satellites programmed to do if an unexpected nuclear attack occurs during DEFCON-II?"

The stunned Larrabee did, in fact, know the answer to that. "Th—they take over the Minuteman launch codes. They take them away from NORAD."

Ephraim nodded. "They take over the launch codes," he said, and he pointed at the contrail-streaked skies outside the wall of mushroom clouds encircling them. "And that happened about forty minutes ago, at which time our satellites launched a massive, irretrievable, all-out 'counterstrike' at Russia. A few minutes later, I'm sure the Soviets detected our inbound ICBMs, and they've long since launched their own.

"That was a while ago, so it's a safe bet that theirs will reach us within, say, the next few minutes—at most. You haven't taken possession of *anything,* colonel. You've destroyed civilization. Five *billion* people will die today."

The soldiers nearest them looked confused, whispering frantically between themselves. Man by man, the panic set in. It spread through the ranks like wildfire. They forgot their assignment, began milling about, panicked, no longer with purpose or focus. They ceased pointing their weapons at anyone. Jeff and Ephraim were desperately aware that they had mere minutes—or by this time, perhaps only seconds—in which to retrieve Rose's crew and leave.

Rose and her hop crew, abandoned by their panicked guards, exited the truck bed, and pushed toward Jeff and Ephraim through the crumbling, disorganized soldiers.

Ephraim saw them approaching, and called out, "Rose! Are you guys okay?"

"We're fine," Rose said.

"Will your hop work?"

"No. It shut down when the nukes went off. We were just landing, so it wasn't damaged. We shut the power down."

Ephraim said, "It should start now. You have to try it. We're out of time. If it doesn't work, pile into ours."

"Got it," Rose said, as her crew headed for their hop.

Larrabee jumped in. "Wait a minute, I didn't say—"

"You're not listening!" Ephraim yelled, and he pushed his face up close to Larrabee's. *"You're. Already. Dead!* Do you understand? Everybody you *know* is already dead. *Everybody.* But, *we* aren't supposed to die here. So we're leaving—and we're leaving *now."* He turned to Rose and snapped, "No time, gotta go. *Move."*

Larrabee looked up, and that was when his blood ran cold. "Oh, my God," he said in utter horror, and began to tremble uncontrollably. Overhead, hundreds of southbound contrails traced their way toward them through the northern sky. This man, Ephraim Caine, had told the truth. They could only be what he claimed.

Larrabee knew he couldn't save himself or his men. But, he *could* give these people—these Americans—a chance. He knew their time machines were fast. If they launched right now, they stood a chance of outrunning the holocaust that was fast coming upon them. It was just a slim chance, but it was more than he and his men had.

He waved Rose and her crew aboard their hop machine. They scrambled aboard, and hastily prepared for departure.

As the crew picked up the checklist to do the startup sequence, Ephraim yelled, "No checklist. Start it now, or you'll die! Start it-start it-start it!"

They fired it up. Jeff dropped his fields momentarily to allow Ephraim to climb aboard.

With fields established around Rose's machine, Ephraim looked over his own machine's rising fields at Larrabee, and said, "Thank you, Colonel. Sorry it had to end this way."

To the north, innumerable ICBM contrails filled the sky with lazy arcs, all incoming over the polar ice cap. Each contrail had split, or was in the process of splitting into several more trails. They were initiating the last stage of their flights—their target runs.

With the fear and desperation of imminent death in his eyes, Larrabee yelled, "Go! Get the hell out of here! Go on!" He raised a finger upward, rotated his hand, and pointed up and away.

They didn't need to be told twice. Lifting off, they pointed the hop machines to the sky, and accelerated steeply to the south and east, away from the ICBMs. Seconds later, they shot between two of the now-withering columns from the first detonations, and toward the outer atmosphere.

Back on the ground, one of the men asked, "Colonel?"

The colonel's attention returned to his men. Numb with terror, and shaking, they'd gathered together and around him instinctively, for protection. It struck him at that moment how very young the men's faces appeared as they looked to him for guidance.

He was all they had. But he had led them to this. He regarded himself as wholly inadequate to lead them further. The fear in their faces reminded him that they had no one else to turn to. There *was* nobody else. He would have to rise to the occasion.

For his men, he raised his arms, spread them wide, and spoke in a strong, clear voice. "Men, let's take a knee, and spend a moment, shall we?" Kneeling with them, he led them in a simple, sincere prayer. As he prayed, many of the men sobbed. Faced with such a tragic and certain end, none felt any shame in it.

Two minutes later, high above the earth, Jeff asked, "How much time do you think until—" but he stopped when he saw Ephraim pointing back at the vista below. The ICBMs had reached North America. The attack was already well under way. Across the continent, dozens of brilliant flashes blossomed every second. He couldn't tear his eyes away from the bedlam.

Across the ocean, a dense, angry cloud covered the entire Soviet Union. Russia, as it had been, was gone. North America would soon look the same. The planet below crumbled into fire, smoke, chaos and death. Both hops slowed to a hover, and from the cold safety of the exosphere, the crews looked down in agonized silence upon the Armageddon they had tried so hard to prevent.

An emotional voice from the headset broke the silence. "Jeff? Jeff?"

"I'm here, Rose. Are you okay?"

"We are. Thanks to you. Do you see—oh, God …" she tried to say more, but her voice caught and broke in a sob of sorrow, so great was her grief.

He saw it, and like her, it was all he could do to speak. "I don't think—I don't think I've ever *not* wanted to see anything so badly in my whole life."

After a moment, she said, "Thanks for coming for me—uh, I mean, for *us,* Jeff. Tell Ephraim thanks for us too, would you?"

"I will. Oh, uh, Rose?"

"Yes?"

"Rose, I—I don't know what I would have done, if I'd lost you. I'd rather die than live without you."

"Me too. Jeff?"

"Yes, Rose?"

"I've missed you so much," she whispered.

"I've missed you too—uh, what, Eph? Oh. Okay. Rose, Eph says that we have a stop to make along the way. He's dialed in another destination. I guess I'll see you back at the fortress?"

"You'll call me?"

"You know I will. As soon as I get back. Be safe."

"I already am. Bye."

He raised his hand toward the other hop, and imagined Rose inside, waving back at him. Turning to Ephraim, he said, "This had better be good."

Ephraim knitted his brow and scowled. "You finally get to crew on a hop machine, and all you want to do is go home? Shut up and enjoy the ride."

"All right. I will. Where are we off to?"

"I believe you mean *when* are we off to, and the answer is 2080."

"But Eph, that's within our own lifetime. That's not allowed."

"Neither is this machine, Jeff. The problem with the Board is that they think in too-few dimensions. We're not allowed to go back in our own lifetime because they only allow hops *from* our time. They *must* be seventy years minimum, and they're required to return straight back to base. But we know it can be done, because that's how we originally recovered several of the old hop machines. We're going to 2080 from 2015 via 1929. After that, we're going to drop in on 2010 for a visit. And *then* we'll return to 2099."

"Why 1929?"

"I chose the year randomly. The outbound passes I'm using exceed seventy years from each time I'm planning on visiting. I think they used to call it being a Sunday driver when you'd just cruise around for fun."

"Cruise around. Okay. What about 2010? Why there?"

"Why not? Are you game?"

"Are you kidding? I'm already strapped in. Hit it, mister."

# 32

*Late autumn, 2080*
*Somewhere over Casco Bay, Maine*

From the air, Portland, Maine looked much the same as Jeff remembered. He wasn't sure he wanted to be there. 2080 was a bad year in his life. But Ephraim insisted that they go to Portland in 2080. It was late in the year, and the weather was already chilly. The bright foliage had faded, so most of the leaves would already be on the ground. Everything would almost certainly be brown and damp.

Jeff shivered in the damp. He knew this weather, and his instincts told him that this was the year it happened. *This weather is similar to the day I rode shotgun in that truck. At this very minute, my young self could be crushed, and my back broken. Maybe I'm out in the country, lying in that wrecked truck right now. I remember feeling so certain that I'd never make it home alive.*

*No. Why would we bother coming, if we're already too late? Ephraim knows when it happened. This must be one of the days just prior to it. Maybe we can stop it.*

But, how?

There weren't rules for meeting yourself, except for the single rule dictating that it wasn't allowed, under any conditions. *As long as Ephraim had the hop machine out, he couldn't resist breaking the rules. I*

*can't say as I blame him. They'll probably take it away from him when*
*he gets back. We might as well push it as far as we can while he's got it.*

By all appearances, he seemed determined that Jeff should meet
himself; something Jeff was certain would go over quite well with the
Board, should they ever find out.

He suspected the discussion would be more along the lines of an
inquisition. Still, if he were to be completely honest about it, the
concept of cutting loose for a while appealed to him, even if there
would more than likely come a time of reckoning for it.

Ephraim was fearless, and already had a plan to fly into Portland
proper. Jeff couldn't understand how he thought he would get away
with landing in a city. He was curious to see how his friend would
accomplish such a feat.

Ephraim manually dropped the upper fields and cages, and flew
just feet above the ocean, and maneuvered through Danforth Cove,
between South Portland and the islands. Rounding the point, he
entered the harbor. The protected waters had less chop and required
less height, so he lowered and maintained a hover at 6 inches above
the water, and minimized the fields. They appeared to be gliding on
top of the water.

He drove in slowly across the bay, and into the port, where he
exited up the boat ramp in the old port. Jeff felt a panic attack
coming on when Ephraim set the hop machine down in front of fifty
witnesses, many of whom came over to learn what it was. Not
unexpectedly, dozens of questions followed.

Ephraim was unshakable as he strutted around the machine,
patting it proudly and gabbing on about it. "It's a prototype
hovercraft I've been working on. It's in the experimental stages right
now, of course. I'm still working the bugs out, but it's getting better.
It runs all the way across the bay and back now without a problem."

The growing crowd ate it up, while Ephraim, the wild man,
parked his top-secret time machine in plain sight, and told them it
was a hovercraft. Nothing to hide, right? Instead of disbelief, the
onlookers were excited to be among the first to see this 'prototype.'

One man offered to provide the intrepid inventors with a locked garage bay to store it in while they moved about town—in exchange for a ride on it on the way over to his garage, of course. After some introductions, Ephraim was happy to comply.

Not long after, with the machine safe and secure in the garage, they were off. Ephraim rattled on as he strutted over his inspired plan. "Simplicity is where genius is found, my friend. Give the people what they want," he said, with an exaggerated, puffed-up swagger, waving off Jeff's admiration, despite the fact that his smirking friend had offered none, and wasn't buying a bit of it.

Truthfully, he hadn't expected him to. "No? All right, then. Come on, we have an appointment to keep."

Off they went, but he wouldn't say where they were going. They remained in the old port, and soon found themselves in front of the truck terminal offices, where Ephraim asked Jeff to wait outside.

After a short while, he emerged from the loading docks with a younger man. As they approached, the young man's ragged appearance struck Jeff. He remembered being that poor when he was young. Then he realized why this man's walk seemed familiar, as they drew closer. It was then that Jeff realized what Ephraim was up to.

"Jeff Waldron, I'd like you to meet my best friend, Jeff Waldron."

The young man stared, gaping at the mid-thirties-aged man in the wheelchair, not knowing what to say. The older Jeff spoke first, "I'll bet this seems pretty strange to you."

"Yeah. You have the same last name, and you look just like me, so we must be related, but I didn't know there were any other relatives with our name."

Jeff looked at Ephraim. "Eph, is tomorrow the day—?"

He received a nod of affirmation.

The following day, this young man would climb into a truck, and lose the use of his legs forever when hijackers overturned the rig. They needed time to talk to the young man, so Ephraim, who knew Jeff's proclivities, made a suggestion. "I have an idea. How about we talk over a few beers? I'm buying!"

That did the trick. The three wandered along the harbor together to the ancient Ri-Ra Pub, and found a table, up some steps in the front corner, where they could discuss how the two Waldrons were related.

Once the beers and shots arrived, Ephraim told his favorite stories while they roared with laughter.

"So what did her old man say about that?" the young man asked.

Ephraim shrugged and said, "I didn't stick around to ask!" which set them off again, their laughter reverberating off the walls of the old pub.

By Ephraim's estimation, the younger Jeff was by now sufficiently plied with alcoholic lubricant. They stood at least some chance of broaching the sensitive subject without him wigging out. He nodded to the older Jeff, indicating it was time to talk to himself—literally.

Jeff started in as easily as he could on his young counterpart. "Jeff. I know how we're related. I can tell you, but I'll need you to keep an open mind. Can you do that?"

Young Jeff nodded amiably. He felt sure that his mind was open. The next minute or two would determine that.

"Okay, here we go. Jeff ... I— I'm you. I'm you, twenty years from now. I work in the field of quantum physics, and I work for the government, up in the county, in the fortress."

"You're me," young Jeff repeated affably, drunk enough to be amused. "I'm a quantum physicist. Right."

As nonchalant as his voice sounded, he couldn't escape the uneasy feeling that this man was speaking the truth. And even drunk, the fine, analytical mind that would help him to become a quantum physicist probed, questioned, sought the truth. Small details stood out, told him what he needed to know. Or as in this case, told him what he didn't want to know, and certainly didn't wish to admit. Not when his gaze fell upon the wheelchair.

He didn't need to look down to know that he was wearing little more than rags; threadbare clothing, worn until they could no longer be stitched together by candlelight at night. That was the norm, here in the city, and across most of the country.

Even though the older Waldron lived his life in a wheelchair, he wore clean, almost-new clothing. *Both* of these men did. Young Jeff couldn't remember the last time he saw anybody without at least *some* ragged clothing adorning them. Without so much as casting a glance around the bar, he knew every other individual there was wearing clothes as worn and tattered as his. And there was more.

He and the man looked alike. *So much* alike. The man spoke like him, with the same inflections in his voice. The eyes—though older—were so like his, it was downright spooky.

What about the man's choice of careers? Sure, it could be a coincidence, but quantum physics? Science had always captivated and intrigued him, but he never had the education needed to follow that dream. Had he found a way to pursue it? It might explain the clothing, if he worked as a physicist for the government up in the fortress. All of those thoughts passed through his mind in a matter of seconds, but none were lost on him.

Jeff nodded to him. "Yes, I'm you. And I'm not surprised that you didn't ask what a quantum physicist is."

Young Jeff had no good response for that, but he did find one thing disconcerting, especially if this man really was him. He asked, "Then why the frick am I—are you—in a wheelchair? And how did you get here if you're me, and you're twenty years older?"

"Because tomorrow morning, when you're on the road, riding shotgun in the back of that truck—"

"*Whoa,* there, guy," young Jeff interrupted, looked around quickly, and raised his eyebrows. In hushed tones, he asked, "How the *hell* do you know about that? It's a secret run."

"I know it because I'm *you,* okay? And I can't tell you how, but I'm here, in time to warn you. Now, listen; when you get on the road, about an hour north of here, you'll—"

"But we didn't tell *anyone* about that run," the tipsy younger one objected to his older self again.

"But *you* know about it, right?"

"Well, yeah."

Well, I'm *you.* Twenty years ago, *I*—" he said patiently, and pointed a finger to himself, "was *you,*" and then he pointed at his younger self. "And, *that's* how I know about it. Get it?"

His young drinking buddy took a swig as he gave their association some deep thought, and then, through the increasingly thick mist of alcohol, it clicked. "Oh. Yeah. You're me. I get it."

"Ahhh. Great. So, okay, here's the deal. *IF* the truck gets hijacked—and it *will*—then **you** end up in this chair when it wrecks." He pointed again, repeating his words for emphasis, "**You** end up in *this* chair for the rest of *your* life, Jeff. **We** end up in this chair for the rest of **our** lives. Get it?"

The young man absorbed the information in sober silence. No matter how much he drank, and no matter how much bravado he tried to summon or feign, the withered legs in that wheelchair knocked the wind out of him. He understood, and even accepted that this was him in that wheelchair—to an extent. Looking at those legs, he couldn't summon a reply.

The older Jeff remembered how hard he drank when he was younger, and at that moment, he regretted it— more than ever. He wasn't making this very easy on himself. Damned hard, in fact.

He knew both versions of him were smart enough to do this, and pushed ahead, determined to break through, or at least get his young self to respond. "Okay. I need you to do something to help me out. By doing that, it means you'll be doing something to help *you* out; are you with me?"

"Sure. Okay."

"I need you to *not* ride shotgun on any trucks, ever again. No more jobs where you can get shot or killed. Can you do that for me?"

Young Jeff gave him a look of incredulity. "You want me not to *work?* How the hell'm I gonna make my money?"

"Not working at all isn't what I'm asking of you. It's okay to get out and work, but you need to find safer work. You need to start studying the books at home. Spend some time with Mr. Salls, the teacher who lives in the building with you."

"I can't just quit. I've got responsibilities. Hey, how do you know about Mr. Salls?"

"I'm you, remember? And being you, I know that what you've

got *isn't* responsibilities. You spend most of your time and money drinking too much, and chasing Mary what's-her-name over there on Congress Street. You need to get a handle on all of that, and you know it. She doesn't work out. Take it from me. When you run out of money, booze, and especially when you're fresh out of legs, Mary will be *gone*.

"If you don't stop working at the dock, if you don't stay out of those trucks, you won't have your legs. I know you like having legs that work, Jeff. You see, I was you, and I *really liked* having them. Ride shotgun on that truck tomorrow, and *these* will be your legs from tomorrow on. You *will* be in this wheelchair for the rest of your life."

Jeff leaned forward, laid his fists on the table and opened them in an appeal to his young self. "Please. Go home. Study. Become a quantum physicist. A quantum physicist with working legs. You're smart as hell. You're great in the sciences. You love them, it turns out."

"And you suck at women, anyway," the tipsy Ephraim offered, perhaps believing something about the cutting remark was helpful.

"Look, thanks for the drinks, but I gotta go," young Jeff said, and reached into his jacket pocket for some money to pay for drinks. The other two watched his hands shake as he counted out some coins.

"I'm buying, remember?" Ephraim said.

"Oh, yeah. Okay, thanks," the young man said, and started down the steps, headed for the door.

Jeff had done what he could to stop him, but it was clear that his young counterpart was freaked, and about to bolt. He called out to the young man, and said, "Promise me you'll at least give it some thought, Jeff. Please."

The young man didn't turn back to acknowledge him.

Ephraim spoke up. "Here, take this, Jeff." He held up a cinch-bag. The young man turned to see what he had. Curious, he climbed back up the steps to the table, and took it from him, regarding it cautiously.

In a low voice, Ephraim said, "It's money. Go ahead, count it."

Young Jeff turned his back to the crowd, poured the coins into his hand, and counted them. He looked up, astonished. "There's over four hundred dollars in here!" he said, in an excited whisper, eagerly slipping the coins back into the pouch.

"Four hundred and fifty," Ephraim said, "and it's all yours. But you'll have to promise us you *won't* ride shotgun on the trucks anymore, especially tomorrow. *And* that you'll look for safer jobs. We'll need your solemn word on that."

Young Jeff looked at the two men. "You're really serious about this, aren't you? It's so important that I don't ride shotgun anymore, that you'd pay me all this money?"

"It is, but don't worry about the money. It's a loan. I'll make you pay me back when you're *him,*" Ephraim said, and jerked his thumb nonchalantly at the older Jeff.

The young man's eyes moved to the wheelchair, then to Jeff, and back to the wheelchair several times, and a flash of real fear showed for a moment in his eyes. He walked over and asked, "You're really me? You *swear* it?"

"I swear on that funny you-know-what-shaped birthmark on both our butts, Jeff. I'm you. I'll swear it on anything you need me to swear it on so you'll believe me. So you'll keep me out of this damn chair."

Young Jeff's eyes widened in surprise. *Crap. The birthmark. Not a whole lot of other ways he could know about that.* "Okay. Okay ... I— I promise. I'll stop riding shotgun." Pocketing the hefty bag of coins, he turned to leave.

He stopped for a second, and glanced over his shoulder, half expecting them to come after him to take the money back, and gave some thought to something else he considered saying.

He walked back over to Jeff. "It was good meeting you," and extended his hand.

Jeff smiled and reached out to shake hands with his young self. When they touched, a strange surge of energy ran between the two, cementing their meeting.

Neither would forget this day.

Without another word, young Jeff wheeled, and walked quickly down the steps and out the door.

Through the front window, they watched him leave. Jeff wheeled to the edge of the steps, and step by step, let himself down. Ephraim settled up at the bar, and they exited the pub.

On their way back to the garage, they walked along the water.

"You know, Jeff, you were kind of a humble bumble when you were a kid. Not too swift at all."

"Don't remind me," Jeff said, as he reached down and felt his legs. He slapped them, and pinched them. "Hmm. Nothing. How long do you think it'll take for them to come back if my young self stays off that truck?"

Ephraim said, "How should I know? Hell, there's no telling if it'll even work. Just being here, we're setting a precedent for someone trying to change something within their own lifetime. You haven't returned to our time yet, human nature is a factor, and the list goes on.

"Whatever happens, the important thing is that you came here and tried. You did your best. It's sort of encouraging that your young self at least took the time to listen."

"It *did* look like he—err, I—was taking it seriously there at the end, didn't it?" Jeff said, with hope in his voice.

Ephraim said, "Money is a strong negotiator. I brought it along just for this. I knew you were dirt-poor. We all were, before we made it to the fortress. I figured; why not just bribe you if talking common sense didn't appear to be working, right? You'd told me that riding shotguns on those trucks was all about the money."

He scratched his head, and said, "Of course, there is *one* statistic probability we're up against here. The vast majority of all our corrections fail, typically for unrelated reasons. Mostly human nature. Then there's the very real possibility that, if you never lose your legs, you could disappear from our lives, and end up in another life, working in some factory, never knowing Rose or me. There's a price for every single move we make in life."

"Never knowing Rose?"

"Or me."

Jeff looked a little worried about that, but then he looked up at Ephraim and said, "You know; I never thought I'd get the chance to talk to myself; to do my best to change my mind, or my path. I'll never be able to tell you what it means to me.

"And now," he said, shrugging his shoulders, "now we wait. Maybe I listened, maybe not. Maybe I'll get my legs back. Maybe not. Whatever happens, you made it happen for me, Eph. Now, all I have to worry about is how stupid I was at that age, and hope I'm just a little smarter than I remember being."

"Not too smart at all, from where I sat."

Jeff snorted. "Yeah. I was there today. Twice. Either way, my chances are a *hell* of a lot better than they ever were before."

Ephraim smiled, and said, "Sounds like cause for celebration. How about a trip to 2010? Can't go home without it, you know!"

Jeff said, "Sure, why not? Say, did you notice? I'm a fair bit taller than you, Eph."

Ephraim stopped in his tracks and gave Jeff a hurt look. "Oh, sure, let no good deed go unpunished. What a putz. Some friend."

As they continued up the street, Jeff said, "Well, I was taller. I saw it. So did you. Several inches, at least."

"Next time, I'm leaving the parachutes off."

"Some guys just have to have the last word all the time, don't they?"

"You owe me four hundred and fifty dollars."

"See what I mean? They say it's an affliction."

# 33

"This won't go well for you, will it?" Rose asked.

Jeff shrugged. "No, but we knew what we were getting ourselves into when we took off. I'll never be sorry we went. Our mission was to save you, and you're safe. You're *all* safe. Besides, I don't think the colonel will let anything too bad happen to us. We were acting under his orders.

"Of course, there was that little side trip where we went off the radar for a few days. That part probably won't go so well. It would have been nice if I'd gotten my legs back. But I always was one stubborn son-of-a-bitch. I never *would* listen to anybody."

She kneeled, and looked at him. Her amazing, liquid-dark eyes never failed to melt him. Giving him a fierce hug, she said, "I won't lose you now. You're going to be all right. I won't believe anything else. They'll let you stay."

Looking in his eyes, she saw the love returned in kind. She pulled his head closer and kissed him softly. When she stood, she said, "I'll be right behind you."

"So will I," Sam said, "I'll be right there with Rose. You two remember that."

"Yes, ma'am," Ephraim said, in an unusually polite tone. "We're counting on it."

The crowd murmured around them, and parted ways as Colonel Clayton arrived in his dress uniform.

"Mr. Waldron. Mr. Caine. Are you ready to face the music?"

"Yes, sir."

"We are, sir."

"Good. But I see something missing." He snapped his fingers and held out his hand, and a sergeant placed something over his arm.

"Due to the severe nature of the offenses, I was unable to stop the inquiry proceedings. But these should send a clear message to the Board. It's the best I could do. My brother's pulling for you on that side, as well."

He continued, "No members of my hop crews will face the Board without their Hop Ops crew jackets. Is that clear?" he handed each of them a jacket adorned with a patch showing T.I.T.O.R. boldly emblazoned across it.

The last-minute show of such support meant everything to Jeff and Ephraim. Jeff looked up at the colonel. "Crystal clear, Colonel Clayton, and we'll be proud to wear these. Thank you, sir."

Ephraim choked up at the unexpected show of support, but managed to nod, and mumble, "Um-hmm. Proud."

Sam helped him slide his jacket on, took him by the arm, and said, "Everybody in Ops is proud of you two, and we wanted you to know it. C'mon, we'll walk you in. Jeff, are you okay?"

He was sweating, and looking uncomfortable. "Yeah, fine, I'm just a little sorer today than usual. No surprise, with all the activity in the past couple of days. Let's get this over with."

The Board was already in session in Port Angeles, attending the proceedings remotely. They were larger than life on the Ops chamber view screen. Behind them, seated away from the board table, was General Clayton.

As people took their seats, the general walked toward the camera, and said, "Hello, Samantha."

She looked up and smiled. "Hi, Daddy. It's good to see you. I miss you."

"I miss you too, dear," he said, and held his hand up to wave to her, then returned to his seat.

Moments later, both rooms fell silent as the proceedings were called to order.

The morning wore on while every individual involved stood and gave testimony; several of them a number of times.

"It's your contention, then, Mr. Caine, that the nuclear war could not have been avoided?"

"I didn't say that, and it's not my contention. I said—"

"But you said we caused it with the time machines."

The Board had an irritating habit of calling the hop machines 'time machines,' which grated upon everyone at Hop Ops.

"I said that the U.S. *military* in 2015 caused it by trying to steal our hop machines. And I'd like to remind the Board that neither the designation nor the terminology for these pieces of equipment has *ever* been 'time machines,' and I ask that the Board show a modicum of respect for the hard work we do and expend the minimal effort required to call them hop machines. It would at least make us believe that you're paying some attention to what we have to say."

"Very well. So, you claim that the military was trying to steal one of our, uh, *hop* machines."

"No. Their military was trying to seize *two* of our hop machines by force, and I don't *claim* anything; we have proof of it."

The speaker placed his hand over the microphone and conversed with the others, who nodded. He returned his attention to Ephraim. "I believe we now have a sufficiently clear picture of what went on in Wyoming in 2015. Our presence did not provide a solution. You were fortunate that both crews escaped with their lives. Do you agree with that assessment?"

"In exactly that context, I agree with that assessment."

"Good. Then let's move on to your unauthorized hops."

Ephraim struggled with the urge to roll his eyes. *It's amazing how they can remember what to call them when they want to.*

He said, "I'd like to point out that the hop machine in question was not mounted on a vehicle body, because it was not officially in service. It was called into emergency service, never having been formally registered; therefore it was neither authorized nor unauthorized. As the pilot, I did take advantage of the situation to make an attempt at restoring Jeff Waldron's legs to him."

"By traveling within his lifetime so he could meet himself at a younger age. Is that correct?"

"It's correct if I can finish what I'm saying. Otherwise, no, it's not correct."

"Continue."

"I'm considered valuable to the program, so valuable that I've never been allowed to crew on a hop machine. You know that. Jeff Waldron, another pivotal member of the hop program, is also not allowed to crew a hop machine. Because he is in a wheelchair, he cannot pass the physical portion of the tests. His score is one hundred percent on the written test. Yet, because he can't stand or jump, he's automatically disqualified.

"All I have ever wanted, and all Jeff has ever wanted, was to crew on a hop. Even a small, unimportant hop, the ones the crews call 'milk runs.' We had this one chance to go, and we went. I can't apologize for that. We had completed our assigned mission successfully, and it was worth taking the chance to restore Jeff's legs, even though it didn't work. Both Jeff and I are keenly aware of all the inherent dangers of hop travel."

He continued, "I also wish to point out that most of the rules of hop travel you enforce were adopted subsequent to recommendations submitted to you, primarily by myself and Jeff Waldron. They were geared toward the safety of the hop teams, and paradox prevention. If anybody would know when it's not dangerous to sidestep a rule, then we would.

"One rule Jeff and I *never* recommended—or agreed with—was the rule forbidding time travel within one's own lifetime. That was a rule the Board itself established due to their wholly unsubstantiated belief that meeting oneself is a recipe for disaster. The 70-year minimum on hops should in no way prevent us from exploring the recent past, as we have demonstrated here. Why not expand your beliefs? Our experience has shown us that we can go much further."

The speaker scribbled, and looked up. "Thank you, Mr. Caine. We in no way wish to impugn your heroic rescue of the other hop crew and their machine. Whatever way you may choose to describe it, however, we are less than comfortable with what can only be construed as your joy-ride after the fact. Let's see. Yes. We still have one or two more questions for Mr. Waldron."

Jeff rolled forward. "I'm here."

After reading some notes, the speaker said, "We should like to continue this matter after lunch, if there are no objections."

There were none.

Sitting down with Jeff, Ephraim, and Sam at the lunch table, Rose looked anxious. "What do you think they want with Jeff?"

Ephraim looked unconcerned. "They're probably just dotting the I's and crossing the T's. I don't think we're going to be in any deep trouble, even if they did try to call it a joy-ride."

Jeff, lacking Ephraim's certitude, didn't feel as confident as his partner-in-crime at that moment. "But it *was* a joy-ride, Eph. Do you really think they're going to just look the other way and say; "*Boys will be boys?*" This wasn't a Humvee or a motorcycle; we took a machine built to travel through time, and we used it for just that purpose. Sorry if I don't share your optimism on this one. What do you think, Sam?"

Sam said, "I think Jeff's right."

Ephraim shifted uncomfortably. Sam didn't often disagree with him.

She went on, "And I think Ephraim is right, too. You guys *did* screw up in a big way, and I don't want to hear either of you denying it. You had your reasons, but you still broke rules. On the other hand, you were untrained, yet you still accepted a risky mission, where you saved a hop machine and the lives of its crew."

"A very *grateful* crew, I might add," Rose said, and kissed each of them on the cheek. Ephraim blushed. Jeff grinned.

Sam said, "I think you'll be in some trouble, and there'll be a lot of finger wagging, and yelling at you, and decrees stating that it'll be a long time before you take a hop machine out again."

"As though we ever intended to," Ephraim said.

"Yeah, especially when you feel this bad afterward. I never thought about this part of it," Jeff said, rubbing his sore lower back.

Sam said, "Agreed. You should tell them that. But I doubt you'll even get a cut in pay. Remember; hang your heads, and at least feign some sort of shame, or remorse."

Jeff and Ephraim glanced at each other and smiled. That sounded good to them.

Catching the impish gleam in their eyes, she said, "Okay, you two. Maybe it's just me, but that doesn't look a lot like remorse. I think you'll need some practice to bring off that part."

The inquiry reconvened with Jeff's continued testimony.

"Mr. Waldron, you are a civilian contractor?"

"Yes. I've been with the program for nearly thirteen years now."

"Mr. Waldron, the Board has discussed this matter at some length, and we find it particularly disconcerting that a civilian contractor had ready access to such a sensitive piece of equipment, and was able to take it out on an unauthorized hop. What do you have to say about that?"

Ephraim stood up. "I'm the civilian contractor who piloted that hop machine, and initially, we took it out under orders, under extreme circumstances."

"That's different, Mr. Caine. You're the creator of these hop machines."

"And Jeff is the yin to my yang, the other half of the formula, my man in the Ops center who helped me build this program from the dust and obscurity of the prior programs."

"I'm sorry, Mr. Caine. We see it differently. Now, Mr. Waldron, do you have a response?"

"I have access to everything on this base, every nut and bolt, every single one, and every single zero in every computer program. And yes,

I have access to the hop machines. I helped Ephraim build this machine. This has been the case for the past twelve years and some months; there is nothing remarkable about it. I offer no defense or excuse for the trip I took with Ephraim, but I have no regret for taking it, either. We brought Rose's crew home.

"Had I returned with my legs, I would have petitioned for a position as a hop crew member. As you can see, I now have a crew jacket, and, official crew member or not, I appreciate the confidence placed in me by Colonel Clayton and the rest of the team. It's doubtful that I'll ever have the opportunity to crew a hop again, so any reservations you have are likely superfluous, once that's taken into account."

"So, you have no regret for what you did."

"I won't allow you to take what I said out of context. Please rephrase the question."

"I would like Mr. Waldron's testimony read from, here, to here."

The stenographer read, "But I have no regret for taking it, either."

The speaker said, "I think that answers the question to our satisfaction." He placed his hand over the microphone again, and spoke briefly with the others. At the back of the boardroom, General Clayton's face clouded as he listened to them, and his anger was evident.

The speaker turned back to Jeff, still scribbling as he spoke. "Please stand, Mr. Waldron."

Jeff said, "We can see *you*. Are you blind, or are you unable to see *us?*"

"Without looking up, the speaker said, "We can see you, Mr. Waldron."

"The *HELL* you can, buddy." Jeff's normally calm demeanor slipped. There were two kinds of people. One kind of people looked at you, and the wheelchair disappeared in favor of you. The other kind saw the wheelchair, and *you* disappeared. Clearly, he was dealing with the latter. "*LOOK* at me!"

Taken aback by the abrupt response, the speaker stopped writing and looked at Jeff, and red crept into his face. "Oh, ahh, I'm, ahh, sorry about that, Mr. Waldron. You may remain seated."

"Oh, *thank you,* thank you so *very* much. *So* kind of you," Jeff responded, the contempt in his tone unmistakable. "You know, you're supposed to pass judgment on me here today, and you've listened to what I said, and watched me, and paid such rapt attention throughout these proceedings that you still didn't even know I'm sitting in a wheelchair, until I forced you to look at me.

"You're stacking up all your little facts and adding them up, and you think you see somebody who is going to hop up on one of these machines and just ride off on it. I deserve better than that. This program, and the Board that governs it, both owe me a great debt for all the work I've done. I demand that substantially more thought be put into this decision."

As though Jeff had said nothing, the speaker said, "Jeff Waldron, we have the right to exercise at any time our right to dismiss you as a civilian contractor, without further explanation. Your services are no longer required. You will receive one month of severance pay, and you must vacate your base housing within three weeks. That is all."

"If Jeff goes, *I* go," Rose said, standing and facing the speaker.

"If Jeff goes, *I* go," Sam said, and stood to face the speaker.

"And me," Ephraim, said, standing.

"Me too," Fred said.

One by one, every member of the Ops team stood, and quit. And then, every member of every Ops crew on base stood, and quit.

But it stunned everyone on both sides of the screen when Colonel Clayton stood, and said, "If Jeff Waldron goes, I go."

The general stood up, astounded. Bird colonels in charge of entire bases didn't just quit. Especially his little brother.

Colonel Clayton continued, "I'm no longer addressing just the Board. I'm addressing the general as well, because I no longer have confidence in the Board, and until this is settled, I will not recognize their authority. I have some things I need to say."

The speaker sputtered, "This is *outrageous,* an—"

The general interrupted. "That's enough from *you.* You've had your say, and look what it's brought about. Go ahead, Marcus; I'm listening, and I'm inclined to go along with you on that."

The speaker's face burned dark red with silent fury as Clayton continued, "I guess what I'm saying is that I'll be gone anyway, if Jeff goes. Please, take a long, hard look at these people standing here before you today. I'm sure you think that look is defiance. Maybe it is, to some extent. But the plain truth is, without the people in this room, I have no program, and that means I have no job. Jeff Waldron, Rose Rios, Ephraim Caine, Fred Arnold, Samantha Clayton; these people are the best anywhere, and I need them. I need their minds, their hearts, and their unflinching loyalty to me, to this country, to this program, and to each other.

"You believe you can just discard my people. If you do, then you endanger this program. Losing any one of them means you put me and this program at tremendous risk. Whatever happens here, Jeff Waldron will have a place to live and food to eat within the walls of this fortress, as *my* guest, as long as it *is* my fortress.

"It's my belief that the Board has lost touch, and no longer understands our objectives and goals—if they ever did to begin with. We've reached a crossroads with this program. The Board has decided that, rather than assign our best people to identify and seek solutions, they want to assign blame to my team members to draw attention away from the undeniable fact that their leadership to this point is what placed us in this dangerously untenable position.

"I *know* my team can handle the job at hand, whatever we are assigned. But I feel that we've outgrown the Board. We know our objectives. We know how to reach them. The Board doesn't have a clue what we're doing, or what's truly at stake, and now they're trying to cover their collective asses, hoping nobody realizes what a supreme mess they've made of things."

The members of the Board, already furious, recoiled as though they'd been slapped in their faces, shouted and cursed as they expressed their disbelief over the colonel's stated position of no confidence.

General Clayton waited for the furor to die down, and when he spoke his voice was quiet, and authoritative. "With the evidence I have before me today, I find the colonel's assessment of the situation to be astute, accurate, and to the point.

"Therefore, for the time being, we will maintain the decision to suspend operations until further review of the efficacy of the Board. Period. Mr. Waldron stays. Not only because of all the votes of confidence he received here today, but because I personally know what kind of person he is. What do you think, Mr. Waldron?"

The northeastern fortress crowd burst out in applause, and backed away, with excited shouts and grins, making way so the general could see Jeff.

Slumped over in his chair, Jeff trembled uncontrollably, facing the floor.

Rose rushed to him, crying out, "Jeff? Jeff, what is it? What's wrong?" She reached down, and gently lifted him upright in his chair. His head dropped backwards, the cords in his neck were strained and stood out, emphasizing the grimace on his face. His eyes would not stop moving, and didn't focus on her at all.

Slowly, his teeth unclenched, and he opened his jaw just long enough to snatch a deep breath. "*Pain,*" he gasped. "*Pai— AAAghh!* Oh, God, make it stop. *Make it stop! Pleeease,*" he pleaded, as his eyes locked with hers.

Blacking out, he fell limp, rolled sideways, and had not so many caring hands reached for him, he would have fallen from his chair.

Clayton took charge. "Get him up to Medical now. You. Call ahead; tell them what we have here. Rose, stay with him. Move it, people. Come on, clear the way."

The room emptied quickly, and Clayton turned back to the screen, where his brother stood, also alone.

"You're having one helluva day, little brother," the general said.

Clayton nodded. "Looks like yours isn't much better. You still have to report all this to the president, don't you?"

"That I do."

"You win, then. Your day is worse. I'd better go see what happened to Jeff."

"He didn't look good. Give him my best when you see him, would you? You were right; he's a good man. Oh, and Marcus?"

"Hmm?" Clayton responded, clearly distracted as he turned back to the screen.

"I think you're right. Our biggest problem *has* been the Board, and I'm going to recommend to the President that they be removed from power immediately. We should make T.I.T.O.R. a self-regulating entity with minimal oversight. Once we map out a new mission plan, it's my belief that T.I.T.O.R. will shine."

That should have been the best of news, but Clayton was distracted, and said, "I've got a man down right now. I'll trust whatever you decide to do. I always have." He turned and hurried from the room.

"Right back atcha, kid," the general said, and reached for the button on his center console. The picture shrank to a small black dot in the screen's center, and disappeared.

# 34

"Do you know what's wrong with him, Doctor?" Rose asked.

The doctor shook his head. "We've got him on a Morphine drip. The normal dosage did very little, and now we've exceeded the safe dosage, but he's still in considerable pain. It doesn't seem to be helping much. It's the strangest thing, though ..."

"Yes?"

"Um, he's a paraplegic, right?"

"That's right."

"Well, that's what's strange."

"What about it?" she asked.

"The pain. It's all from his waist and lower back, downward. Hips. Legs. Buttocks. Feet. All of it. He says it's like ten people are beating on him with hammers from the waist down. It's almost as if— as if his nerves are regenerating. We'll occasionally see nerves regenerate in a paraplegic, to a limited extent. Usually, it's something small. Certainly nothing like this.

"With an injury this severe, and with nerves regenerating, it would require *bone* from the spine to suddenly start repairing itself, which is, well, it's— it's impossible. But there's no other explanation. Don't ask me how. I've never heard of this before. It's unprecedented."

"Does this mean he'll be able to walk again?"

The doctor raised his eyebrows. "Damned if I know, ma'am. Your guess is as good as mine. I've never seen anything like this before. Right now, he's bearing up under terrible pain, and it seems to be increasing, rather than lessening. His body is under such severe strain right now, it might fail—" he hesitated.

"When can I see him?"

"I don't suppose it would do any harm to see him now, but don't expect him to be too chatty. That's a heavy dose."

His eyes were open, but bleary. When Rose approached, he smiled weakly. She loved the way he smiled at her.

His voice slurred when he said, "Hey, boss lady. You got some work for me to do, or is this a social call?"

She picked up his hand, and stroked it gently. "You know me, I'm all business. I brought some filing for you to do."

Neither spoke for a few minutes. She continued to hold his hand and stroke it.

Finally, he broke the silence. "I know this looks bad. But don't worry, I'll be okay."

Her brow knitted. "Oh, Jeff. It *does* look bad. They don't even know what's wrong with you."

"No, but I do. And it's not what's wrong, it's what's right."

She looked perplexed. *"You* know what it is?"

He managed a wan grin, feebly attempting to look cocky, or at least confident. "Yeah. I'm getting my legs. I think I convinced myself not to ride shotgun that day in 2080. Or, maybe Ephraim's bribe worked. Either way, I'm walking out of here, Rose. On my own two legs. And, until I do, I'll bet real money it's gonna hurt like a bitch," he laughed, but the motion brought on more pain, causing him to wince and moan.

Though he was sure it was going to turn out all right, and confident that his legs were coming back, he was unaware of how critical his condition was, and she struggled to subdue her own fears and remain cheerful for him, to keep his spirits up.

She had to put on a good show for him, and let him know she was happy for him. "I'll be walking out with you, love."

His eyes lit up, and though still dopey, he grinned. "Rose. You called me *love*. Do you know how long I've loved you? From the first day I ever saw you."

"Same here. I wonder why we never did anything about it before."

"We're a lot alike, I guess." The morphine had another effect upon him; he was relaxed enough to say what he felt and thought. "You're the only thing in the world worth living for, Rose. The only thing that matters to me. The only thing that ever did."

Tears flowed freely down her cheeks. She grasped his hand tighter, and kissed it, and then leaned over and kissed his forehead. "Then *live*, Jeff. I want you to live through this. Fight hard. Win. Come home to me."

He said, "Marry me, Rose Rios. Say you'll marry me if I walk out of here. Say yes."

"I love you, Jeff Waldron, and I'll marry you any way you come out of here, whether it's walking, rolling a wheelchair, roller skating; any way you come, the answer is *yes.*"

"I don't have a ring handy right now. Will you trust me for it?" he asked, his eyes shining.

There was a knock on the door.

"Are you accepting visitors, Mr. Waldron?"

They turned to see Ephraim and Sam in the doorway, grinning like Cheshire cats.

"Eph! Sam! Come in, you're just in time, guys."

"Why, are you dying in a minute, or something?" Ephraim asked.

"No. Rose just agreed to marry me."

Sam said, "Ignore Ephraim. We heard the whole thing from the doorway. That's *wonderful*. Congratulations, you two!" Excited at the news, she hurried over and hugged Rose, then leaned over and gave Jeff a kiss in the forehead. "You two belong together. You make a great couple."

It was then that Rose realized just how good a friend Sam was to Jeff. What Sam had told her was true; he had never, ever loved anybody else but his Rose.

Ephraim quipped, "I especially liked the part about the roller skates. Yep. It painted a *vivid* mental picture for me."

The others cracked up, including Jeff, who promptly regretted it when pain wracked him again. They leaned over him, worried, but he said, "It's nothing, don't worry about it. I'm gonna be fine. Just wait. I'm starting to remember."

"Wait for what?" Ephraim asked.

"For my legs to come back. That's what this is, you know."

"You think it worked?"

"I *know* it worked. This pain is just my legs becoming normal again."

Ephraim had an amazed look on his face, and he walked over to the bedside. "Do you know what this *means?*" he asked, his eyes full of wonder.

Caught up in the moment, the girls said, "No, what?"

His look of wonder melted into a wicked grin as he said, "It means Jeff owes me four hundred and fifty dollars. How great is *that?*"

*   *   *

"Come in, Colonel Clayton," Jeff said. "It's good to see you."

Clayton walked over to Jeff's bed. "How's our hop crew member coming along?"

"Ready to spring into action, sir."

"Is that so?"

"More or less. Kinda less right now, but I'm getting there."

"Well, don't make me wait. Let's see," he said, focusing his gaze on Jeff's legs. "I can see from here. They're filling out again."

"They are indeed, sir. Watch this." He spread his toes apart and back together again, three times. With a concerted effort, he lifted one leg a couple of inches, and then the other. By this time, sweat was beading up on his face.

"All this, after just four days? I'm impressed."

"Thank you, sir. It's pretty exciting. Something else, too, sir. I want you to think about my wheelchair. Do you remember it?"

"Your wheelchair? What wheelchair? You're in here for muscle problems with your legs. I hadn't heard that you were going to need a wheelchair. Is this getting worse, or better?"

Jeff grinned. "Oh, better, sir, much better. I'll be dancing a jig before you know it."

It amazed him that he remembered both lives right now. His own personal forced-paradox. His old life was quickly fading, and his new one was growing stronger. The hospital personnel had somehow changed his diagnosis from unknown ailment, to muscle atrophy due to an unknown cause, and now, rapid-moving recovery from atrophy. Everything was in flux, all around him. Sam, Rose, and Ephraim only mentioned aspects of his old life reflexively, unaware of it when they did so. Only their subconscious minds remembered him in a chair now, and that changed constantly, fading by the hour. When questioned, they could consciously remember only his new life— which, ironically, he couldn't ... yet. Not completely, anyway. At that moment, he *could* remember being younger and meeting his older self in the chair when he was young, and that memory grew stronger by the hour. His memory of his recent visit back to meet his young self was rapidly fading. Ephraim had already forgotten the trip to Portland, but still remembered their rescue mission to 2015.

Charlie Troyer, the generation one hop pilot—and the only other human who truly knew what Jeff was going through—had paid him a visit, to let him know something about what he should expect. There were many aspects of this he'd have to deal with, but the most important would be that others would know him from an entirely different past than the one still in his mind, and until their memories matched his, their expectations might seem strange to him. He'd have to go with the flow. And before long, just as he said would happen, even Charlie had no idea why he was visiting the hospital. It was a lot for Jeff to keep straight in his mind. He couldn't write it down. He'd tried, but the writing disappeared in spots, leaving odd blanks on the page. Probably the oddest thing of all was the new memory of his leg ailments coming on, which he, at the same time, knew hadn't happened to him.

Clayton said, "Keep up the progress. I expect to see you walking out of here soon. I hear there's a lot on the line."

At least the wedding plans hadn't changed.

"Yes, sir, I'll do just that. Count on it."

"There's news from Port Angeles. I thought you'd want to hear about it. The Board was disbanded. Hop ops are suspended until further notice. We expected that, anyway, as it'll be a good four to six months before Ephraim has all four machines recalibrated. But if all goes well, when operations resume, T.I.T.O.R. will be self-governing, reporting only to General Clayton and the President. I have some bad news for you, though."

"You couldn't save my job?"

"That's pretty much the gist of it."

"I guess I saw that one coming."

"You'll be too busy anyway. What hop pilot wants to spend all his time at some station in Hop Ops, am I right?"

Jeff's mouth dropped open. "Me? I— I'll be piloting hops?"

Clayton nodded, and looked strangely at him. "Why *wouldn't* you be? You were only filling in at the command center while you worked through your leg muscle issues."

*Well, that's the first I've heard about it,* he thought. "Oh. Uh, sure, of course, sir. I guess it was starting to feel like I'd never get out of there."

*Going with the flow...*

"It may not matter. That's all dependent upon whether we resume ops. And right now, that's a big *if.*"

"Thank you, sir, whichever way it turns out."

"Don't thank me. The rest is up to you. You say your legs will be back up to snuff, and I expect you're as good as your word. You'll have to be able to pass your physical again, so I don't want to see you lying around here, milking it. Is that clear, Mr. Waldron?" Despite his gruff demeanor, he couldn't entirely hide his affection for this young man.

"Crystal clear, Colonel Clayton, *SIR!*" Jeff barked back, beaming ear to ear. He didn't care that the sudden exertion hurt.

Clayton looked around at the other patients in the room, and said, "Well, I've wasted enough time on you slugabeds. I've got work to do. If you'll excuse me." He stood, and marched briskly out the door, putting a little extra 'colonel' into it for Jeff's benefit.

Jeff couldn't help but grin as Clayton exited, and then, inspired, he looked down, and lifted his legs. Just an inch or two. One at a time. He now had *two* reasons to walk out under his own power. And the sooner, the better.

# 35

Colonel Clayton entered the cluttered building, and followed the sounds of voices out back, toward the lab.

"Mr. Caine. You requested my presence? Was it something important?"

"Yes, Colonel. We came across this file. It's not pretty."

"Summarize please, if you would."

"The photos in the file have enabled us to confirm that Flash was captured, and interrogated. We can be fairly certain that was how they got the information that helped them intercept Rose's hop machine. They did some pretty horrible things to him, but before he told them everything, he escaped, and died in a firefight in the process. It's all here." Ephraim said, and handed the file to Clayton.

Clayton solemnly accepted the file, and said, "I'm sorry to hear this, Ephraim. I know you liked Flash. We all did. We'll send these files to the research team. If he can be found, we'll find him, and bring him home. Full military honors. I'll authorize the manpower. Was that the only reason you sent for me?"

"No, sir. There's more. Going through the last containers of items from the warehouse, we found something unexpected. It took some time to check it against the data we have, and we ran a number of tests as well. You really need to see this," he said, and placed some shiny gray, flexible material in Clayton's hands. "Go ahead, try and stretch that."

Clayton tried to stretch it, but it didn't give at all. He bunched it up in his hands and pulled hard, with the same results. With raised eyebrows, he said, "I can't."

Ephraim smiled, and said, "Look where you bunched it up in your hands, did it leave any marks, or wrinkles? No, see? Go ahead, try and fold it; try and leave a crease. Lay it right down, and really press on the fold."

Clayton pressed hard, but the material relaxed, and laid as flat and smooth as when he started. "What *is* this?" he asked.

"I think I know what it is, but you have to see some of its more remarkable properties first. Stretch it out like this—that's right— now, I'm going to hit it with this propane torch."

Clayton complied, as Ephraim held the torch flame against it. From his side, Clayton saw a slight glow through the material, but the second the flame was removed, the glow stopped. Touching it, he found the material to be cool to the touch, with no visible signs of burn damage. "That's remarkable," he said. "The material is still perfect."

"There's more," Ephraim said. He took the material from the tabletop, and clipped it to the sides of a framework. "Take that radar gun in one hand," he said, "and that laser radar gun in the other, and point them right about here, and squeeze the triggers." He took the framework, and swung it through the spot Clayton was monitoring with the radar guns. The radar readout displayed 27 miles per hour, and the laser gun's readout showed 28 miles per hour.

"Okay, so it shows up on radar," Clayton said.

"No, that's just the point. All you got was a reading from the frame. Give me a minute here to change frames." Ephraim grabbed a smaller frame, and moved the material over to it. He had to wrap the material around the frame edges to keep it taut and flat, and clip it behind the frame, out of sight. "Okay, ready when you are, Colonel."

Clayton pointed the guns, squeezed the triggers, and said, "Go."

Ephraim swung the framework through the target spot, stopped, and looked expectantly at Clayton. "And?"

Clayton looked at the screens on the backs of the guns, and his brow knitted as his eyes went back and forth. "Nothing. Do it again."

Ephraim swung it again, and this time Clayton was certain he had aimed correctly. But when he looked, the readouts were all zeros.

"Nothing. On either. It should have at least registered on the laser gun. That'll register *something*, even on stealth materials." He looked at Ephraim and said, "Are you telling me that none of our sensors can pick this up?"

"I'm telling you *exactly* that, Colonel."

"And this material came from the warehouse?"

"This came from the pieces of the wreckage. There were a lot of bits and pieces of this material found at the site of the wreck. We know that *none* of it came from Hop 206. Colonel, I think we may have found the reason for 206 going off the screen."

"You have my attention. I'm listening."

"One more thing I need you to see before I continue." He took the material, went over to the drab concrete wall, and hung the material on two clamps, flat against the wall. He clamped some jumper cables onto the bottom of the material. Next, he turned one of the work lights toward the wall. "Watch the material now," he said, and clamped the other ends of the cable to a car battery he had nearby.

In front of their eyes, the material disappeared. "Whoa," said Clayton, surprised. "It's gone."

"That's what I thought too, the first time. Look closer. The clamps didn't fall."

Clayton walked closer, and as he drew near, he saw that, indeed, the clamps were still clamped to the material, which had not disappeared. Instead, it had gone into chameleon mode, and now matched the wall so perfectly that it was detectable to the eye only under close scrutiny, mostly by finding the edges.

"It camouflages itself?" Clayton asked, though he saw it for himself. "It's amazing, I'll give you that, but what does it have to do with the crash?"

Ephraim said, "Hop machines 101. Our hop machines have auto-detect and auto-evade devices built into them, due to the escape velocity speeds required, and the need to evade potential pursuers or interceptors. They react faster than any human can. We equip them with the latest in laser detection technology, a setup approximately the same as this gun, but on a much larger scale, with many emitters and sensors.

"Because a laser is the only type of light that can freely pass through our fields in both directions, it became our default primary sensor system. Let's say the sensors detect an attack or interception attempt, or an impending collision. It punches out, even if it's in mid-arc. If it happens in mid-arc, it means it ends up somewhere else, maybe even in another time, but at least it arrives there intact, and leaves the crew in one piece. They can reset, make their way back home, and try again."

"Standard stuff. I'm with you so far."

"Let's put a twist on that scenario, and imagine that there's an object out there orbiting our atmosphere. Something somebody doesn't want us to see, maybe an outpost for observing our species undetected. This material is as close as I've ever seen to a true cloaking device. Turn out the lights, shine a bright light on it, and it doesn't even light it up. You have to check your flashlight to make sure it didn't go out on you.

"One of its two main characteristics is the total absorption of any type of energy, which is then converted into usable power. It even channels the power in one direction through the material. The light of the sun behind it, and the light reflecting off the earth in front of it would have supplied such an outpost with much of the energy it needed to run, perhaps enough to power the entire rig. Certainly all it needed to cloak itself. It's conceivable that it could remain in orbit, and power itself indefinitely."

"The crash, Mr. Caine?"

"Oh. Right. Sorry. The connection. I was getting to that. It would make sense to assume that this material cloaked their orbiting observation outpost, and I think Hop 206 had the bad luck to run smack-dab into it. Well, more like an indirect or glancing blow. A hop machine can detect and evade something the size of a tangerine at full escape velocity, but no evasive action was taken, because it detected nothing.

"But, here's where it gets interesting. Once it impacted, it didn't default to anything else. Why? Because, with such an advanced detection-evasion system, we never designed impact or collision response features into its design. When the hop machine impacted at that speed, even though it was just a glancing blow, the speed, combined with the singularity fields—which are probably the only tools we have capable of slicing through this stuff—took away quite a bit of its covering when they collided. It took away some of the framework as well."

He held up a small piece of I-beam. "Here's one of the pieces we've heard described as having some sort of glyphs running along the girder. That describes it exactly, but these; they're not ours, colonel. The material and framework tangled up in one, maybe two of the quadratic singularity field generators, partially disabling them. With the built-in field redundancy of systems we have, the crew wasn't exposed to the vacuum of space or the re-entry burn. But it was more than sufficient to cause fluctuations in the field generators and destabilize the arc, and affect—or even disable—attitude control.

"Without attitude control, it couldn't be manually controlled, and I'll venture a guess that the impact with the undetected mystery outpost may have disabled the auto-evade system. With control compromised, it dragged these parts all the way back into the atmosphere, to earth, and to Roswell, New Mexico, the crash point."

He raised his hands apologetically, and said, "We *never* accounted for the possibility of a cloaked ship orbiting the earth. I wouldn't have ever considered it, and I wouldn't *believe* there could be technology like this if I hadn't seen this for myself."

Clayton raised a skeptical eyebrow. "I hesitate to even say this… you're saying that … *aliens* wrecked Hop 206?"

Ephraim looked at Jeff, who nodded. Then he said, "In a manner of speaking, Colonel; it sure looks that way. It would appear that we're not alone out here in this big ol' universe after all. And, what we have here, well, it indicates that they know a *lot* more about us than we do them. Their technology is astounding. They can see us, and they can remain *invisible* to us."

Clayton said nothing for a minute or so, and remained lost in deep thought for some time before he finally spoke, "Okay. Say there *are* aliens. There's little doubt that they had front row seats to watch us while we ruined our own planet. They may even know they had an unintentional hand in it. I'll bet they've been watching us for a long, long time. Think about it. At any time within the past century, they could've taken this planet with almost no resistance, so they're almost certainly not hostile. This technology tells us that they were *observing* us—a comparatively primitive species—from a distance."

Jeff said, "We agree. That's why we asked you to come and see this, Colonel. Maybe *they* could help us. Odds are, they're still watching. As far as time travel goes, I'm starting to think that we're wasting our time, and we *know* we're playing with fire. We seem to do more breaking than we do repairing with it. Most of the corrections we make are damage control from some other mission we screwed up. The more we try, the more trouble we get into. It's becoming something of a slippery slope. But if these beings could help us …"

Clayton agreed, "I can't argue with you there. But there are questions. *Will* they help us? Are they still up there? Did they pull up stakes and leave after the collision?"

Ephraim said, "All fair questions, sir. Here's what I think. I think they've been waiting for us to ask for a hundred and fifty years, Colonel. They've known for that long that we have these bits and pieces of their technology. They could have come for them anytime.

"Just throwing it out there, I'm guessing they have a non-interference policy, or perhaps some sort of prime mission directive that prevents them from doing so. Most importantly, I think it's always been up to us, to contact them, to say we know they're out there." Laying the material in the colonel's hands, he said, "And to ask for their help."

The evidence was incontrovertible. Feeling the material, lost in thought, Clayton wandered away, through the building, and outside. They followed him, waiting for him to voice his thoughts. He stood under the obsidian black, jewel-encrusted sky, looking upward, as though he might glimpse something there.

"So, you believe they've been up there, watching us the whole time. Damn," he said, wonder in his voice. For several more minutes, he wandered in circles, stargazing. With a growing sense of awe, he gazed at the age-old, ever-present night sky, a sky that now held new meaning, and with any luck at all, a second chance for the planet. Finally, he came back to earth, and turned to the others. "Got any ideas for talking to them, Mr. Caine?"

"I sure do. First, I thought—"

"Get on with it, then. You've got the lead. Mr. Waldron, Ms. Rios; I assume that you'll want to be a part of this new project?" he asked, as he returned the materials to Ephraim.

Using his forearm crutches, Jeff walked over to Rose, and reached for her hand, to find hers reaching for his. "As long as we're together, we wouldn't want to be anywhere else, Colonel."

"Good. I'll see you all in the conference room tomorrow morning. Ten o'clock. Bring your ideas and proposals, and I'll call Port Angeles and notify the Board, err, sorry—General Clayton— that we'll need a satellite linkup." He took a step or two, stopped, and looked up again. "Maybe there's still hope for us."

As so often happened, whether he was talking to himself or not, none of them knew. He climbed into the passenger side of the Humvee, and before giving the go-ahead to his driver, he said, "Oh, Mr. Caine. I believe there's one more thing of great importance that you wish to discuss with me?"

Ephraim gaped for a moment or two before he found his tongue. "Uh, yes, sir, Colonel, there is. I, uh, would like your permission to pursue a, uh, serious relationship with Samantha."

"You mean you'd like permission to *continue* pursuing the relationship you and Samantha have been engaged in for some time now?"

Poor Ephraim's face burned red, and he was thankful for the

darkness that shrouded them. "Uh, y-yes, sir. That's what we'd like to do."

"My brother, General Clayton, will want assurances that your intentions are honorable. Are you asking permission to court my niece with the intention of marrying her in the near future?"

"Yes, sir, as near in the future as possible. But I can—I can only *ask* her. She has to do the deciding. I'm just a guy who, uh ..." and finally, in surrender, he said it. "Who loves her, sir."

"*That* is what I wanted to hear, Ephraim. Permission granted. Driver, drive on."

The taillights and motor sounds faded into the distance, leaving the three shivering in the frigid silence of a black, moonless night, alone with the stars in the sky. Their eyes—and their imaginations— remained glued to the sparkling pinpoints of light. For quite some time, no one moved, and no one spoke.

"You dog," Jeff said. "Not *one* word about it, even to your best friend.

"Yeah, I know. You were *really* wrong about me getting the girl. That must bug the hell out of you."

"But you'll notice that I *am* taller than you by several inches."

"*And* that you still owe me four hundred and fifty dollars."

"Yeah? Why?" Jeff grinned, wickedly, and thought, *this can be fun!*

"Because, I, uh, you, ah ... hmmm. I don't remember. That's weird."

He'd pushed it far enough. "Good for you, Eph. You done good. I'm happy for you and Sam."

Rose asked, "So you think there's somebody up there, Ephraim? You're really sure we're not alone?"

"I *know* it, Rose," he said, "I know we're not alone." He threw his arms over their shoulders, and as they returned inside, he said, "You know what? I think we make a great team, guys."

Rose rolled her eyes, and sighed, "Why do I get the feeling that I'm going to regret this?"

# 36

Ten o'clock the next morning found all the technicians and command center personnel gathering at Hop Ops, which they found to be guarded, and the doors locked. Minutes later, the team was granted access, and filed inside. There they found the colonel already conferencing with his brother. But something was wrong. They could see both Claytons were clearly agitated, and from all indications, a heated argument had just concluded prior to their entry. What they couldn't know—yet—was that the argument wasn't between the brothers.

General Clayton looked on, his face clouded, while the colonel faced his people.

"Good morning, people. I have news for you, and not much of it is good. Earlier, after reviewing the dismal track record the T.I.T.O.R. program has accrued in the field of late, the President dropped in on our conference, and came down on us, *hard*. He didn't want to hear our arguments or look at our evidence regarding the board's poor decisions. Some of the board members have powerful friends and it's no secret that a few of them were seated on the board *because* they have his ear. In light of that, this wasn't entirely unexpected, but we had hoped we could hold our own. We tried to argue that as we drew closer to solving the mystery of why and how the war started, we could *expect* the degree of difficulty to escalate, and our job to become tougher. And yes, even some losses and casualties. This *is* a military program, after all.

"That didn't matter. He was determined to focus on losses, rather than gains. With Rose's hop placed in jeopardy during that September 15th mission, and worst of all, losing Hop 206, all the heat fell squarely on us. The President is holding us responsible, and as one might expect, the Board got a free pass.

He looked at the faces present, faces who had become his extended family, and closed his eyes for a second before he had to deliver this to them. "And so we come to the real bad news. There will be no more hops, for any reason. The T.I.T.O.R. program has been shut down. All of the hop machines are to be dismantled, and all of the plans are to be destroyed. All scientific research related to our program—especially any aspect of time travel—is to be destroyed along with them."

Groans sounded from across the room. For a substantial number of the people present, the development of this program had been their entire life's work. They had no idea what they would do if the program closed down.

Colonel Clayton held his hands up, and said, "I know, I know, people; this is bad. But we're still the team in charge of saving the world, and our goal hasn't changed. Every last one of you still has a place here, and you'll be pivotal in implementing a *new* program designed to contact another civilization that we believe may live in our corner of the galaxy, a technologically advanced race of beings that we've only recently confirmed the existence of."

The others murmured and whispered among themselves, and Clayton gestured at Ephraim and Jeff.

"Our resident intrepid wild men, Jeff and Ephraim, will bring you up to speed. I want all team leaders in here for a conference tomorrow morning, to develop plans and ideas on how we might restructure T.I.T.O.R. into humanity's greatest hope, by finding ways to ask our celestial neighbors for help."

Looking downcast, he said, "I'm sorry about the program, people. We lost our focus with T.I.T.O.R. We all knew we were going at it in the wrong way, and none of us voiced any objections or did anything to change that, until it was too late. That was my fault."

He stood, and said, "From this moment on, we will no longer lie to ourselves. Nor will we entrust this sacred duty to coddled, protected, supercilious board members who live in luxury, remaining purposefully ignorant of the doom facing us all."

He made a fist and punched the palm of his hand with it to emphasize his words, and said, "We're out of time. We owe this planet our best effort, our absolute *best*; we *must* find a way to save it, and ourselves in the process, if it isn't already too late for us all. From now on, we will check our arrogance at the door, and we will face our mortality with realism, and grim determination."

He turned to his brother, up on the view screen, who until now had said nothing. "General, would you like to add anything to that?"

Looking grim, weary, and more weighed-down than his younger brother ever remembered seeing him, the General said nothing at first. Finally, he said, "There's nothing else to say, Marcus, except— God help us all." He nodded solemnly at his brother, reached forward, and the screen went black.

T.I.T.O.R., the earth's last, best chance, was suddenly gone, to be replaced by a backup plan that involved contacting and working with beings they'd never seen, never spoken to.

Not a sound was uttered by any of those assembled.

His demeanor grave, Colonel Clayton gestured to Jeff and Ephraim, and said, "My office, one hour, gentlemen." With that, he rose and exited the command center.

An hour later, the two entered the colonel's office, and he gestured for them to be seated in the chairs opposite him.

Jeff said, "That was a good speech, Colonel. Very inspiring."

"Yes, it was," Ephraim agreed.

Leveling a gaze at them over his reading glasses, he said, "It was bullshit, and you know it."

The two resisted a powerful need to squirm in their chairs.

Removing his glasses, Clayton dangled them, and for a moment or two, chewed absently on one of the rubber earpieces.

He said, "Let's talk reality. What we spoke about last night. These beings are probably up there, sure. But what are the odds that they'll actually respond to us, much less answer our questions, or extend a helping hand?"

Ephraim shrugged. "Honestly, sir? I'd say about even-up that they'll even respond. The odds that they'll actually take that extra step and help us? Much worse."

Clayton twisted his mouth into a slight grimace, and nodded his head in bitter agreement. "I agree. But we have no choice. We *must* continue to try to find ways to get them to respond and help us."

Laying his glasses down, he gestured toward Jeff and Ephraim. "I want you two to revamp this program; get it on the right track to pursue these new goals. Repurpose the equipment we presently use for tracking hops telemetry, if you can. Otherwise, you'll need to remove that equipment from service. Our orders are to dismantle and destroy all three of T.I.T.O.R.'s hop machines, so that they can never be reassembled and used again."

"You mean, all *four* hop machines sir," Jeff said.

Clayton was in a dark mood, and when his stone-cold gaze locked on him, Jeff wished he could crawl under the desk. The colonel reached out, picked up a paper, and slid it across the desk it to Jeff. "This is an official list. There were four. Hop 206 was destroyed. How many hop machines does this program now list as assets?"

Nervous, Jeff studied the page, and found what he was looking for. "Uh, thr— three hop machines are listed here, sir."

"And how many of those hop machines have I been ordered to destroy, Mr. Waldron?"

"All— all of them, sir."

"All three remaining hop machines created for this program are to be destroyed. Those are my orders, and they're the orders I'm giving. I don't like when my orders are questioned, disobeyed, or modified, Mr. Waldron. Perhaps you remember the dim view I take of that?"

Jeff weighed his answer. New-Jeff question time. Had he been good? Bad? Whatever his past now, he'd probably managed to get into some trouble with Clayton, especially if Ephraim had anything to do with it. He decided to wing it.

"Like it was yesterday, sir."

"Good. Mr. Caine, do *you* have any questions for me?"

"Just a few procedural items, sir. There will be, uh, odd items, unspecified on that sheet, items that we'll be … removing from service. I assume you have a place in mind for them?"

"See the Lieutenant on your way out. He'll have all the details for you. There's an empty hangar not far from R&D."

"Do you have a timeframe in mind for all of this, sir?"

"Three months at the outside. That should give you enough time to set the team in motion here, and to get your affairs in order. You have a lot of work to do between now and then."

Ephraim looked at Clayton, and their eyes locked, without a word. He didn't want to misunderstand what wasn't being said. Then, he nodded, and Clayton nodded back.

Ephraim said, "Thank you, sir. I just want to say that it's been my privilege to serve under you."

"It's been mine as well. But it's not over yet. Dismissed."

They picked up their papers from the Lieutenant, and Jeff couldn't remember being more confused in his entire life. As soon as they walked outside, he said, "Okay, I know I'm missing something important here. Bring me up to speed."

Ephraim looked at him, and thought a moment before answering. "This doesn't go beyond us. Not to Sam, and not to Rose. Spend the next three months doing some nice things with Rose, whenever you can. I'll do the same with Sam."

"Okay. And?"

"And work really hard on getting your legs into shape. You're going to need them fully functional. No crutches. Got it?"

"Check. Already hard at work on that. Anything else?"

"Yeah. I've got a machine to recalibrate, and we're going to need a *bunch* of ballistic chutes. As many as we can find."

# 37

Jeff read from the list. "Money?"

Ephraim responded, "Check. A whole bag of it, separated in five-year increments."

"Thirty pounds of small gold ingots, and precious gems. Really?"

"Really. Gold and gems can be converted to money in any era. Check."

"Gotcha. Makes sense. Okay, next on the list – weapons and ammunition?"

"Holsters and handguns, rifles, lots of ammo, crossbows, checked and double-checked."

"Camping gear?"

"Right down to the food."

"ID's?"

"Check. For three different decades."

"I can't believe we're doing this, Eph."

"Can you see any other way?"

Jeff sighed miserably, and said, "I finally get my legs back, and I

285

finally get together with Rose, just so I can go play Kamikaze." He muttered, "Juuust out-*standing.*" He shook his head.

Ephraim said, "I understand. I do. But we're doing this for them, Jeff. It's the last, best chance for the planet."

"I don't suppose it's crossed your genius mind that, if we fail, we'll probably die, and if we succeed, if we're lucky enough to find them afterwards, we'll find a Rose and a Sam who never so much as *knew* us in the world we'll come home to. By climbing into this hop machine, there are no maybes. We're saying goodbye forever to everything we know and love."

"And we'll be protecting them from ever having to suffer this living hell."

"I know it. I do. I just … I just wish I didn't have to leave her behind."

"I'm with you there. It kills me to leave Sam here."

Voices spoke from a dark corner of the bay. "I dunno. Looks to *me* like there's enough room on that hop for two more. What do you think?"

Another voice spoke. "I'd say so. Evening, boys. How about a table for four?"

Sam and Rose stepped into the light, wearing crew jackets.

The color drained from the boys' faces. Ephraim, trying to speak, stuttered and mumbled something unintelligible.

Sam looked condescendingly at the two. "What? Do you two *really* think you've been secretive about this? *Paleeaze.* We both knew you were up to *something.* I pried it out of Uncle Mark when I threatened to tell my dad. Looks like there are four of us sworn to secrecy now, boys, 'cause we—" she said with a smile, passing a duffel bag to Ephraim, hard enough to make him catch his breath, "*We* are going with you."

Rose did the same with Jeff, who caught his, stunned at her sudden arrival.

"I call pilot's seat," she said, smiling.

Jeff, already sporting an unbearably happy look, broke into a grin from ear to ear. He stood there, unmoving, with his silly look, still holding the duffel bag.

Ephraim finally found his tongue, trying his best to object, to sound irritated. "We— we're all going to die on this mission. You *do* understand that, don't you?" he snapped, more worried than angry.

Sam grinned and shrugged. "Everybody dies. Looks to me like Jeff's gonna die happy. What about you, *cowboy?*" she said, emphasizing her question with a slap to Ephraim's behind as she walked past him.

He dismissed her with a cool wave of his hand, his index finger straight up into the air. "Uh-uh. No. You're gonna have to do better than just showing up." He turned back to the hop machine, and stopped in his tracks. Then he rolled his eyes skyward, leaned his head back, and appeared to be in excruciating pain as he cried out, "Oh, *God,* why is this happening?" and shook his head mournfully. "This is not *fair.* This is just *wrong.*"

Jeff could see where Sam might get the wrong idea at that, so he explained. "Not enough room for Esperanza now. Months of planning, straight down the drain."

The three of them attempted to stifle their snorts and chuckles as a heartbroken Ephraim offloaded his beloved still, moaning and grumbling as he removed the three meticulously-packed crates he'd stowed with loving care in one corner of the hop machine.

After Rose and Sam strapped in and adjusted their harnesses, they unbuckled to help finish the checklist.

Colonel Clayton walked in as they checked off the last few items.

Ephraim said, "Colonel. Thanks for coming to see us off."

"I wouldn't have missed it, Ephraim," he said, shocking the younger man by addressing him by his first name, probably for the third time since he'd known him. "Of course, my niece here has put me in an impossible position. I now have to tell my brother where she's gone, and that there will be no way to retrieve any of you. We all know this is *not* a sanctioned mission. I hope you appreciate the gravity of this, and the trouble I'll be in, young lady."

"I do, Uncle Mark. Tell Daddy that I went with the man I love, doing the work I love to do."

"Don't worry, I'll tell him, dear," he said, and stepped closer to address the four of them. "This is it. Barring an absolute miracle, or at the very least some extraterrestrials willing to unveil themselves just so they can help us, this is the only other chance we have to reverse the damage done to the planet."

He looked away pensively. "Hell, to tell you the truth, this hop machine shouldn't even exist, and this will be the second time I've sent it out in a last-ditch effort to save our asses."

He turned to Ephraim. "Where's the support equipment for the hop machine? Did you already destroy it?"

Ephraim shook his head. "No. I already transported it to the past, to a secure facility I plan to use as a base. I went back, bought the place, hired contractors to build it into a secure facility. It took years of work to set up. Support equipment, tools, everything is there now," he said, then looked at the three crates that held Esperanza, and sighed. "Well, *almost* everything."

Clayton looked stunned. "I'm impressed. Good work, Ephraim."

Turning his attention back to the rest, he said, "Now, listen up, all of you. I can't overstress the importance of you surviving this mission. And now, I'm giving you an *order*. Whatever happens, *don't* come back here. There's nothing left to come back to. The Earth is played out. We're struggling to breathe.

"Once you've done what you can, find a quiet, out-of-the-way place, and settle down, maybe in the 1950s. Whatever suits you best. Destroy the hop machine, and forget what we've been trying to do. Stay out of history's business. Make a good life in a living world. Grow old together, and die peaceful and happy."

He looked at Sam, "If I can take that to Conrad, and make him understand what you're going back to do, I think he could live with that. You're his little girl, Sam, but because I helped raise you, you're as close as I've ever had to having a little girl of my own."

She hugged him tightly, and nodded. "And you're a great uncle; the best a girl could ever hope for. I promise, Uncle Mark. We'll try our best to do just that. I'm sorry that we put you in a corner with this."

He put his arm around her shoulder, and shrugged. "I should fess up. I'd already decided that I was going to tell you about the mission, because I *wanted* you to go. I wanted to get you away from this. You four are young, and smart. You're in love. You deserve a shot at a real life, not … *this,*" he said, gesturing in despair at the world in decline all around them. "Try and find something better. For all of us."

They all murmured promises that they would.

"And Rose," he said, turning to her, "I don't think I could be prouder of you if you *were* my own daughter. I think I'm going to miss you most of all. You made us a family."

Rose smiled tearfully, wiped her eyes, and said, "I'll miss you too, sir." She sat up straighter in her seat, took a deep breath, and said, "Colonel, I think I speak for everyone when I say I wish there was room onboard for one more."

"Hear, hear," the others chimed in.

Clayton raised an eyebrow. "Don't think I hadn't given it some thought. Too bad this hop isn't mounted to a truck. You might have found me later on, stowed away in the cab."

He smiled and hugged Sam closer. "But you don't need some old codger slowing you down on this mission. I'll be with you, anyway; right here." He gently thumped his chest over his heart. "Go on now, Samantha. It's time to go."

He wasn't the only one fighting back tears as Sam climbed aboard, and not another word was said as she strapped in.

Rose pointed to the overhead door, and tossed the key fob to the colonel. "Sir, if you would?"

"It would be my honor, young lady," he said, and before he pressed the button, he paused. He took one last look at each of them, and then gave his last order as their colonel.

"Do us proud."

She nodded, and fired up the machine. The aluminum links rose, locking together above their heads, forming the protective cage. The fields rose next; first the base fields, allowing her to raise the hop into a hover and exit the building. There she set down, and engaged the full fields, which gave the machine the classic "flying saucer" look so often seen in the twentieth-century skies.

As the fields rose, the colonel saw much more than two men and two women on a hop machine. These four carried with them the fears, the hopes, and dreams of an entire world.

As a species, humanity had shown itself to be a spectacular failure. Individually, as with *these* four remarkable souls, man held a promise of almost limitless potential. How fitting, then, that they alone should be chosen to carry out this last mission.

Not long before, the dusk had slipped away, leaving the dark northern skies blanketed with stars, sparkling like diamonds. Now, the northern lights erupted, splashing across the sky, painting the night, sending spectacular, undulating waves of color skittering through the heavens; a magnificent and timely blessing to their final mission.

As Clayton waved, Rose lifted the hop into a hover, and pointed the craft skyward, her course taking the hop directly into the brightest eruption of color.

Seconds from then, they would become nothing more than just another diamond in the sky, just one more shooting star to wish upon, and just perhaps, the last, tiny glimmer of hope for the beaten, weary, careworn remnants of humanity left in their wake.


End

# Afterword

A good story is never about the answers. It's all about the questions. If the right questions are not asked, how can the answers be correct?

The Roswell incident. UFOs. Wreckage. Aliens. Secrecy. The cover-up. It's exciting, stimulating to think about. Though not a conspiracy theorist, I've never been so naïve as to think our government wouldn't lie to us. Perhaps that means I've leapfrogged over being a conspiracy theorist to something more compelling. To me, FACT means that it's no longer theory. We all know our government—or at least, representatives of our government—have lied to us before, and they will lie to us again.

Welcome to America.

I've been asked why I wanted to write a story about Roswell. The short answer is; I didn't. Beyond the everyday laments about politicians, I had no particular bone to pick with the government, and my views on Roswell were decidedly neutral. At best, I had a passing tourist's interest in it. Sure, maybe it happened, maybe there *was* a cover-up. Maybe not. That's how I saw it.

But my perspective was that of an author telling an interesting tale, and the Roswell incident provided critical elements I needed to weave the story I pictured in my mind.

Shift to the other side of my tale. I was fascinated by the story of a man called John Titor, who appeared in chat rooms and forums in late 2000 through early 2001. He claimed to be a time traveler from 2036. He made a handful of predictions, and talked about our future before he disappeared. After reading his posts, I questioned what motives a traveler from the future could have to visit "our" chat rooms, and to casually disclose that he came from the future. Who would do that? Why would you risk letting people know you're here? Why risk the government finding you? They'd almost certainly confiscate your time machine, and they'd be willing to use extraordinary measures to achieve that. That got me thinking.

It's probable that the John Titor visiting those chat rooms was merely somebody with too much time on his hands. Even so, it would be amazing to imagine the story behind it if he wasn't.

And I did. Imagine it, that is. That's my job. Authors look behind every interesting story to see what *other* stories might dwell there, hidden in the shadows, and I'm the type who loves to turn over rocks, to ask every kind of question you can imagine. It's not my fault; I was born that way. Whereas most two-year-olds incessantly ask "Why?" to their parents, driving them crazy, I did it until I was eight. In the minds of my beleaguered parents, curious George was not a monkey.

While imagining the story behind John Titor, things got interesting. Researching Roswell, I sifted through massive amounts of available information. For my purposes, the Roswell crash was perfect, with wreckage, bodies, and the essential components to support the premise that a crash occurred.

I parsed the conflicting interviews, corroborators, and naysayers, compared witness interviews, information, and photographs. I studied reams and reams of information.

Then, one day, I stopped in my tracks. The jigsaw catalyzed, forming a clear picture, and I suddenly knew beyond all doubt. There was a cover-up! There it was, as plain as day. *All* of the witnesses agreed upon the properties of the material in the wreckage. When crushed, it laid out flat and returned to a smooth state. It wouldn't fold, and it wouldn't hold a crease. No matter who handled it, virtually everyone who touched it made those claims.

In the photos, Major Jesse A. Marcel was shown holding material from a weather balloon. He always claimed he was ordered to pose with that material, and was consistently unwavering and resolute in his affirmation that he was *not* photographed with the material found at the crash site. Indeed, one need only look to see in those newspaper photos that he is holding *heavily wrinkled and creased material.*

Marcel was telling the truth.

There's more. They first used a massive B-29 to move the "weather balloon" from Roswell to Fort Worth, and on its second leg a C-54 to move the same items to Wright Field.

All military estimates during the period I call 'after-coercion' put the total wreckage volume as perhaps enough to fill a good-sized garbage bag, or maybe two. Yet, they assigned a plane designed to deliver atomic bombs to carry that small amount of material, when the smallest Piper Cub in their air force should easily have carried every bit of it, plus the pilot's dog, girlfriend, picnic basket, and a blanket with room to spare.

To give you some perspective, the B-29 had *four engines,* a wingspan of 144 feet, and a length of 99 feet, tip to tail, with a maximum payload carrying capacity of just over *sixty thousand pounds!* The second plane, a C-54, also had four engines, and was nearly as large. These certainly would *not* be my common-sense choices if I needed to deliver a shredded weather balloon that amounted to one or two small bundles of wispy material and sticks.

Wrapped around the President, maybe. Otherwise? Uh-uh.

And just like that, my imagination was sparked. Whatever happened there, whatever their motivation, the government absolutely drew a veil of secrecy over the Roswell incident. Heady stuff!

Then I was drawn in by the ensuing tragedy that unfolded there in New Mexico in 1947. The more I researched, the more I saw how the real-life Mack Brazel and his family were affected, as well as others living in and near Roswell at the time. Nobody can deny that within a year of the crash, most of the people involved experienced radical changes in their lives. The radio station manager ended up living in another state within a year, far from Roswell. Things happen to people, it's a fact of life. But the odds of that many bad things happening to virtually every member of that precise group of people are incalculable. It saddened me when my research revealed how many lives were adversely affected.

Young Vernon grew up, moved away, and changed his name. At each new location, the locals somehow learned his real identity, and he was forced to move on. Early in his twenties, far from home, he died. It was reported as a suicide. Was it? Perhaps. Perhaps not. He was among those most profoundly affected, one of the first, yet far from the last.

Dee, Vernon's best friend, developed a unique response to people coming around and asking questions. Wherever he was, should somebody start talking about the Roswell incident, or start asking questions, he dropped whatever he was doing, and quite literally *ran* away from there, as fast as he could. This he did even as an adult.

I don't blame him.

So many witnesses—and their families—had their lives shredded over the Roswell incident. Few remain. It's almost ancient history now.

Ancient history; that's where I usually come in. History is my thing. So I decided to write about the real tragedy—as much as I could weave into the story. I maintained as much accuracy as my story would allow. I had no intentions of making any sort of a statement; it's far too late for that. But I thought it might be a treat to allow my readers to view these people as I did.

Once we remove the word Aliens from the Roswell incident, we find that it changes nothing. There's no doubt that the government wanted to cover *something* up. A rancher—even a stubborn one who sticks to his story—isn't taken into custody and questioned military-style for a week because he found a weather balloon. There would be no reason for the military to escort him into a newspaper office and a radio station under guard and force him to make public retractions. Can you even *think* of a scenario where that would be an appropriate course of action?

I could end those sentences with the word 'today.' If no other good came of it, I believe Roswell became the focal point wherein our government learned and formed—through trial by fire—protocols to dictate policy for when our military secrets become inextricably tangled and intermeshed with the lives of our private citizens. I believe in my heart that Mack Brazel's family and the Proctors—and many others I never touched upon—paid the dearest of prices for the military's learning curve during the inept handling of the Roswell incident.

I also believe, within the military, that, however brief, a struggle of another kind occurred. As I tried to convey in my General Ramey's character, most of the men and women in our military were good people even then. The protection of American citizens has never been optional for our military. After such a monumental faux pas, an internal uproar would be virtually mandatory, though you and I will likely never know about it. I believe the policies created in the aftermath of Roswell help to guide our military forces today; in every country in the world, every village, every trail where they set boots on the ground.

Land-mass wise, the United States is a small nation, whose population steadily increases. Its citizens and military secrets must coexist within this shrinking parcel of land, and as such, this uneasy cohabitation will never cease to be a work in progress. We've come a long way in the nearly seventy years since the Roswell incident. We still have a long way to go.

But, as my friends from the UK are fond of telling me, the United States is a young nation.

It takes time.

J.M.

# About the Author

J.M. Surra is also the author of Angels and Their Hourglasses, and is winner of both the 2011 & 2013 eLit Awards in the category of Science Fiction & Fantasy, as well as the winner of the 2011 Global Award in the category of Popular Fiction.

J.M. wishes to thank the many readers who write to tell him how they enjoy his books. Please take a few minutes to drop into Goodreads and your bookseller's site, and leave reviews to let others know how much you enjoyed T.I.T.O.R.

For more information, visit www.jmsurra.com and see what other releases J.M. has in the works.

www.ingramcontent.com/pod-product-compliance
Lightning Source LLC
Chambersburg PA
CBHW020555260626
47157CB00003B/705